LEAVES *AND* CIRCLES

BY SPENCER THOMAS

TABLE OF CONTENTS

EPIGRAPH

T HE WORLD ISN'T WHAT IT *used to be, but then it's never what it used to be.*

Allen Saunders once wrote that life is what happens when you're busy making other plans; that's what happened to the world.

Where we were recently, events still echoing, things we were celebrating victory over or saying *"Never Again"* about while slipping into things we'd be saying *"Never Again"* about in another half-century.

Where we were, or seemed to be, that space of time often called the "extended present," seemingly inescapable no matter how much we tried to touch history or create it, especially in America.

Where we would be, the future, or rather, the non-future, due to accelerated innovation beginning to devour it.

Then something comes out of nowhere, bringing it all to a screeching halt while we're wondering who we are, where we are, *when* we are, forcing history and the future to recede out of view, warping our view of time and eras, forcing those concepts to take on a new shape, a more indeterminate one. Forcing the now into an even *more extended* present. That's where, and when, we are now.

PROLOGUE

What I write here constitutes a continuation of part the work I've done—we have done—since we started our "research" last year. Some parts of the work are based on news reports, personal discussions, and social media postings. Other parts are based on memories of personal experiences, my own analysis, or just conjecture. At times the text may jump back forth, interjections thrown in as I remember important things. I've added dates in order to reduce reader confusion. This work is a synthesis of the information contained in the copious notes I've kept since it all began, which I've tried to put it into a higher-level, more narrative form for better understanding. I assume that anyone that has access to this work will also have access to the raw data.

This is likely the only record of what's happened here.

BAR
251
SUNNY'S BAR 253

CH1
KOMOREBI

It's been over a year since it all began, a series of events that altered everything so dramatically, so completely, upending thousands of years of human society. That's what the stretch-banded digital watch-slash-calendar I've been using implies; I'm not actually sure how long it's *really* been. Ever since late last autumn, time has seemed to sometimes behave in unpredictable, disorienting ways. No laws of causality or thermodynamics have been broken, and time's arrow has been in its usual forward motion, but there have been punctuations and mismatches that have tested my view of things, my view of what's real. If other nearly incomprehensible events hadn't occurred since then, I might be questioning my perception, and possibly even my sanity. However, due to the things I've observed and continue to observe on a daily basis, I have to believe those perceptions are correct. For instance, the makeup of days and the weather have changed in noticeable ways. I'll start with those.

Nights are longer than they used to be, seeming to last until seven or eight AM on typical days, though not all days are what I'd call "typical" anymore. Dawn starts later, and goes on much longer, manifesting as a gray, limply hanging half-light that lingers until around noon. Thankfully, I have a healthy collection of digital watches and those little batteries that you might associate with old-school, tube-sided hearing aids, that allow me to continue to determine and record the time.

Days tend to be heavily overcast; the last time I saw the sun itself until very recently was during the middle of last fall. A blanket of brooding clouds are ever-present during most days, and some form of falling precipitation is not unusual. Most days and nights themselves are dank and soggy, with cottony fogs and mists swirling through the streets, reducing your range of vision to essentially nil. Visibility wasn't something that people in the modern world (which I'll call old-world) that weren't behind a steering wheel or the bow of a ship generally needed to concern themselves with. In new-world, however, it's become more important for the day-to-day.

Daytime is warmer than other times, but the thermometer never reads above seventy anymore, even on the balmiest of days; most hover in the fifties, occasionally pushing into the lower sixties. Overall, it's warmer than it used to be during times you'd expect it to be colder, but never hot, and never quite reaching that Platonic ideal of temperature and humidity that the west coast always seemed to manage and some east coasters secretly envied; certainly no San Franciscan ever spent any days living above anything like the concrete-and-steel quasi-swamp that this place has become. What passes for "full" daylight rarely lasts past six or seven PM, with one exception, and six hours of steady illumination are now standard.

The black and blueness of twilight, at first pale, then a darkening periwinkle, finally giving way to a deep ink-like indigo, stretches on for five, sometimes six hours; always my favorite time of day, the best time to wander the streets without any particular destination in mind. Why the angle, amount, and duration that the sun hits the earth can have such a strong emotional impact is still somewhat of a mystery. Sure, we understand Circadian rhythms and light levels affecting mood, but there's something more to it. Why do certain times of day feel like magic to some people? Why does it seem the perception of the world to one filled with secrets or hidden, ill-defined powers? How does it create the feeling of excitement and possibility, but with a lining of fear? In new-world, unlike the old, twilight has become the time to take shelter and get out of the streets rather than a time to wander, as those secrets and ill-defined powers have become dangerous realities.

The darker parts of days, ominous before widespread use of gas lighting and electricity (as during the times of *"Nightwalking"* and city watches in London) have once again become associated with threats. I would say I have some inkling of what they experienced, but new-world is far beyond the comparatively benign one of cutpurses or highwaymen. That, and the fact that daylight eventually returned them to a softer reality, relatively speaking.

Nighttime tends to start at nine or ten and end at the aforementioned times, when the dead gray sky returns to finally push it back aside. Nights are also often cloudy, a hazy round ball of bone hanging cold and silent up in the amorphous blackness. Occasionally, however, cloud cover breaks up so that you can glimpse our smaller neighbor clearly, now impressively eerie due to the lack of light drowning it out; the electricity went out last winter.

There have been a few notable exceptions to the above: periods where a languid daylight hung around for days on end, the new-world version of a midnight sun, and a crystal-clear, moon-flooded night that lasted for more than week, patterns only familiar in those northern countries that birthed Black Metal and government that actually worked. Two things you wouldn't expect to see in the northeastern US, but you could say that about a lot of things now.

Humidity is near-constant. There's a dampness to everything that seeps into you, grips you. Sometimes I think I dream about lying spread-eagle in the middle of a dry, ruddy desert, like the *Killpecker Sand Dunes* with its sagebrush and stubby slabs of granite just to counteract it. I've never actually been there, but what I've read makes it fit for purpose; my own version of "think happy thoughts" is "think dry thoughts." Streets are perpetually slick or at least damp, matted with leaves of maize, deep orange, or woody brown, exquisitely pretty in their autumnally grim, waterlogged way or floating in unevaporated roadside ponds or riding next to curb edges on tiny, oft-flowing rivers in miniature. Trampled castoffs from every deciduous forming a squishy carpet underneath your feet, looking at times fused with the asphalt and concrete.

Preparation for surviving in this altered environment, as you may have already guessed, is very important. For example, layering clothing: generally a long sleeve thermal shirt and a hoodie under a thinnish overcoat does the job. Or you can double up on the hoodies. I tend to go for those wicking, super-thin, insulating thermo-tech fabric coats that were all the rage, as they seem to work as advertised. Considering the state of things, you really have your pick; one giant department store with every style, fabric and color you could ever dream of, and none of the acrid mixes of perfumes and colognes that seemed to follow you from escalator to food court and back again. (It's easier to get used to the scent of soaked literfall and *Inceptisols* everywhere you go, if not rain-soaked piles of garbage of every kind.) A high quality canvas backpack or solid gym bag are must haves, too, for both your peeled-off layers and all your standard equipment: plastic water bottles, police-style flashlights, and dried snacks, among others.

The locations and basic edifices of the city remain largely the same: buildings, streets, sidewalks and other trappings of an urban landscape—excepting those that were destroyed outright—are in their proper places, though many are in a state of disrepair, which, without regular maintenance, happens faster than you might think. The perpetual dampness probably doesn't help, either. Vehicles sit, usually haphazardly and hastily abandoned, idle and uncared for, and have become so commonplace and familiar in their arrangement that you could almost forget that they weren't always part of the landscape, like rock piles made of steel and wet, round rubber. The city is still a city in the strict sense of having the basic physical and topographical features that define what we think of constituting "cities," but run through a filter with unsettling, often difficult-to-fathom qualities.

New-world is both telluric and alien. It elicits the feeling of visiting a place you've known inside and out for your entire life, but that has had key things rearranged, shifted, twisted; a house once lived in with the furniture swapped out and different scenes depicted in the art on the walls, but still surrounded by the same picture frames. Expected objects replaced by similar, but not identical objects. A conflicting feeling: the deeply familiar mixed with the deeply unfamiliar. *Disconsonant.*

I don't understand much of what we've observed at a deep level, as we have had only rudimentary abilities to perform tests; that means I'm forced to speculate on certain aspects of what's occurred, especially root causes. Our ability to try to do anything resembling modern science has been extremely limited; nearly everything now is based on direct, high-level observations and reasoning. We're far from the world of microscopes and high-performance computing clusters, and we aren't scientists in any case, though one of us has had some formal training, which has helped.

Until very recently, I'd studied it all with a measure of enthusiasm; now my interest is a bit more subdued, more utilitarian, even though in some ways it's more interesting now than it's ever been. Getting

Leaves *and* Circles

a better understanding to aid in survival was a large motivator, but plain curiosity and the desire to unravel the what, how, and why of the many strange changes played a large part as well. At present, my time is spent on organizing and synthesizing the data I've collected into this work, trying to transform it all into something resembling a coherent whole, rather than just a haphazard collection of notes.

I feel sad today.

CH2
NICHE LIVING

It's funny how you can remember what things felt like before you really understood them. How you can compare that certain feeling, the feeling of having only a fragmented, disconnected version of the truth to the more complete one you have at the end, and can peel back each layer of understanding, seeing where connections were made and each nugget of enlightenment showed up. What I write here reminds me of that periodically, giving me brief moments of satisfaction when I mentally deconstruct and reconstruct the things I didn't understand, but now do. My understanding of the overall picture remains incomplete, however.

Since I have only fragments of information about what happened to the world outside of New York (and really just Brooklyn and Manhattan, the only places I've been able to reach or observe), I'll be starting this account with what I have direct knowledge of: where I am now. I don't know what form the changes in other places may have taken, but it seems unlikely to me that they could have gone on as they were, with people sipping their macchiatos and juice blends, strolling through parks and snapping pictures of cupcakes on top of dogs on top of trees and posting them to Instagram. What I've seen here is just too radical for that to be a possibility.

Where am I? A quaint, riparian little part of southwestern New Brooklyn is the area I presently call home. Here I'm surrounded by bronze steel encrusted cranes; dilapidated, crack-laden cobblestones; and narrow, two- and three-story brick-built structures of mahogany, cherry, charcoal, and white. Not the old Red Hook, a sleepy, but still completely recognizable place of human settlement, with the rare trundle of car wheels on uneven stone, or the semi-frequent rumble of a van picking up another order of Steve's Authentic Key Lime Pies. Red Hook felt less changed than many other places; it wasn't free of the after-effects of what's transpired by any stretch, but it was more limited, muted. It was comforting.

The lack of subway access, small population, low number of stores and street activity, and occasional stone road all contributed, in old-world, to the feeling of it being a place out of time (the rest of the city now feels, in one way or another and to varying degrees, as somewhat of a place out of time, but that's for different reasons), and that feeling remains. One thing that it does have in common with other neighborhoods is a lack of presence of actual human beings. Red Hook, New Brooklyn; known Human Population: one.

In addition to its relative remoteness and the fact that it was less affected by the events than some other neighborhoods I could have chosen, proximity to water was one of the reasons I decided to settle here. They—and I will detail who they are and what they do at length in the coming text—studiously avoid entering bodies of water, and not, I think, because of something to do with the salt content or unprobed worries about fish. They don't display any particular fear of it, nor any noticeable aversion to water or wetness itself, as they operate round-the-clock in the ever-present damp and frequent drizzles. They simply seem to lose interest once they've gotten near any body of water that isn't inland, as none of the "work" I've seen them engage in involves it.

On an occasion that I observed one of them fall in (accidentally), something strange happened: the robe-clad body landed on the water surface (with no languid arm tosses or flailing as you would expect of a drowning victim, as many of their reactions to things are often what might be considered robotic), and after a short pause, disappeared beneath it, rather than slowly being carried on down east, right past old-world beasts of transport and commerce, steel-toothed and rusting, that dot the waterfront. None of that is what you'd expect to happen after a person drowns: we sink when we're alive and float when we're corpses. After I witnessed this, I decided to test the physics involved in this puzzling, worrisome phenomenon. I picked up a jagged piece of wood that looked like it was once part of a shipping pallet and lobbed it underhand into the East River and watched the event repeat itself. *Something about the water isn't right.* There's virtually no surface tension after a brief moment of normalcy; any ideas I might have had about attempting to swim away or build a boat to leave were dashed in that moment. To this day I have no idea what may have caused this change in the behavior of these bodies of water, nor what purpose, if any, this phenomenon serves.

Finally, parks and other urban pockets of nature, the seeming hubs of their activities, aren't found in abundance in this neighborhood, giving me much-needed distance between me and the bulk of them, contributing to the aura of relative safety. All these apparent advantages, taken together, made the choice to reside here seem sensible at the time.

About where I live, specifically: my building. It has cherry red brick on the top two floors, with a black gated-up first floor that houses, or housed, an uninspiring antiques-slash-knick-knack shop. Inside of the store itself is fairly sparse, just a few old tables with items of no present utility or particular visual appeal. An odd collection of items, the kind of quasi-kitsch appreciated in certain quarters as having a sort of oblique appeal that might wind up at a yard sale or nailed to the wall in a quirky Bushwick bar: an old rectal thermometer with its mercury removed; a coffee "percolator" with no cord; a misshapen tan mug with an insipid inspirational quote and a jagged crack running down its side. The store was left abandoned early on in my estimation; whoever owned it was likely not a resident of the area and never bothered to come back.

The gates securing the front doors weren't even pulled across when I found the place. Only a simple, unremarkable lock kept anyone out, though it was probably redundant: no one else, similar to myself, likely saw much value in this place, as it was completely

untouched when I first found it. The slide-across gates serve as my current doorway. The north side on the first floor has no window, thankfully. It appeared to have had one at in the past, but it's been covered over with thick horizontal slats of well-worn wood painted a dull, charcoal black. The other side (and street-facing) window also has a gate on the inside part of it, obviating the need for much additional fortifying. That one was down and locked for some reason and so I've left it as-is. The first floor mercifully has no other windows to defend, and there's no fire escape in this, nor many other buildings around here, so all access is through the gated front.

The area has many buildings identical to this one in nearly all basic respects: two or three stories high, brick, pretty, quaint. Precious, but with a hint of past Brooklyn grit filled with eggs-and-sausage breakfasts; stale coffee and the hint of fish-washed cigarettes; and rough hands performing rough work with cranes, wood, steel. Coming to this place even back then felt like being on the edge of the world, even though so much was happening just a river-width and change away. That effect is magnified in new-world.

I'm on the second floor just above the shop, near a window, shut tight, thick black curtains drawn on all but the one I sit by. Mine is halfway open to give me light and a good view of the street at all times, though my worries about actually being spotted up here are presently subdued. I probably have enough food up here to last for three months if I'm careful, and in my experience, they give up far sooner than that anyway, though I wouldn't characterize them as impatient by any means. Far from it.

It's still outside today, with no wind to speak of, dead silent. All the sounds of the city, which you would expect to hear an occasional smattering of, even in this typically sedate area, are totally absent. No blaring car horns or foghorns; no gentle whoosh of passing cars or buses, that comforting sound like an oscillating floor fan, set to rotate on low speed; no sounds of others coughing or the persistent hum of old incandescent streetlights. No hint of birds, squirrels, or rats, nor anything else small and furry anywhere. That's not to say there's no life. There's plenty of it again, having all come thundering back after an extended semi-disappearance. Just not any that makes noise here, at least today.

CH3
YOU'VE GOT TO START SOMEWHERE

Early April, year one

The firs t signs of t he events that were to come began in the spring of the previous year, though at the time—and certainly at the very beginning—no one took them as a sign of anything other than the strange, disquieting behaviors of a certain brand of unsavory people; the usual, or sometimes less-usual suspects; or potentially explainable, if notably odd, natural phenomena. The unpredictable product of the thousand shards of desire, played out on the streets of one of the wealthiest cities in the world. Things that could happen almost anywhere. That particular assessment wasn't wrong, per se, just utterly inadequate. Based on what I know, it *didn't* just happen anywhere. No, I believe that it started here. Right here, in fact. In Brooklyn, New York, the borough right next to the one of my birth, and the place I spent many of my early years.

Something about that fact, or maybe assumption, struck me as outré, fanciful, like there was no possible way that it could be *here* that all this would begin. Brooklyn? Manhattan, maybe. London, sure. Los Angeles? Okay. But Brooklyn? The place where *GIRLS* was filmed; where Paul Sorvino grew up; or where *Last Exit...* was written. The place that birthed Jay-Z and late night punk shows, and brought artisanal-handcrafted-everything to the world stage. The place that once had black and boot-clad teenagers lined up around the block in Bensonhurst to see their favorite bands, and that gave us one of the world's first rollercoasters. This was the place where events seemingly so inexplicable and macabre would originate? The incongruity and surreality of it amused me, drowning out any revulsion when I first considered the idea.

It all started with animals: they began going missing. Squirrels, those furry little creatures that would follow you around waiting for some bits of fresh pretzel or a soggy, grease-soaked French fry, regarded alternately as a nuisance and an adorable symbol of urban naturalism, were to be the first bellwether for what was ahead. Then it was pigeons, our "rats of the sky" no longer delivering their slimy white gift to unsuspecting park-goers or the windshields of cars. Then insects: one by one parks fell silent, no more songs of grasshoppers after dark, nor those crescendoing spin sounds from bugs everyone called locusts, but that were actually cicadas. Bees vanished. No flies hovered around hot summer garbage piles outside fruit stores, the source of the quintessential eau de summer, trying to get another meal.

The local media characteristically delighted in faux-end-of-days speculation. Crass, but morbidly entertaining stories and gallows humor based on an amalgam of popular apocalypse tropes presented by the heads-in-boxes with a glossy, tongue-in-cheek tone and barely contained laughter. Just like *The Seventh Sign!* Except animals died rather than disappeared in that one. How many variants of *"Which Sign of The Coming Apocalypse Are You Most Excited About?"* listicles were written that month, I wonder. No one in the media seriously, or at least openly, believed anything was really wrong, but I thought I could detect an underlying sense of unease. There was worry behind all the jokes.

The prepper industry was a different story; they probably had their best quarter in years when it all started, people buying up fortification materials, bottled water, canned goods, and solar chargers, not to mention more guns and ammo than at any time since the last president was elected. The big gun organizations were all over it, too, switching the rhetorical flavor to a more eschatological (rather than political) one, always in sync with the times, always ready to pounce on the latest scare or tragedy. Media organizations had become masters at capitalizing on the latest horror story or crime-wave, able to turn on a dime when the tragedy-of-the-week broke, even if they themselves weren't buying it. Scientists and conservationists were brought in for interviews to proffer their own theories, from city noise to some kind of cross-species Colony *Collapse Disorder* to *El Niño* to climate change. Fire-and-brimstone preachers were in virtual orgasm on kook-radio with every announcement, trying desperately to fit the facts to their preferred narratives, and raking in donations that would have made a presidential candidate blush. The rumblings and speculation continued, enthusiastically and unabated into early summer, everyone trying to make their nut with a wink and a smile while the spooky was still going down.

On the streets, the sudden lack of nature sounds was unsettling, alien, their absence especially glaring in leafier parts like parks and quasi-suburban areas where you'd usually only hear the sounds of passing cars or people. No nervous little bodies scuttling through leaves or cooing noises from underneath rattling, precarious-looking window-unit air conditioners, those objects of every New Yorker's Looney Tunes-inspired nightmares. Those were still the early days, though, so the impact and reaction was limited for the person on the street, more flavor-of-the-month or "well, that's the zeitgeist," rather than a cause for widespread alarm.

Things got more serious once summer arrived.

Early June, year one

People's pets (in addition to the aforementioned city wildlife) began disappearing, just a few scattered ones at first. The news stories in tawdry local rags jumped right on the occurrences with their typically clever headlines: *"Napping Terrier Nabbed"* or *"Pug Thief Now on the Lam."* Stray cats, too, began to vanish according to some short-run alterna-press papers and local blogs, though how that particular piece of data was verified or quantified, I have no idea. Things deteriorated further just days after the first reports, starting with a rash of break-ins in apartments and houses with nothing taken except the family pet. Doorpersons and security cameras alike gave up no useful clues, though one widely hate-read shock-media web site claimed the former were being bribed to allow entry in order to support "a booming underground dogmeat trade in the city's Chinatowns," the veracity of which turned out to be completely unsupported by a subsequent official investigation.

Houses wealthy enough to have in-house servants, like some of the tonier parts of the Upper East and West sides were hit in the pet-theft wave, with said servants being charged by their owners with everything from negligence to conspiracy, rapidly followed up by actions like firings and "anonymous" calls to ICE; you do not want to be in the line of fire when someone's favorite Retriever disappears,

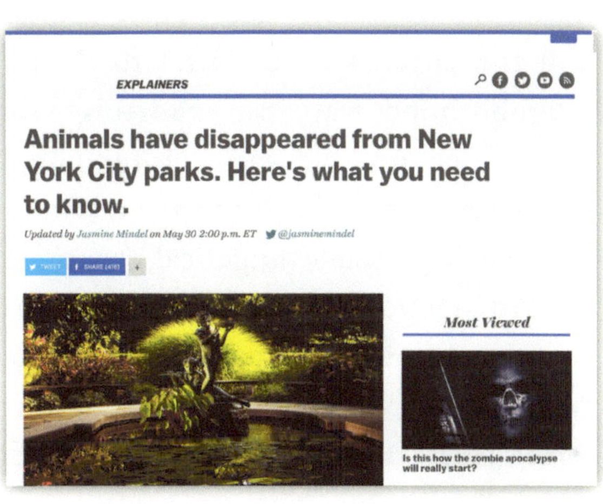

especially when said Retrievers are liked more than the households' actual children. A hint of alarm was starting to grow citywide, moving the worry level from yellow to a light orange in short order, though the actual color-coded national terror alert system was long gone. People started walking their dogs in pairs, then larger groups. Veterinary practices and pet stores started offering boarding services in lieu of grooming, converting every inch of empty space in their establishments into areas for "safe" pet housing. Cats and dogs in dwellings were put in heavy metal cages secured with locks while their owners were at work; local pet shops ran out of them

Leaves *and* Circles

in days. The police formed an *"Animal Investigation and Protection Unit"* with a dozen officers spared to look into the cases. Headlines started taking a more serious tone, with local blogs dispensing with the joke headlines. Reporters began to look somber during their broadcasts.

Next up were pet store break-ins, with no living creatures other than fish left behind. Animal health clinics were hit daily. The newly launched boarding services themselves became prime targets and were often emptied out. The Bronx Zoo didn't have a tiger or bat left in it after June. Community and local religious groups, most of whom openly rejected apocalyptic explanations for the events, asked for donations and began to pool funds for private security, and the latter were the first to float the idea of round-the-clock neighborhood watches, exhorting fellow believers to all become "watchmen on the walls." Inter-hood and interfaith cooperation was at an all-time high, though a few unexpectedly eschatologically-minded Christian evangelical groups, ones that traditionally tended toward symbolic interpretations of scripture, unexpectedly banded together to pick up sticks and head upstate, perhaps thinking their Messiah would be more likely to rapture them if they were on their knees in East Syracuse. It all seems so outlandish, even knowing what I know now: mass pet theft, funds for private security, gorillas just swiped from the zoo like they were a brand-new iPhone sitting on the lap of a dozing straphanger. Interestingly, these efforts seemed to work, at least for a time; I think it was because it forced

people to pay attention, to become fully engaged with what was happening around them. The five boroughs almost felt like a unified community; as overused as that term was, it really applied, more than any time in my memory. It felt real. Or maybe that's all wrong, and I was just projecting. *I* was certainly fully engaged (with every scrap of news I could find.)

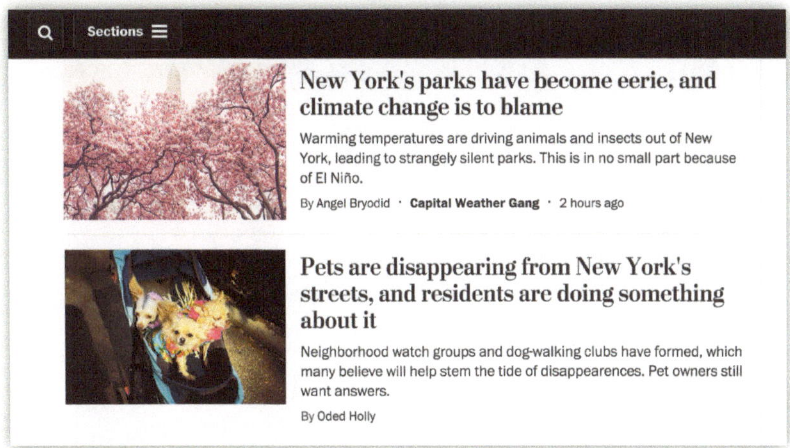

Soon after that, pet disappearances dropped significantly, something like eighty percent in a week according to media sources. The police investigations had so far gone nowhere, occasional discovery of animal bones by a park notwithstanding, but at least no more were going missing for the moment. By the latter half of June things felt like they might finally be under control again, and everyone certainly *wanted* it to feel that way, that's for sure. Worry was there, but receding, if very slowly.

During that period, things felt tentative, transitional, not completely defined.

CH4
DETOUR: DESTINATION IMPORTANT

I'm going to back up here and add some things about two incidents that predated all the previously described ones. One is a popular story about an incident from before the start of the events proper (but it could be that said incident *was* the start of the events), but that nobody, including me, connected to any of the subsequent occurrences. The other is something I personally witnessed, something unnerving, but that I wasn't able to realize the significance of until later on.

Back in the nineteen-eighties and -nineties, and especially the mid-nineties, there was a semi-underground revival of interest in the United States around nature-oriented belief systems like Wicca and dozens of semi-personalized or regionalized variants of what's loosely called "Neo-paganism." Devotees ranged from groups of music fans that had a spiritual awakening or thought it fit well with their forest-goth aesthetic, to teenagers disillusioned with their parents' restrictive form of quasi-suburban northeastern Catholicism. They'd engage in informal rites based on something they'd read on Usenet in places like Prospect Park or Flushing Meadows, things like practicing *Handfasting* or *Cone of Power* invocations, or even the occasional leaf-necklace-only orgy under a copse of sycamores. Mostly an obscure, if oddly appealing, footnote to the era.

Six months prior to the start of the events, five twenty-somethings were discovered mutilated in the area near the Queens Museum in Flushing Meadows Park. It was initially called a mass murder-suicide, then a murder after further analysis, which caused a larger investigation to be launched. On the scene, authorities discovered an *Athame*, a traditional tool in Wicca, covered with the blood of all five victims. The bodies had full autopsies and medical inspections performed, and bodily fluids were found in and on all of them. No fingerprints were found on the blade, but bits of latex residue were found along the hilt, which is what helped change their minds about the first theory. After an extensive investigation involving a multi-borough search, interviews with everyone close to or living in proximity to the victims, and a second set of autopsies, along with a trace of the tool used (which led to an eBay listing from a novelties seller, some kind of neo-hippie surfer making his living out of a beachside house in Far Rockaway), the authorities were stumped. The victims were practicing Wiccans (notably, one of the group was a social worker for teenagers with drug addiction problems, another was an environmental sciences major), had no known enemies, no history of violence, and were apparently well liked. Inter-Wiccan feuds were essentially unheard of, with others in that community expressing shock and even holding a semi-public memorial in the area of the murders in the aftermath. It stopped making sense, and no longer fit any popular narrative.

There was an iconic photo taken at the scene, the sole one related to the investigation that was released to the public: the unmarked upper quarter of a porcelain-skinned girl, with long, curly, fire-red hair laid up against a tree, looking strangely peaceful; it was shown on every story in every newspaper and online post about the case. The other bodies were apparently in such grisly condition that no photos were released, and the details of their disposition were kept purposely vague at the request of those close to the victims. The story petered out after a few months of speculation and rumor, then faded from public consciousness.

The other incident occurred in Prospect Park, the less storied and smaller, only marginally less compelling sibling to our Central

Park in upper mid-Manhattan, itself nestled next to the regal stone pads of the rich and occasionally famous. Though dwarfed in size and prestige, it had its own set of attractions like dense thickets of old-growth trees, unexpected clearings, a hand-shaped peninsula, and an abundance of wildlife. It was a gem of the borough, majestic and haunting, a mix of the semi-wild and the civilized, something attractively gritty about it, just along the edges: Stranahan's masterpiece. It had a magical quality about it, difficult to define.

I was there exploring an area in the central part of the park dense with elms, accessible only by simple dirt paths. I wasn't looking for anything in particular that day, or any day, really; I frequently spent time wandering New York's streets and parks, looking for the unseen, the unexpected, and the haunting, but nothing more specific than that. At one point during the jaunt I heard voices close by, to my right, past a thicket of trees still dressed in full summer green. Guttural, throaty, with long, ragged breath-sounds and streams of repeated syllables, spoken softly. Hebrew, maybe Arabic? I crouched down, listening intently, trying to aurally pattern match the sounds. Having heard both languages on plenty of streets and in countless bodegas before, I was pretty sure it wasn't either of those. I wasn't scared at that point, though I probably should have been. Instead I was intrigued, eager to identify the maker of the gutter-babble, and to discover its nature and possibly its meaning. As gently as I could, I moved aside a small handful of low branches, half-kneeling then, squinting, and peeked through, trying not to make a sound, wary of interrupting.

Curiosity vanished, poof, turning to frozen horror and naked, dry-heaving revulsion. Five individuals were present: a person kneeling on a blanket, covered in a hooded, crimson cowl, facing away from me, that was doing the babbling. Two others, also in cowls of muddy brown and a deep, earthy pine, sat next to a pile of short, neatly cut logs, which they were carving with machine-like precision into perfectly round circles, hollowing out most of the center area of the wood without so much as a ruler, cutting them roughly as thick as a horseshoe. Another of them, also in a muddy brown cloak, was face down in some longish, unmanicured, red-stained grass with haunches up in the air. Near those doing the carving was a pudgy, mustachioed, olive green-uniformed parks department worker leaning against his deep forest green truck adorned with the white leaf logo. He was the only one not robe-clad, and the only one with a visible face. Then there was the dog.

Hanging above a wooden container by both legs, split open from neck to tail, was a full-grown greyhound, thin, yet muscled, with bloody, dog-spaghetti insides just hanging down towards the ground. It was mangled, having the vacuous look that dead things have in its solid black eyes, and what was left of its blood dripped down in intermittent plops into the container below it: a short, half-barrelish thing that resembled those baskets that crabs were forever trying to make their escape from on every corner of Chinatown, but thicker and sturdier.

I was immobilized for a good minute-and-a-half, knee joints locked in place. Once my muscles began cooperating again, and without a breath, I did an immediate one-eighty. I walked on the tips of my toes, gingerly, slowly, trying not to perturb a speck of dirt. Straight ahead. Slowly, slowly, one deliberate, considered step after another. Then, as fast as I could, I ran, unable to remember a time prior to that moment where I had any reason to move that fast. I dashed west, hopping low iron fences and barreling through shrubs, everything a green blur until I reached the edge of the park, where I nearly bowled over a couple of children just beyond the tree line who were sitting on their bikes. I was out of breath, heaving, shaking, shaking, bent over, arms akimbo. The children were terrified then, too, and pealed away from me, away from the park. Away from *that*. Good. Good. Run the hell away from this, I remember thinking.

At other times, I probably would have alerted the authorities like a dutiful citizen, but at that moment I just wanted to get as far away from there, away from that, away from them, as fast as I possibly could; civic duty wasn't anywhere in my thought process just then. As was typical in that area, there wasn't a yellow cab to be found, and I was shaking too much to hold my phone straight enough to summon one in an app or make a phone call. I also couldn't fathom the idea of waiting for a train anywhere near the park after the dog-show-gone-wrong I'd just witnessed.

I caught my breath and did another run straight down Prospect Park West, almost blindly, until I saw a shiny, new, blue-and-white city bus, one of those long accordion-style ones, idling for a brief moment at a stop right near maple-lined Bartel Pritchard Square, which isn't square at all. More of a fancy park-cum-traffic circle. I ripped my Metrocard out of my wallet and leapt up past the entry steps, landing right on the solid bus floor with a semi-hollow thud. I must have had the maddest look on my face just then, grimacing, terrified, brow creased as far inward as it could possibly go, probably aging my forehead roughly a year in just minutes.

Those drivers had likely seen everything in their days—from IPA-soused late night revelers to old, disheveled men smelling of cheap whiskey reciting their theories on who *really* got JFK or how you-know-what was an inside job, so he barely paid me any mind, hardly even looking up from under his MTA baseball cap. I popped the card into the fare slot, nervously tapping my foot during the half-second it took to come out, then sat in the seat closest to the driver, trying to put as much space between myself and the park as I possibly could, though I think I would have preferred flattening myself against the windshield to get even further. I sat there without moving for the rest of the trip, until I was satisfied I was finally far enough away to think, brain refusing to cooperate until we crossed some arbitrary distance threshold that only it knew.

The bus was nearly at Coney Island by the time I felt safe enough, far enough, to disembark from it. The driver gave only the slightest nod as I jumped out, just another nut getting off the bus on his late-ish, typically sleepy little route. Never before had I so badly wanted for Coney to be an actual island again, filled with rabbits and a stretch of water between me and the mainland, detached from anything touching that shambles made of trees and benches and butchered greyhounds. It took several minutes to regain my composure, and I realized that I'd been kneading my phone between my palms like a plastic rock between two pieces of hard dough while squatting down on a street corner. I probably would have looked like a madman, but not many people were outside there at the time, as it was starting to get dark, the liminal tail-end of a ghostly blue hour tapering off, ruining every local photographer's day. I looked up to the sky, which was unclouded, serene in its ghostly blue, and saw a leaf float down from a tree I didn't see. It transfixed me, that leaf, bisected into equal parts deep orange and sienna with veins matching on both sides, vacillating from side to side before falling down into a sewer grate in front of me, causing me to bend my head down to look for it, a sense of deep fascination, but it had already faded out of view, making me feel a gentle sense of *mono no aware*.

Shaking a feeling of enthrallment, I exhaled a long breath through the tiny "O" I made with my lips, hoping to will out all anxiety that was suspended for a moment from my body. I then tapped "Kat" on my phone contact list. She picked right up.

CH5
KAT

Kat, short for Katherine, had been a close friend and itinerant companion of mine for the past several years. Kat worked as a paramedic, which, strangely enough, is what led to us meeting initially. I got doored one day while walking down a seemingly empty back-alley side street in Chinatown, one of those places that always looks like a movie set in a cop show, one where they open the first scene with the coroner placing a body bag over a bullet-ridden corpse or the big bad's secret hideout containing a weapon stash large enough to supply a South American paramilitary. The only vehicles you'd typically see there were vans for some video production company or ones delivering donuts to offices of companies you'd never think would even be there, because you

wouldn't think that there'd be offices there in the first place. It always seemed like the kind of place that existed in a kind of hollow nether-state, having no inhabitants or actual function except to serve as a backdrop.

There was a stout tan car with a hand-painted white stripe painted sloppily around it on the horizontal, and no plates. It was a Yugo, of all things, probably the best car to get doored by if you're planning on getting doored at all, which I don't recommend. No one appeared to be inside it when I first saw, but as soon as I approached, wham, a flash of white-striped metal slammed right into my torso, knocking me flat on my back and causing me to see spots. The door closed and they sped off.

No one was ever caught despite an actual investigation, with a detective following up with me just days later proving that one had taken place. I'd guessed that the usual alley parkers were helpful in ensuring the investigation happened, putting pressure on the cops; they apparently hated having anyone park there who wasn't part of their crew, especially their neo-paparazzi competitors trying to get fresh shots of the local mini-celebrity for their Instagrams. Yugo ninja probably thought I was paparazzi, too, and wanted to send a message or maybe return the favor for a previous slight; the competition in that business was apparently fierce, and I inadvertently got in the middle of it.

I wasn't hurt too badly, the extent of it being a dull ache in the abdomen and chest with some buzzy ear ringing, more mosh pit injury than hit-and-run. Kat treated me; she was thorough and very patient, staying until she was sure I'd gotten my bearings (and maybe guarding me in case my attacker returned) so I offered to take her out to coffee to thank her, and she said yes. I found out she was a fellow lover of Roasting Plant, Lower East Side's best coffee spot, and a friendship was born; after that, we were mostly inseparable. We had the strange ability to communicate without saying many words, though it was more one-way; she said she'd learned to read facial expressions and body language by watching TV with the sound off when she was a kid, staying up late after school trying not to wake her father, when he was there at all. Whether that origin story was true or not, I don't know, but I enjoyed the thought of it. Though initially on the tight-lipped side, subjects like local history, how neighborhoods were changing, or where to get great Pho tended to get her talking back then. I miss those days.

For background, Kat was "raised" by her father, her own use of air quotes, but there's not much to tell since she was always rather brief on the subject, and I had no desire to push it. He ignored her almost completely as a kid, rarely present, then nearly completely absent when she was a teenager. She wasn't even sure if he actually still lived at the apartment at all, but someone was paying the rent. She'd been attending school in Queens part-time when the events started, adding some extra medical courses she hoped would help with jobs down the line, maybe physician's assistant or RN. Always in demand, apparently.

She wasn't planning on staying at the apartment much longer, either, with it serving just as a place to sleep until she was able save up some money and finish the round of classes she was taking. She had no particular attachment to the place (she was thankful to be living rent-free, though), and she didn't expect that it would be ghost-paid forever, so she was already planning her subsequent moves. That was essential Kat, always thinking three steps ahead.

After the events got serious our interactions grew more terse, Kat's microexpression and slash language reader turned up high to substitute for speech, and her EMT procedure training kicked in hardcore. Kat was always extremely organized and focused, which helped us survive, especially at the beginning when I was so *unfocused*, less human and more *William Infovorus*. Topics of conversation narrowed, becoming things like where we should sleep, how we should fortify, what supplies we needed, how much food was left, which routes seemed safest, and later, them. She was the exact right person needed, doing the exact right things at the exact right times: the antidote to the chaos and uncertainty unfolding around us, especially for me, who was largely blind to the hard facts on the ground until later on. Kat was the *Realpolitik* to my academe.

CH6
BACK ON THE DETOUR

"William? You haven't called. Are you OK?" I told her I wasn't, flipping phone from ear to ear. No, not really. Not at all. After a brief moment of silence, she informed me that she was coming to pick me up, then summoned an Uber with me still on the line to make sure I wasn't *completely* losing it. She had the driver race to where I was: "Big tip if you beat traffic," I heard her say, and she got to where I was in record time; Mr. Nassir certainly earned his Benjamin, and in cash. I sat diagonally across the black leather seats, barely able to hold myself up straight, slipping on the smooth material, head slumped against the window, trying to use it to hold myself up.

While we sped towards the Williamsburg Bridge, Kat relayed to me some strange recent happenings at her school, and I felt like it was the first real conversation we'd had in a month. Apparently, many people had stopped showing up over the prior weeks: a couple of students in a class here, a TA there, some professor. The school administration was concerned, and had launched a formal investigation into it; they were apparently hoping it was either an illness or some sort of defection to another institution. Something they could either explain easily, or explain easily *and* get outraged about. On that day, it was discovered that an entire research department, a professor, several grad students, some lab techs, and a group of undergrads involved with the department had apparently disappeared some weeks prior, their research vanishing along with them: hard drives gone, paper notebooks missing, a couple of databases wiped clean, and some unspecified school property stolen. Which department wasn't named, but Kat said the rumors were about it having something to do with historical research. Of what nature, she wasn't sure.

We arrived on the street my apartment was on, a rundown studio right on the edge of Chinatown, not far from *"Lighting Row"* on the Bowery, that glowy, ever-blinking stretch of avenue that seemed to have every possible permutation of lamp and sign display, with names like *"Lighting by Jim," "Lights Give You Lighting,"* and *"Lights for Lights Sake."* As we turned the corner, a backlit sign the color of dusk pulled me back to that sewer grate and that leaf, such a lonely object, probably not seen as a distinct entity before I glimpsed it in that brief instant before it disappeared into the subterranean void. I felt a flash of pity for it, but the tire screech as the cab came to a halt brought me back to the present, causing me to slide forward on the smooth seat and nearly slip into the footwell.

Not many apartments like mine left at the time, but I lucked out, having once fixed the landlord's servers at a local gambling joint disguised as an innocuous-looking tea parlor, weirdly stereotypical in an imagined American Chinatown noir-movie kind of way. Definitely not what I was expecting when I answered that Craigslist ad offering "great money to repair a hard drive," which actually turned into "great money to attempt to get as much illegal book-keeping data off a dying hard drive before it wound up in a blast furnace at a steel factory in Buffalo." He appreciated the work (and discretion), and so gave me first dibs on the place. I tried not to think much about how the landlord made his money, but I wasn't going to say no to cash and a cheap apartment in a market like that; I opted to laugh it off, with no small amount of unease, instead.

The apartment itself was a functional, if minuscule, fourth story walkup in a run down, faded-brick building above a restaurant equipment store featuring a huge faux-wood sign printed with

     Leaves *and* Circles

bright orange type. Abutting the store's entrance was the door to my building, which was designed, with some humor, to resemble a door leading to a restaurant kitchen, shining silver with round, criss-crossed windows near the top. The outside looked decent enough, perfectly adequate to impress the local restaurateurs who frequented it, but inside was a different story.

The stairwell had a shabby set of walls in peeling chunks of gray paint, revealing underlying layers of white, lime-green, and mauve underneath. No graffiti or other human markings, but enough dried, multi-colored gum to seal a hole in an aircraft carrier along the edges of the steps. A lack of railings was another less-than-handy feature, especially when ascending six flights straight up after a twelve-hour shift crawling on hands and knees plugging in Ethernet cables. The apartment itself was decrepit, far from the shabby-chic so popular on hip real-estate blogs at the time. No, this one had the real deal shabbiness, with red bricks exposed intermittently from underneath a thin plaster wall of ambiguous white-gray, probably last painted while Clinton was still in office. Two windows were bricked over, exposing no light from outside, leaving the apartment perpetually dim. The others worked fine, not drafty at all, but with a bevy of scuffmarks from endless opening and closing over the years. The place was fairly sparse anyway, with just a mattress on the floor and a shiny new Macbook, whirring softly, with a sleek three-button Logitech mouse on a plain white, wheeled wooden table sitting nearby. It was dirt cheap, too, bookie landlord refraining from squeezing me on the rent, figuring I'd come fix his broken server whenever he wanted me to. Recent events have put that on the "things to never again worry about" list, however.

"What happened?" she asked gently, trying not to show too much urgency, trying not to rattle me further, but she was clearly concerned. I was still shaking, clenching and unclenching my fists like I was holding an invisible stress ball made of some inexplicably squishy gel. I told her to wait until we got upstairs, as it was just too much to summarize. I hobbled, one arm around her neck, to the curb, stiff leaves cartwheeling by and crackling, air unexpectedly dry. We pushed through the door, Kat practically dragging me up the steps, then finally into the apartment. I staggered into the bed, eyes glassy, laying down flat across the mattress to face the ceiling.

She did a short bunny hop into the bed and turned herself around to face me, ending in a muffled plop, seating herself cross-legged, leaning forward with her palms on her chin. She listened intently, occasionally nodding or taking a mental note, sensing that I needed to get it all out at once; I didn't really explain it, more like expurgated it, everything in painstaking detail, reading off memories from a film reel, frame by frame.

It's amazing how something like that, lasting only a moment could have so much to describe, have so many pieces to ponder and analyze, with every single object in the frame possibly holding a deeper meaning, some clue as to what it all meant. What was the parks worker doing? What was it about a circle made out of wood that had him staring so intently? What were the circles about, anyway? What was the language, and what were they saying? Are we talking psychotropics or some new synthetic drug that the Feds hadn't managed to make illegal yet, rebel ex-chemists seemingly always a step ahead of them?

At the end of my monologue, she breathed out a long, rounded breath, and didn't speak a word, her brain in full-on processing mode. A siren wailed in the distance, nothing out of ordinary for New York, dovetailing with a previously unnoticed ear ringing, then collapsing into the cacophony of the city night. I collapsed into the bed, utterly spent, dreamless. I didn't wake up until half a day later.

She was crouched over my laptop, feet on the chair underneath her, eyes half-squinted, left hand gripping her chin, with a long-sleeved, black-and-charcoal sweatshirt with some kind of half-faded human face on it pulled down past her knees, reading intently. Focused, scanning. She must have had twenty tabs open, all varied sources by the look of the favicons, round and colorful. I sat up, dazed, blinking, but at that moment I was serene, like that feeling you get just after getting over lying in bed with the flu for a week: buoyant, comfortably empty. She was there sitting at my Macbook like she did most weekends when she would wake up before me, like nothing unusual was happening, the same old feelings of comforting familiarity you come to expect when noticing those kinds of unconscious, regular habits. The previous day's events hadn't yet entered my mind.

"I did some searching," she said flatly, eyes still fixed on the

LCD. That's when it all came rushing back: cloaks, circles, running madly, fear, panic, the bus ride, the dog. The dog. Agh. I tend to pet every dog I see on the street, so that particular memory put my stomach on the floor, somewhere halfway between the bed's edge and the front door. I imagined that she must be reading blog posts with names like "Semiotics of Hood-Robed Dog Murder Cults: A Treatise" just then, wondering immediately what she'd managed to find out.

"I found a bunch of forum posts, people posting about weird shit happening in parks. People in colorful cloaks, dead animals, squirrels, mostly, and—"

"And what?" I asked, tentative, almost not sure I wanted to know the answer just yet.

"Circles carved out of wood, just like you saw." At least there were no dogs involved, which had a measure of comfort to it. I sat there, thinking intently, hand across my mouth squeezing my cheeks, lips pursed tight like a politician trying to weather a question on a tough topic they'd rather pretend didn't exist, trying to make some kind of sense of it all, vexed.

"This is going to be a summer of some kind," she mused with purposeful understatement and a terse snort.

CH7
MIDSUMMER, NO DREAMS

Early July, year one

The middle of summer, quite mild, no scorching ninety-five degree days or record energy use remarked breathlessly by the local heads in boxes. Animals (the few that remained, anyway) had stopped disappearing, but people were still agitated, twitchy. It was long a popular trope to moan about a return to "the bad old days" of the eighties, but no one could have envisioned anything like that. In the span of a few short months, those burned-out shells of buildings, those ghastly symbols of supposed liberal urban policy failure that haunted Democrats for so long would become a reality once again, but not because of fire department cutbacks or alleged insurance scams. No, the old version would probably seem comforting compared to what was coming, since as bad as events were back in those decades, they occurred in a world that was horrible in ways that were at least graspable by anyone who'd spent any time as a functional adult with access to a newspaper in the past century. This was very different.

The lull in the events came to an end early that July, first with the homeless. Those long regarded—or, more typically not regarded at all—as the most vulnerable among us began to disappear from the streets in a pattern no one likely knew and few even really cared about. In waves? In bursts? Drunken park sleepers in Greenpoint, gone. Subway panhandlers who liked to start their speeches with an

City Officials Play Down Animal Disappearances

By PHILIP THEODORE SCRIMMIN   JULY 3

The Mayor, City Council, and Police Commissioner declared at a joint news conference in Lower Manhattan yesterday that the spate of pet kidnappings were the "work of independent individuals and groups trying to cash in on the growing New York 'Luxury Pet' trade." Officials maintained that monitoring of city pets and their owners would be continued, but that the threat was temporary and should warrant only awareness and heightened vigilance, rather than a full-scale

always-polite, "Good evening ladies and gentlemen," were nowhere to be found. Stories about what was happening to them were initially fragmented and scattered, still far from being noticed by mass media, but indicating a clear trend; I picked up this information from small, local blogs and neighborhood-level forums, so it's anecdotal and very likely incomplete.

The Bowery Mission, with its beautiful stained glass windows and fire-engine red, doublewide door, long a refuge for those discarded by society, was generally filled with people. With the Great Recession and the spiraling housing cost crisis, its numbers swelled almost daily. After the disappearances began, it was nearly empty whenever I passed by it, with few drawn faces, weathered by the streets and long

lives of addiction or bad luck. This fact went largely unremarked upon, too, even though actual people were disappearing; the local rags we euphemistically called "newspapers" generally only complained when homelessness appeared to be going up, not down.

Next, older people started vanishing, with an article here or there about an independent elderly person mysteriously gone missing from their apartment or someone at a care home wandering out due to "dementia" and simply never returning, a few choice quotes taken from some distraught relative to round them out. Concerned that people might still be raw from the previous incidents, the police, the city government, and unusually, the local media started to take great pains to try to separate the new spate of disappearances from the prior ones, dialing back the hysterical headlines, taking on an uncharacteristically balanced and sober tone, trying to manage the public's reaction (alerts from the municipal Silver Alert system were telling a very different story.) Reports on the homeless and elder disappearances, though initially sparse, continued percolating up from the local level to the mainstream. Not front page material at that point, but working their way up, and increasing in number on a daily basis, squeezing through a news-pipe that was being throttled to the width of a straw. It didn't work, though.

People knew something was up.

Mid-July, year one

Cracks in the info-dam started to appear. It was clear that the administration and media were coordinating, increasingly keen on preventing outright panic, providing daily messages of reassurance and constant updates about the efforts of authorities. They made careful use of language and tone, a throwback to a previous age of the media, Cronkite-esque; "Criminals" rather than "Terrorists" was the standard moniker used in titles and copy to describe the abductors—a conspicuously understated choice. That instinct was probably a good one, but the bleak tone of user-created posts and comments belied the under-control narrative of officials and reporters.

The city mood was by measures sober and tense again during mid-month, wound just tight enough to keep people alert, but without yet spilling over into the streets, though things were deteriorating daily. You could see it people's faces, in the way they looked at you, looked over their shoulders, held their bags just a little bit closer, a little bit tighter. As the month progressed, the mood darkened, and a twitchy, quivering fear became palpable, everyone wound tight, suspicious, like we were all expecting everything to just suddenly come apart at any moment, ready for the metaphorical blood in the streets. The Guardian Angels, long dormant, were patrolling neighborhoods around the clock, in addition to the aforementioned ad-hoc watch groups. Many members were young, obviously new, membership rolls swelling along with the crisis. It was a new-old era, with all our troubles compressed into the short time period of a few months rather than building to a boil over most of a decade, when the blackout gave

Cordon Evacuees Are Not Victims

By **THE EDITORIAL BOARD**   July 3

Email

Share

Tweet

Save

More

Over the past few months, New York City has been facing its most serious crisis since the Sept. 11, 2001, terrorist attack on the World Trade Center. A large number of New York City residents, which experts estimate to be roughly twenty-one hundred, have disappeared with few clues about the nature of, or motive for the crimes.

Recently, the mayor of New York ordered a mandatory closure of city parks and beaches due to extreme safety concerns, which we believe was the most sensible course of actions to safeguard New Yorkers.

While we sympathize with those forced to temporarily leave their homes and take shelter elsewhere, we believe the continued public attacks on the mayor's policies are misguided, and the veiled threats directed towards City Hall should be considered dangerous in these difficult times.

In particular, those residents calling the cordons "unjustified" or "completely unfair", several of whom are implicated in scandals involving schemes to surreptitiously or forcibly evict tenants from their homes to pave the way for their own real estate projects should be regarded as engaging in rank hypocrisy. Instead of calls for the mayor's resignation, these citizens should heed the mayor's call to lend resources to the way to the crack epidemic and people watched the inexorable slow-motion slide.

Things really started to turn as the month wore on. It was no longer just some person no one knew anymore, a stranger, a hermit, a derelict, or a shut-in, living alone. Children were disappearing. Teenagers. Adults. No one was immune, and we all knew it.

That was the point when the mayor ordered parks and beaches closed and cordoned off, with a two-block buffer zone erected around them. People living in buildings nearby were part of a mandatory "temporary" relocation to tent housing in places like the Sixty-Ninth Regiment Armory or at expanded city shelters, many of which were being used by the homeless that still hadn't disappeared. There were howls of protest at City Hall from people living along Fifth Avenue or Central Park West, but the mayor held firm. There was no small measure of schadenfreude expressed at this turn of events, and the major opinion pages jumped all over it, making frequent use of the word "hypocrisy."

The buffer zones were surrounded by police lights, the large, round, bright ones you'd normally see hanging off some sort of crane-like contraption in Hell Square to deter drunkards or in high-crime areas to prevent street violence, and steel barricades topped with some kind of taut, "humane" alternative to barbed wire, a kind of mesh. Police were already wildly overstretched, so members of neighborhood groups were deputized, and auxiliary cops were given a one-day training course, armed with batons, a flashlight, and a hand gun. This prompted one of the first waves of departures, many of them high-profile, but with numbers small enough to not cause too much alarm, though I doubt the mayor would have been able to count on many donations from the museum-and-collector set after that. The head of one of the major museums by Central Park, a local resident on Central Park West forced to move, resigned in protest in an open letter to City Hall, and outrage from others in the city's elite similarly uprooted began appearing in local Op-Eds. An iconic photo of a group of officers in full body armor standing back to back in a circle atop a pile of multi-hued leaves while the barricades were being erected near the Apple Store defined the moment, however brief it was.

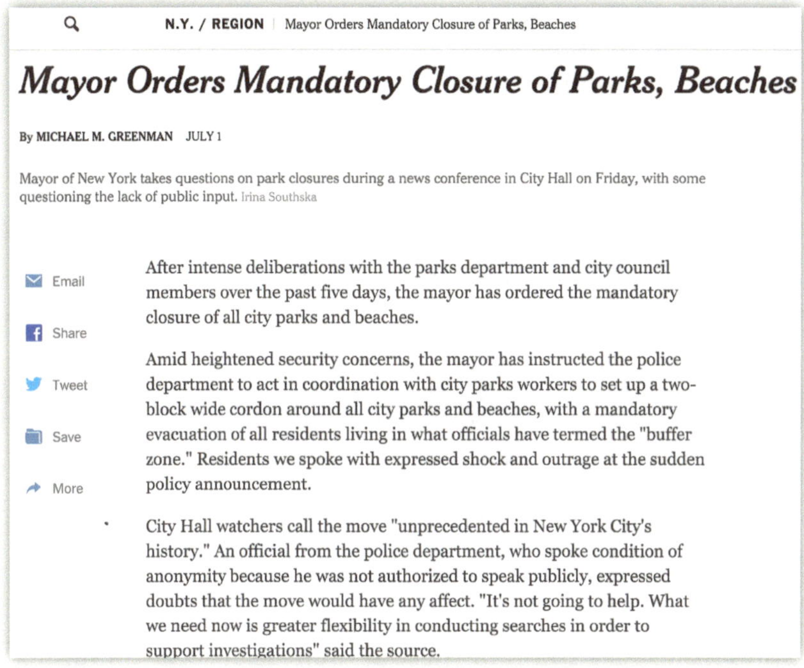

Mayor Orders Mandatory Closure of Parks, Beaches

By MICHAEL M. GREENMAN   JULY 1

Mayor of New York takes questions on park closures during a news conference in City Hall on Friday, with some questioning the lack of public input. Irina Southska

Email

Share

Tweet

Save

More

After intense deliberations with the parks department and city council members over the past five days, the mayor has ordered the mandatory closure of all city parks and beaches.

Amid heightened security concerns, the mayor has instructed the police department to act in coordination with city parks workers to set up a two-block wide cordon around all city parks and beaches, with a mandatory evacuation of all residents living in what officials have termed the "buffer zone." Residents we spoke with expressed shock and outrage at the sudden policy announcement.

City Hall watchers call the move "unprecedented in New York City's history." An official from the police department, who spoke condition of anonymity because he was not authorized to speak publicly, expressed doubts that the move would have any affect. "It's not going to help. What we need now is greater flexibility in conducting searches in order to support investigations" said the source.

So did the cordon work? Sort of, but I think it actually did more to delineate and outline people's fears, rather than lessen them. Intrepid pedestrians who passed by the edges of blocked off areas would report and record the sounds of faint whispers carrying through the air coming from within, and more than one officer asked to be relieved of duty because of it. Lower-ranked staff at multiple security agencies asked to be allowed to investigate, but were blocked from those higher up the chain, with superiors citing an inability to spare additional resources with all the other crises occurring, concerns for officer safety, and a bad risk/reward profile. The mayor reluctantly backed the bans despite well-publicized personal misgivings, but the city council and most top ranked security officials were adamant about them. Helicopter overflights

Leaves *and* Circles

were also banned. Drones equipped with cameras were sent inside the zones by amateurs and professionals alike, but none were able to stream anything for more than a few minutes before the devices were disabled or destroyed by unseen attackers. Most footage that was recovered just showed some greenery or the occasional pile of chopped up logs similar to the ones I saw that day with the dog in Prospect Park.

Stop-and-frisk came back with a vengeance, with all restrictions on the rules of engagement lifted, and there was little pushback that time, though I don't think even a single one of the abductors was caught that way. Checks were completely random, as the security services didn't have anything they could even use for profiling. Searches were more or less constant at movie theaters (even though those were nearly empty by then anyway, a complete waste of resources); subways and bus stops; and right on the street, with no major traffic arteries without a checkpoint of some kind. That was the beginning of nightmare traffic worse than any rush hour you could imagine. Manhattan was generally bad enough before the changes; after the new policy was put in place, we became more Lagos than East Coast, and people were urged to stop driving into the city altogether, which many did. A congestion pricing measure, something that had little traction in the past, was hastily approved by the city council, and the response was mostly just muted grumbles due to the severity of the situation, and the unsurprising fact that fewer people were driving into the borough in the first place.

Cameras, too, were put up on just about every mountable surface, with consultants from Britain's *BSIA* brought in to assist with the deployment. Stocks for facial recognition software companies skyrocketed that week. Protests by local civil liberties groups, much more tepid than in the past, weren't even paid lip service. The head of the ACLU, usually paid some respect by city officials, was escorted out after raising a rather mild objection to the particulars of a certain policy at a Q&A with the mayor. That's how far things had gone.

Scattered flyers for missing persons began to pop up on light poles, like so many band ads in the nineteen-nineties East Village, telling you about ten-band Grunge Night at Coney Island High, and a trope of practically every movie involving the living dead over the past two decades. Most posts, though, were actually made online, where more people were likely to see them.

"Missing Wife." "Have you seen my son?" "Help Me Find My Niece." Facebook was flooded with messages like those, and dedicated pages and groups were being created and updated at a rapid clip; Instagram seemed to have nothing but missing persons reports, and no cats or snapshots of food in sight; Twitter, too, was filled with "last seen" reports, accounts popping up to track missing people by borough, neighborhood, and eventually block, operating twenty-four seven. Dedicated missing persons web sites popped up like so much digital kudzu. Some helped, I think, but far too many wound up being attempts at phishing or money transfer scams.

 Leaves *and* Circles

Painful to think that in even in a crisis of that scale, people were still ready to pounce on the vulnerable and unsuspecting. Grassroots efforts were largely encouraging, if not terribly effective. I wonder now if even

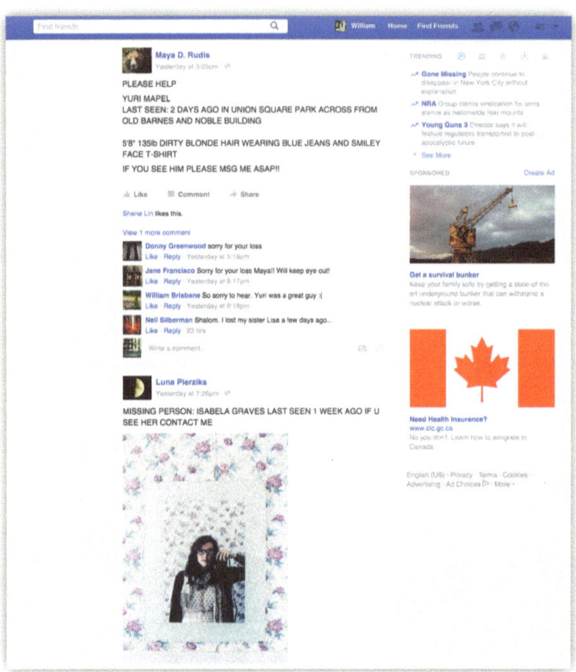

a single person who went missing was ever found; I certainly never heard of any. It did help keep people engaged, though, which in retrospect seemed very important, both to slow the rate of disappearances and to keep people away from the metaphorical ledge. The supply of hope was shrinking along with the population.

It was all out in the open then, front and center, pushing out any and all other concerns on the national stage, with round the clock speculation, analysis, expert commentary, psychic predictions, and offers of help from mediums and just about anyone involved with paranormal "studies." Ex-CIA, NSA, military, doctors of everything from sociology to anthropology were asked (or crawled out of the woodwork all on their own) to provide an answer. Distant conflicts, migration and refugee issues, even terrorism concerns no longer registered with people in the face of the crisis, one with visible effects, but invisible causes.

How exactly enormous numbers of people were disappearing without a single witness or suspect was as puzzling as it was chilling, so collectively, New York was dazed. Police patrols were out in full force, with spotlights and mobile vans running twenty-four seven.

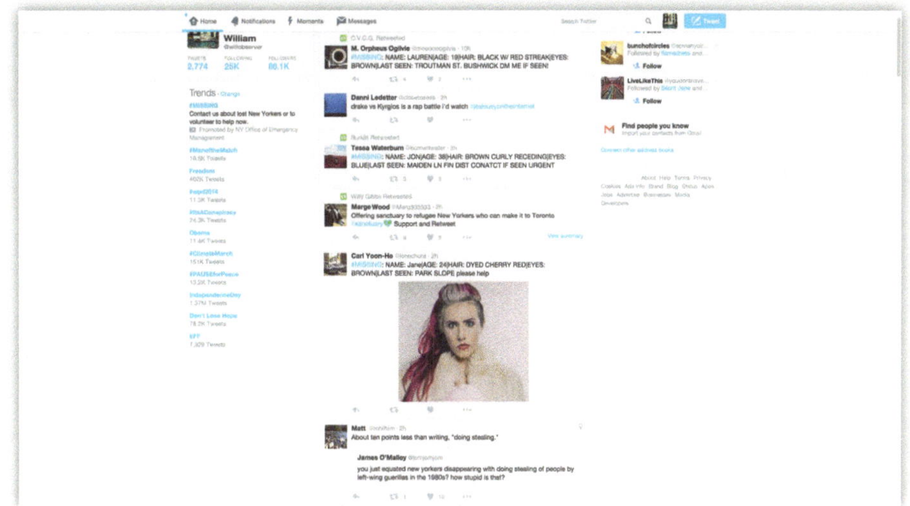

The city council passed an ordinance allowing unlimited overtime for emergency services. They also asked for help from the federal government, who ordered military units in, and from the state government, who called up the National Guard. The Sullivan Act was suspended for the first time in its history. New York suddenly had its own version of open carry: bats, blackjacks, pipes, knives, and just about any household object that could be wielded as a weapon were soon seen at everyone's sides. Seeing a rail-thin fifteen year old wearing a pair glowing black and green Nikes, walking around with a piece of rebar swinging at their hip might have turned some heads just a few weeks earlier, but now no one was batting an eye.

Near the end of July, the NYPD announced that they'd caught a group; finally, we had something.

CH8
GITMO ON THE HUDSON, OR ACTUALLY, THE EAST RIVER

Late July, year one

Three men in Midtown, not far from Times Square, were caught trying to grab a forklift worker from the loading dock of a well-worn warehouse building, one of those probably-was-once-a-Vaudeville-theater ones that looked like it hadn't been washed since that era. Nothing about the three screamed sinister, dangerous, or even remarkable, beyond the fact that they were two blocks from the M&M store dressed up like Friar Tucks. This was Times Square, though, home to a hundred furry red Elmos and walking pieces of candy, so three nondescript people in robes would have barely registered. That is, until they were spotted trying to snatch up one Juan Diego Garcia, thirty-eight, of Corona, Queens, trying to load up boxes of sequins into an off-white box truck destined for a fashion business near FIT. The group tried to escape from the crush, to break through a solid wall of furious humanity, but it was futile with people wired on caffeine and bloodlust. People rushed from the Square, mobbing the scene, with many recording the entire thing with their phones. It was standing room only, a tangle of legs nearly crushing the group underfoot, a mass of people grabbing and tearing the group's cloaks, kicking, stomping, whaling on them with their improvised weapons, channeling the entire city's desire for vengeance, justice. The whole block was a PG-13 version of a Tarantino movie, with the blood splatters to prove it.

Eight uniformed officers, full black and blue, flew from a nearby pedestrian plaza, knocking street umbrellas and tables over in the process, then morphed into urban rugby players, piling on top of the suspects, bearing down on them with nightsticks. People hooted and hollered, elated, pumped; they danced in the streets. "Finally!" "Holy crap this is going on YouTube!" "Don't fuck with NYC!" We were finally getting somewhere.

Or not. According to information leaked to the press from inside sources, the suspects were to be held indefinitely, with *Habeas Corpus* suspended for anyone suspected to be involved with the disappearances, based on an order signed by the mayor and immediately agreed to by the city council. The suspects were subjected to brutal interrogations, every macabre Cheney-esque fantasy method from waterboarding to Iranian Shah-era de-nailing reportedly entertained. "Enhanced Interrogation Techniques" were suddenly back in fashion, with no one in any mood to raise objections this time around. Vengeance, not mercy or adherence to process, was guiding us.

Unfortunately, it didn't work. We know torture doesn't work under the most "ideal" circumstances; it certainly wasn't working with a bunch of mute, robe-wearing, death-cult nutjobs with no known ideology, outside affiliations, or demands who were snatching people out of their beds while they slept. They had a level of discipline other groups could only dream of.

As far as the "leaks" went, some suspected that they were leaked accidentally on purpose in an attempt to mollify the administration's increasingly strident critics, and to try to boost everyone's flagging morale. The suspects were held in a secret local detention facility, rumored to have been hastily erected on the disused South Brother Island, formerly the site of a single house and a mass of trees on the East River. North Brother was considered first, in the old smallpox hospital where Typhoid Mary was held, but a team dispatched there found the site *"unusable"* according to one report, which I suspect meant that something they didn't want to leak was discovered there.

The group styled orange DOC jumpsuits for nearly a week, but they were impassive, with not a single word uttered by any of them the entire time they were held. Nothing. They were then reportedly moved to another facility (likely run by the feds for a second crack at them, or maybe even renditioned, as one rumor had it) for further "processing." Everyone knew exactly what that meant.

As a result of the interrogation failures, the mayor's office and the city council became furious, as they'd been putting serious pressure on the police brass for quick results. People's patience had grown wire-thin in the city, and formerly supportive civil society groups started grumbling about the administration's, and particularly the mayor's, performance. I understood that, with people feeling angry and powerless, but the truth is that everyone probably knew that no one else was likely to accept the job, and snap elections in that environment were a complete non-starter, anyway. What could he do, the mayor, and what could anyone else do better? I didn't envy him his position, and I think even his harshest critics understood deep down that replacing him at a time like that was essentially impossible, so their reaction was uncharacteristically subdued. They may have wished for his resignation, but they were in no position to ask for it.

The group the police caught apparently had no records, no ties to gangs, no prior arrests, and backgrounds that were stunningly ordinary: marketer. Graphic artist. City sanitation worker. They were nobody, but suddenly they were part of a network thought responsible for the largest spate of kidnappings, maybe the first truly mass kidnapping America had ever experienced. The media excoriated them after that, or tried to, with column after column spent exploring the mundane, largely unremarkable lives of three men no one had heard of until that night. Small peccadilloes, college rumors; everything was dredged up. Nothing substantive, and certainly nothing that would indicate their eventual membership in a mass people-snatching cult. I doubt if they even got to see any of it, they were probably buried so deep. I wondered what happened to them.

CH9
PANIC AT THE DUMBO

I slept less those first months than any time in the previous ten years, spending nights poring over forum and social media posts, conferring with reporters and names I'd seen on local blogs a hundred times (but never would have contacted, having no reason to before all this), and updating tracking databases with the latest data I'd gathered. I emailed back and forth with journalists, feeding them updates, and getting interesting tidbits in return, items to add to my own dataset. Lots of people had the same idea, so we banded together, collecting data to source news stories and keep our internal databases (which fed into our dashboards and leaderboards) updated. I consumed interminable posts on Facebook, Twitter, and Instagram, trying to synthesize the different sources into a coherent whole, keeping everything in a spreadsheet, hoping to have a local copy in case the many online tools that were serving the same function went down. I'd previously had it in a local database I'd hosted on my own network connection, exposed via a simple interface I'd hastily thrown together, but it got completely slammed with traffic, forcing me to take it offline and go ultra low-tech.

Sometimes I'd spent half a night going back and forth with people on Snapchat or WhatsApp, just feeding people the nuggets I'd gotten from other sources, and emailing around copies of my spreadsheet. Definitely not the best idea from a data integrity perspective, but I felt like I couldn't trust shared data stores, worried that they could shut down or go read-only at any time.

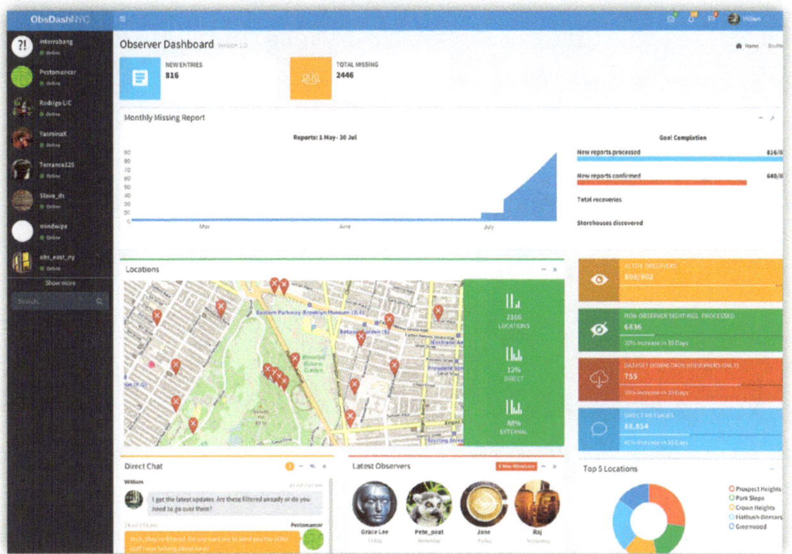

We called ourselves "Observers," but that moniker only covered the barest sliver of what we actually did; we were a combination of satellites collecting data, conduits transmitting to and from appropriate parties, and nodes in an organic, distributed computing system, doing our own cross-correlating, synthesis, and analysis work. In China, they had something called a "Human Flesh Search Engine," a system based on massive human collaboration that was used to find out the identities of individuals being singled out for social opprobrium to dox them, but we transmogrified that idea into something else: a way to try to help find people who went missing (which I think was a total failure); to warn about locations of recent disappearances; to supply people with info on local refugee centers (which did some good, I like to think); and to tell people about where they might be able to get themselves picked up by possible rescue teams. I'm not sure exactly how much of our work actually helped in the end, but I was putting my IT skills to use, real use, instead of just helping small-time bookies save their data from the vicissitudes of magnetic media or troubleshooting someone's server problems, and I felt really good about that. Proud, even.

It was during that mid-to-late summer period that I started making a connection between the Wicca murders and what was happening at the time. One of my contacts, a "forum-watcher" named *"interrobang,"* though his real name was Pavel, started sending me screenshots from invite-only Wicca and Neo-pagan forums that he was keeping an eye on. Pavel was some kind of religious studies student working on his PhD, and he'd spend his days on forums run by local religious groups, earning their trust both by professing to be an adherent and having encyclopedic knowledge of the minutiae of everything from the Old Testament to the Book of Shadows, so he had no problem getting in and being accepted as an insider.

interrobang was getting nervous. He began seeing warnings on Wicca forums he was observing: *"Refuse invitations to meet with people you don't know personally."* Prior to that, the Wiccans were a fairly open, welcoming bunch, meeting up with semi-unknowns to spiral dance in the leaves together or to have inter-group picnics-slash-feasts. Pavel said they were going on complete lockdown, preventing new accounts from being created and banning those people that messaged others without knowing them in real life. Word spread quickly after an admin on one forum admitted reading some old message logs, one of which contained an invitation that said admin confirmed was sent to the environmental sciences student that was part of the murdered group of five; the invitation was sent from an unknown party in the days before the incident. Pavel was emphatic about the fact that the people on those forums were gentle and non-violent, and that, in his opinion, the perpetrators were actually outsiders posing as true believers in order to lure their victims, and I believed him. He still tried to keep me up-to-date with what useful information he could glean, but it was fairly scant after the newer scares; most communication apparently went offline, according to him. That probably wasn't good for his thesis research, but he didn't even care at that point; he was genuinely concerned for their safety, but found himself roadblocked on both counts.

Another notable thing that happened during the events, and that we Observers were plugged into, was the rise of certain themes

Thread	Poster	Replies	Views	Rating	Posted	Updated
Dead animals in Prospect Park Page 1, 2, 3, 4, 5, 6, 7	Uncle Lou	196	6,938	★★★★☆ (47)	yesterday 12:24 PM	today 6:10 PM
DAE see robe-people in Kissena?! Page 1, 2, 3, 4, 5, 6	Anonymous Coward	170	8,802	★★★★☆ (51)	today 6:30 AM	today 6:02 PM
Circles, circles, everywhere: some kind of IRL game [my theory] Page 1, 2, 3, 4, 5, 6, 7, ... 752, 753, 754, 755, 756, 757, 758, 759	Maryann	22,753	1,509,092	★★★★ (531)	05/20/14 9:20 AM	today 6:11 PM
Robe people are just LARPers	Anonymous Coward	3	115	★★★★★ (3)	today 6:00 PM	today 6:11 PM
I found animal guts in front of my house and I'm freaking out Page 1, 2, 3	LadyPorcelain	80	1,846	★★ (35)	yesterday 2:45 PM	today 6:11 PM
Has anyone tried talking to robe people yet?	MindsEye	24	1,264	★★★★★ (28)	today 1:55 PM	today 6:10 PM
My dog (black poodle/beagle mix) went missing :-([Richmond Hill]	The Hoist	27	768	★★★★★ (10)	today 4:37 PM	today 6:09 PM
I stole a circle and here's what I found Page 1, 2	MsBlair	32	440	★★★★★ (11)	today 5:08 PM	today 6:08 PM
Weird whispering/chanting/babbling in Forest Park Page 1, 2	Anonymous Coward	33	1,040	★★★★★ (14)	today 3:05 PM	today 6:07 PM
[Serious] Where can I buy a handgun? Page 1, 2	xxJusticexx	60	4,353	★★★★☆ (6)	today 1:04 PM	today 6:05 PM
I asked my Wiccan friend about them and here's what she said Page 1, 2	allturnswhite	41	1,679	★★★★★ (21)	today 1:03 PM	today 6:05 PM

in what's known on the Internet as "creepypasta," which Wikipedia describes as *"often brief, user generated ghost or alien stories intended to scare readers,"* which is true as far as it goes, but quite insufficient in describing that particular slice of net culture. Across the genre's corpus, creepypasta themes and iconography were fairly loosely connected, without a single set of clearly recognizable, repeated motifs; instead, a loose style and distribution methods were what tended to link works in the genre together. It was this fact, and the anomalies that were appearing in relation to it, that caused one of my journalist collaborators, whom I previously only knew by her real name, to contact me.

Apparently a creepypasta aficionado in her spare time, she spent her nights poring over and inhaling the new works that sprung up daily on those ever-present gray-on-black page backgrounds until the sun came up ("the best time to bail," in her words), and was as close you could get to an expert on the subject. *"Pestomancer,"* as she called herself on the many genre web sites and forums, informed me that newer submissions had begun to acquire a recognizable thread: the subject of circles.

The plots of the stories themselves were still varied: ghosts, mysterious faceless men, odd messages coming through computer screens, but all seemed to now somehow involve wooden circles in some way or another as a central part of the narrative. The connection to the events became clear soon after her first messages to me about it, but how exactly this common thread came about remained a mystery to the both of us. Not a single author of the new pieces that she contacted about it would respond to questions about the subject. Or could respond. Was there coordination between the authors, or was it just run-of-the mill thematic borrowing, authors feeding off each other, playing with the latest iconographic marker? I suspected neither, but I didn't have a good alternative explanation.

I think the reason she sent this information to me was not because she thought that it had a definitive link to anything that was happening, but because she understood well the value of *"Aggregating the Anomalies,"* or ATA as we called it in Observer parlance. Here's how it worked: you'd take information that seemed to not fit any existing patterns, then pass it to others who you think could mix it in to their data, run it through their thought processing or software-based filters, and hopefully spit out compelling, original results that could in turn be fed back into the larger body of knowledge, all in the hopes that some of it would lead to some sort of breakthrough or connection to yet something else.

That was also roughly the point when social networks and image sharing services started to see large numbers of uploads of photos of circles, perfectly round wooden circles, painted various shades of green and purple, or not painted at all, just raw wood. The posts in question were from new accounts that didn't follow anyone and never made any comments, which was always a huge red flag. I'd guessed that photos of circles passed food as the most popular photo subject in less than a month. Many people began to comment on the posts with questions about their origin and meaning, and there was no small amount of trolling, of course, none of which ever received a reply from the original posters. The media had a few articles about the phenomenon, with some analysts trying to connect it to the other events that were occurring, but none of them were successful in creating any kind of link since the content itself was so cryptic, and the posters so unreachable. The police had more pressing worries, too, so queries to them about it was met with *"no resources available for investigations"* statements, which we could hardly blame them for. Vigilantes that managed to crack the ghost accounts weren't able to turn up anything useful, either, all of the source posters having used throwaway email addresses (which would presumably have caused them to open new ones when they lost

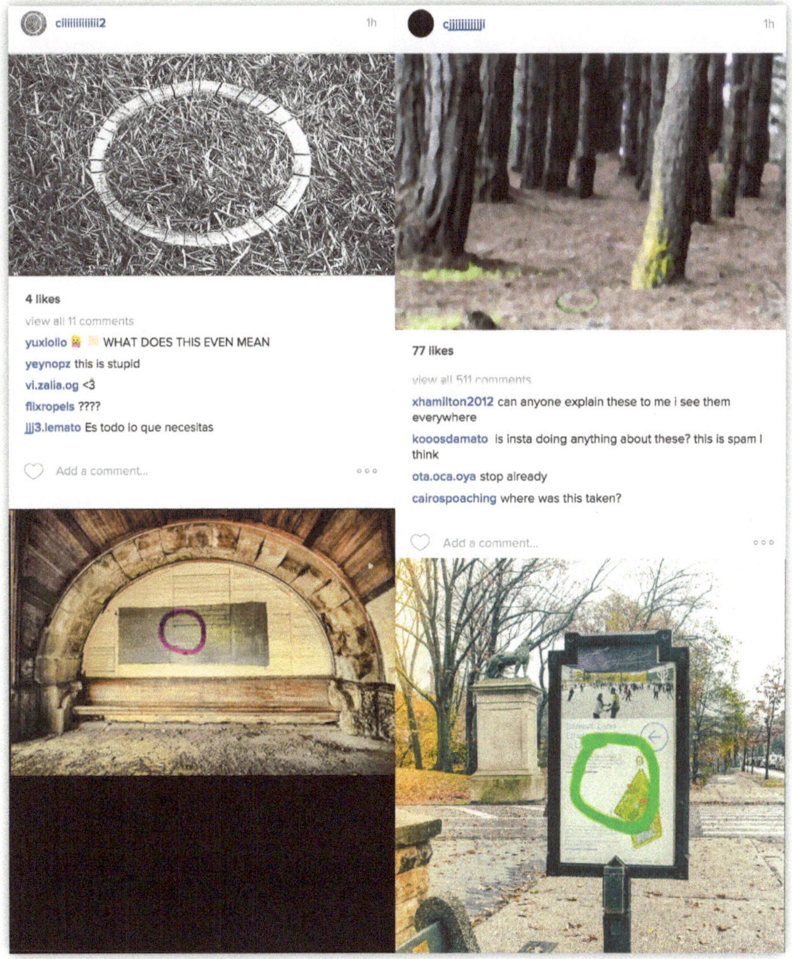

Leaves *and* Circles

control of the old.) Another Observer, a guy involved with Deep Learning for image processing at Google who was running a program to query photo sharing services' public APIs and do image object analysis on them, was the one who spotted the upload content patterns initially, and it was he who gave us the counts; I think that may have been the first time either of us were creeped out by a counter value spit out from a program. I wondered if developers who worked on software at human rights orgs had those kinds of moments.

Early August, year one

Worries ramped up to a fever pitch, even though disappearances had slowed after people became hyper-vigilant and heavily armed. Volunteer investigators, in addition to the police, combed the city, combed the Internet, combed everywhere, looking for something, anything to shed some light on those responsible for the crisis. For all that effort, it was a purely serendipitous discovery that opened up a crack into this heretofore invisible, and it turns out, grisly hidden world. A city building inspector, a Mr. Roger Murthy, demanded to be let into a warehouse (also located in Midtown) that was in a poor state of repair, red paint peeling, bricks scuffed, an unkempt sidewalk outside. Rough, uncared for. (It's also interesting to note that the city still managed to maintain a staff of building inspectors, considering how many other city workers had been transferred to security related work, not to mention the amount of debt the city was going in for security-related services. It turned out to be one of their better decisions.) He banged his fist on the metal pull-down gates, but received no reply. Then it walloped him: a smell. Copper. Feces. Damp wood. He reported it to his superiors, and police were called in immediately. They quickly arrived on the scene with battering rams and K9 units, ready to go full boots-to-doors mode.

That, it should be noted, was a big turning point in the events, the moment when we crossed over from scary, but still fully comprehensible, to ghastly and nearly unfathomable. It felt like we were on the verge of a denouement, but it was actually more of a false ending, a collective narrative tease just when it seemed possible that we'd finally get some closure, or at least progress.

Inside the building Mr. Murthy intended to inspect, rows upon rows of people were found strung upside-down on chains with half-inch thick oblong links wrapped tightly around their ankles, limp bodies swaying over sturdy wooden crab buckets, just like the ones I'd seen at the park during my "encounter" in the park on dog day. Entrails hung out of abdomens and torsos, looking like blood-sodden octopus tentacles, liquid already drained from the bodies. Pallid slabs of human meat, stiffening, mute; most of them already ice cold. Police are trained to see terrible things, things that could test the mettle of even the hardest among us, but that had to have been something not covered in depth in the academy manual. Several went outside to vomit. The rest were frozen in place, eyes wide, faces ashen from horror and disbelief; *The Evil Within* wasn't supposed to happen in real life, and yet there it was, swaying in front of them like so much cattle.

An item of note, the purpose of which eluded investigators, was discovered as well: a three-foot circle, made of some sort of wood and carved perfectly round, was found hanging from a girder on a rust-encrusted chain near the bodies. Information about the scene came from a combination of interviews with officers and Mr. Murthy himself, statements and photos taken by witnesses, and of course, subsequent news reports.

After that discovery, inspections were ratcheted up: warehouses; neglected buildings and basements, some of which still had the two-tone "Fallout Shelter" signs from the Cold War era that always seemed vaguely like a good idea and a laughable anachronism; sheds in quasi-suburban areas; and other disused or derelict structures, all resulting in the unearthing of one gruesome people-shambles after another. Always the same pattern, too: strung upside down, bled out into wooden buckets or barrels, with the stench of blood and that distinctive human feces mixed with gingko fruit smell that slams into your olfactory system, making you in turn want to empty out your own insides all over the sidewalk. It was around that time more specific information was leaked to the press about why the original proposed interrogation site on North Brother was rejected: it was a slaughterhouse, the first discovered by the authorities, and that fact was initially hidden even from the mayor; only a few trusted members of the city council and top brass in the local emergency services were made privy. Apparently the council, full of hardliners more aggressive in their response to the events and distrustful of the mayor's more traditional rights-and-process approach, was keeping the mayor out of the loop. Another report stated that the mayor nearly had a meltdown over that, and almost went public with calls

Dozens of Bodies Found in Manhattan Warehouses; the Police Confirm Wordless Involvement

Credit: Peter Greenman

Dozens of bodies were found hanging from hooks at multiple sites in Manhattan.

By HERBERT BIRKENAU and MELORA FOREST

TWITTER
LINKEDIN
E-MAIL
PRINT
REPRINTS
SHARE

The decomposing bodies of men, women, and teenagers were found at multiple sites in Manhattan yesterday, including one in Midtown and another on the Lower East Side, after what investigators believe were more abductions committed by the so-called "Wordless" cult that continues to terrorize New York residents, the police said.

One set of bodies were discovered after a city building inspector, Mr. Roger Murthy, 31, called the police yesterday about a foul odor. The ground-floor warehouse was being inspected after neighbors complained about a coppery scent

for resignations on the council. Ultimately, he opted to keep it quiet once he was shown the pictures of the site. His animosity towards them and strained relations became an open secret after that, with reports of heated internal disputes, recriminations, and the mayor apparently going on periodic and increasingly caustic diatribes against the council behind closed doors.

Mid-to-late August, year one

The temperature was sweltering, and so was the mayor's temper after what happened next: several more cultists were caught trying to flee a discovered site, and were subsequently interrogated with the same exasperating results (the administration was by then not even attempting to keep up the facade that the insider reports were leaked accidentally.) Imprisoned, tortured, and newly-bejumpsuited, they remained unshakable in their impassiveness. Silent. Useless.

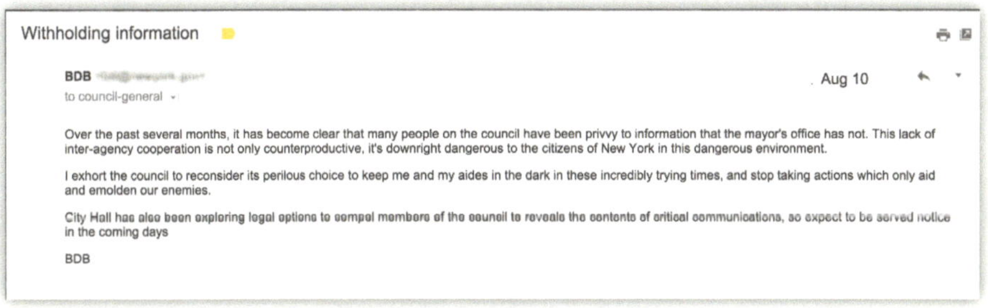

Withholding information

BDB . Aug 10

to council-general

Over the past several months, it has become clear that many people on the council have been privvy to information that the mayor's office has not. This lack of inter-agency cooperation is not only counterproductive, it's downright dangerous to the citizens of New York in this dangerous environment.

I exhort the council to reconsider its perilous choice to keep me and my aides in the dark in these incredibly trying times, and stop taking actions which only aid and emolden our enemies.

City Hall has also been exploring legal options to compel members of the council to reveals the contents of critical communications, so expect to be served notice in the coming days

BDB

Unyielding. It remained a mystery why any members were caught, considering how the rest went undetected; my completely unsubstantiated speculation is that their cloaking system, whatever it was, had occasional glitches.

It was a frenzy after that latest round of leaks-that-weren't-leaks. Protests in the streets began to grow, with the main product of them unfocused terror and rage: no specific demands were made, more just a vociferous, if vague, push to find loved ones or for an even more aggressive police response. People were desperate, grasping at straws. What more could officials do? By that point, the National

Guard and some special army divisions had been called up, armed to the teeth, and were given virtual *carte blanche* to deal with (if you could call walking the streets pursuing an enemy you could rarely even *see* "dealing with") the threat and detain people. Just about every lay citizen had a weapon on them, and police patrols were twenty-four seven, with hardly a stitch of ground without boots on it.

End of summer. It's difficult to believe that most of those developments happened in the span of a little over a month. Unofficial tallies put the number of abductions at over fifty thousand in a city of over eight million, with nearly two million that had already left voluntarily out of fear, and seemingly more trying to get out every day. Streets were clogged with people and uncollected trash, property damage was widespread, and outbreaks of violence between armed citizens had started to become a daily occurrence, half out of suspicion, half out of frustration. Traffic was a standstill, with many people camping out inside their cars with others as a perceived safety measure, a re-imagination of stationary carpooling seemingly inspired by *Soylent Green;* an akraic development considering the scenes from the original movie.

Late August, year one

After two weeks of rising tensions, the bridges were finally closed in a last-ditch effort to restore some semblance of order, with barricades erected and lines of riot gear-clad officers forming a jittery phalanx at the up-ramps and mouths. People continued to clamber out regardless, and protests continued unabated, right out in the open. One day we were a community, the next day everyone was back on their own; that line between civilization and barbarism can be much thinner than you can imagine. The city council countermanded the mayor's order to not use tear gas canisters, rubber bullets, and water cannons on protestors, after months of incredible citizen cooperation and police restraint; the city was approaching full-on panic mode. Luckily, emergency services were on the side of mayor that time, which was fortuitous, as staying focused on the real threat and talking people down rather than going Gaza on them seemed to work once more: abductions again dropped sharply, as sober heads not caught up in the frenzy noted. Community policing effectiveness wasn't just Simonian wishful thinking, **that** emphatically proved.

A slow, nervous exhale was let out of our collective lungs over the next two weeks as things started getting back under control. Nerves were taut, but a fraught calm began to settle over the city, with violence subsiding, and the mood gradually changed to tense-but-stable. The mayor gave a speech one day that August, maybe the most inspiring one he'd ever made, so good that it even drew praise from his longtime critics in neighborhood associations and the city council. People were genuinely moved, and some in the audience smiled through tears, soaking it in. Themes of togetherness were everywhere in the speech, words about being a living whole, of interdependence, of a shared struggle and purpose, allusions to being one's brother's keeper. Concern for the most vulnerable, the weakest among us. Resolute phrases about refusing to let "these terrorists" intimidate us (plain old criminals they were no more.) Exhortations for people to continue to go about their business and lines about staying vigilant. Bold reaffirmations about the importance of maintaining our way of life and about not giving in to fear. The news that the abductions had abruptly stopped helped too, though no one was sure why that was happening. It was the collective Xanax we needed so that we could all think straight again. We could breathe. Maybe we could even hope.

That's when the fires started.

 Leaves *and* Circles

CH10
SUMMER GIRL

How exactly did a city of so many millions, filled with shoppers and tourists, skyscrapers and Uber cabs, ramen shops and dollar slice joints go from a bustling metropolis, the cultural capital of the world, to a city at a standstill, gripped with terror and filled with schoolteachers armed with stun guns and baseball bats? We had plenty of tragedies before: serial killers; four major blackouts; riots; terrorist attacks. The difference, I think, was the amorphous, nearly invisible, and completely perplexing nature of the threat. The fact that no one seemed immune, that it was so insidious and so opaque is what really terrified people. It just lay there, waiting to grab you, no matter who you may have been up to that point. Wall Street, Main Street. Blue, pink, white collar. Greenpoint or Greenwich Village. Orderly or banker. No one felt safe. No one *was* safe.

How, too, did such a large number of individuals go almost completely undetected in a city under constant watch and with ever-present security patrols, managing to thwart one of those most sophisticated surveillance states ever devised—one that would have made Orwell blush? For all the power of the NYPD, the military, and the seemingly omniscient three-letter security agencies of the United States government, no one was able to even get the barest handle on it, it seemed.

How did the Wordless communicate? There didn't appear to be any technical sophistication to their operation; they certainly weren't using encrypted email, remailers, steganography, or hiding behind seven proxies. According to anonymous sources involved in the raids, no electronics of *any* kind were found at Wordless sites. Phones were tapped left and right and there wasn't a peep—all the chatter about the subject was from people talking *about* it, scared out of their minds or proffering conspiracy theories (which, in that environment, now started to sound at least somewhat plausible: aliens; a foreign government with meta-material-based cloaking technology; an elaborate hoax—everything seemed possible at that point.) That the most powerful security apparatus the world had ever known working around the clock couldn't even begin to grapple with this shook the faith of the country, and especially, this city. *"NYPD and NSA Dragnets Called Failures,"* read one pointed headline in New York's paper of record. In the strange vicissitudes of history, even Orwell's worst nightmares couldn't help us.

Mid-September, year one - Early October, year one

People seemed to have lost faith in all institutions that had previously been (for the most part) trusted, at least when it came to big-spectacle incidents, and behavior adjusted accordingly. "Community-based vigilance" and "group resolve" became the order of the day, and "taking back our streets" was the watch-phrase used by those still unwilling or unable to leave. People seemed determined to prevent anyone else from being taken, and the city almost seemed to have gotten back *some* of its resolve, albeit on very different terms than before. Neighborhood and block-level patrols were re-formed, eschewing official organizations, and those groups started getting more formalized and disciplined. The Guardian Angels formed multiple new chapters, and helped train the other groups, teaching them about organization and tactics. Patrols were constant, everyone was well-armed, and better, everyone was focused again, if exceedingly tense.

Lights were kept on at night: apartments, houses, police spotlights, and streetlamps, with ConEd paying double their hourly rate to make sure workers were available to keep the power on. Decorations for Halloween started popping up, just as you might have expected during any other year. Pumpkins on steps leading up to brownstones in Boerum Hill; elaborate funereal scenes on townhouses on the Upper East Side and Dyker heights. It was as if the city were trying to regain a hold on things of by reaching for the familiar terrors, the well-understood ones. Those monsters it could control.

Sadly for us, Wordless were all too good at adapting to the new regime. Unable to make much of a dent with armed citizens, military, and police out in force, and with people resorting to round-the-clock vigils indoors (residents of whole apartment floors were squeezing into a handful of apartments to make sure everyone had

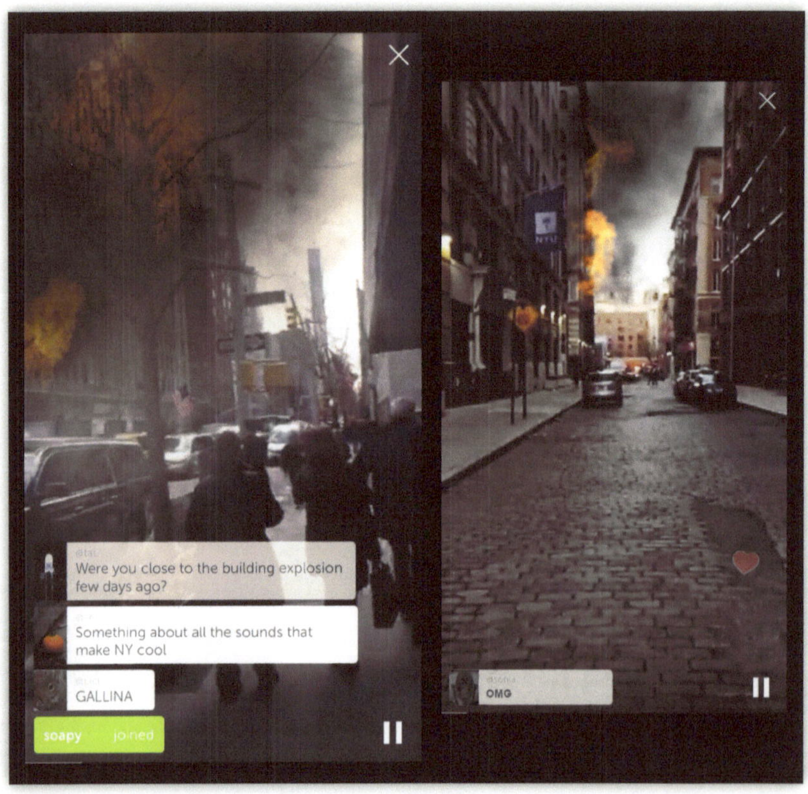

someone looking out for them at all times), the Wordless resorted to a new, but really old, and far more effective, low-tech tactic: arson. A fire would be set in one neighborhood, usually several different buildings on different blocks in roughly the same area. That would in turn draw emergency services and nearby people over to the area, which would create a vacuum in adjacent areas. In all the chaos and confusion, they were able to restart their surreptitious abduction program with renewed vigor.

They used another tactic in the subways. Despite heavy police presence near subway entrances and on subway cars themselves, the Wordless managed to wreak havoc down below by tossing Molotov cocktails and smoke bombs into the open doors, causing people to stream out in terror and confusion. Some of us Observers speculated that the Wordless were using the subway tunnels to get from station to station after getting in through the air vent grilles on sidewalks, or maybe through older access tunnels connected to now-shuttered stations.

The Wordless were very clever with these new tactics, using the chaos and misdirected attention to their advantage. If everyone was running screaming out of a burning subway car or condo, they weren't seeing the people who were pulling up the rear getting snatched up.

If everyone were watching each other out in the streets, up on rooftops, out on corners, trying to make sure no one was spirited away, they wouldn't be looking in boiler rooms and basements, where many fires were started. *"Swarm tactics,"* an increasingly popular set of heterogeneous methods used more often by overseas terrorist groups, were now being used here on US soil. They were playing the new game well, and finding every possible exploitable vector they could.

Every day more fires were set: apartments, skyscrapers, stores; it seemed like in no time at all every neighborhood was burning, and we weren't able to adapt in time, the chaos just too much. The whole of Broadway below Houston was an inferno; every Sephora, Zara, and Lucky Brand was burning all the way down to Canal Street, and people were running in every direction, screaming or rolling on the ground to put themselves out. Hospitals and medical centers were hit especially hard; I'm not sure a single one is still standing in the five boroughs.

One Observer, someone who worked for the MTA itself in the department in charge of repairs and maintenance, showed us a complete subway layout map that included access tunnels, doors, and old stations. He posited that the porous nature of the system (and the fact that all attention had been on events above ground) had been allowing them to travel through the city for some time without being detected, with semi-lit tunnels having minimal surveillance and plenty of places to hide; it would also have explained why track inspectors were some of the earliest people to disappear, something most of us failed to notice. Some higher-up at the MTA must have been looking at the same map and reached the same conclusions we did; the subway fires prompted a complete mass transit system shutdown, with officials calling it *"indefinite."*

It was too late to make a difference, though, with the metaphorical barn already smoldering in the yard. The FDNY was completely overwhelmed, unable to cope with fires breaking out in so many places at once, even with record numbers of volunteers signing up to help. The new tactics gave the Wordless the upper hand again, and the opening they needed to really ramp up their program.

People started vanishing again, this time by the thousands, until the last unofficial tally before they finally stopped counting put the number at nearly half a million. Half a million people whisked off the streets of the five boroughs of New York City, and no one with a clue about where they may have wound up. No more decrepit warehouses or blood-soaked basements in far-flung neighborhoods serving as human meat lockers were discovered, and no more Wordless were apprehended despite a mobilization never before seen in NYC's history, with security services authorized to conduct raids anywhere, anytime, with no warrant or advanced notification required.

A massive exodus from the city began. People were desperately trying to get out this time, causing bridges to be packed to capacity with car traffic, bikes, and people on foot. It was complete gridlock. They got out of their cars and walked, maneuvering themselves around the now-beached vehicles, or scrambling over the roofs, scampering wildly on the sea of glass and metal now flooding the floors of the bridges. The Navy and National Guard were both sending carriers and cutters to pull people out, and some people did make it out that way. Most didn't, though, instead disappearing with the rest. Between the escapees and the abductees, New York was emptying out.

The Staten Island Ferry boats, along with some small-to-medium sized boats piloted by charitable individuals, were repurposed to get refugees—and at this point, we were definitely considered refugees—out, but there was surprisingly little effort from other states or the federal government to commit any more resources to rescue operations. Not sending airplanes I could understand, what with the Wordless managing to torch JFK and La Guardia early, but no Chinooks landing on the east side helipads to take people at least as far as Stamford? I seriously wondered why. Maybe the government, especially the federal government, knew something we didn't about the situation, something that made them extremely reluctant to continue to help. Just another endlessly spinning meat-

     Leaves *and* Circles

grinder, an Iraq on the New York island, a doomed city. People in places not named New York might have had the luxury just then of being outside all the insanity, away from the seeming inexorably expanding chaos bubble, which probably led them to believe that they had a better sense of perspective than we did here on the ground. If they thought they'd seen enough—that they'd just be throwing good money after bad—that could explain the half-heartedness of their actions in the later stages. They'd written us off, opting to focus on areas they believed were still viable. *Realpolitik* took over.

Another possibility was that they were simply short on resources for some other reason, perhaps dealing with their own problems, unbeknownst to us. The news early on had fairly minimal reporting related to happenings in other places, eyeballs of the modern attention economy being spent mostly on NYC, but now I wonder if maybe it all just crept up on them. So fixated on what was transpiring at our new Ground Zero here that they missed the clues piling up in slow motion in their own backyards. By the time it was in their cities, in their parks, in their streets, it was already too late. The same things that happened to us probably happened to them, just shifted forward a few months. *It's like time shifting, but for catastrophes.* This explanation seemed the most plausible to me, even though I have no proof. We already had the police, the army, National Guard, and plenty of private individuals doing their level best to smuggle people out, but those efforts were simply dwarfed by the scale of the problem, and the process itself was incredibly chaotic, beset both by a lack of resources and the geographical limitations of the city itself. Haphazard, self-directed escape attempts by desperate, under-prepared citizens, choked bridges, and widespread fires all but ensured that any sense of order went up in smoke along with the brownstones.

And how exactly did the Wordless manage to abduct people completely unseen? I keep coming back to this question. Did their technology somehow rely on distraction, on us letting our guard down or being focused on the wrong things? (The need for constant vigilance to protect liberty took a very literal turn, it seemed.) Exhaustive reviews of both audio and video recordings by both professionals and amateurs revealed nothing helpful, the only evidence taking the form of a brief blur in most of the footage at the time of reported abductions. No one had an answer, and in the later stages, no one could really afford to look for one. The focus was on day-to-day survival, and getting the hell out of our skyscraper-covered Dodge.

This was the end of the first part of the events. The last official action from our extant government came from the mayor: he gave one final speech, looking harrowed, beaten, wearing the same pit-stained suit with an open collar he'd worn during the previous two briefings. His aides stood behind him, heads bowed, looking grave, a few sobbing pitifully into their palms. The few reporters in the room with him asked no questions, looking shell-shocked or painfully dejected, with their ability to stay neutral, stay outside the frame of the events, evaporating along with most of the people.

The mayor made some meek gestures about keeping up the fight, about doing whatever was necessary, all the usual down-to-the-last stuff, but his eyes said something else: he'd given up, and we were now on our own.

CH11
OCTOBER, YEAR ONE

Power was mercifully still on, and the Internet still worked, but the streets were nearly deserted. Disconcerting to be able to still make toast, turn on a television and get a feed (from non-local networks anyway), and hear the hum of your refrigerator, but then look out a window and not see a person walking down the street for days.

That first October was when the events started spilling over into my little Observer world. We, the Observers, were so focused on our mission of gathering, collating, and processing data; looking for patterns; continuing our feedback loops; and trying to get people information they needed to escape that many of us barely even left our houses. I'd been in my apartment for at least three weeks, with my company having ordered a mandatory work-from-home policy until further notice. There honestly wasn't that much to do at work anyway, and many, maybe most, of the other employees weren't even logging in remotely; too many had fled or disappeared. Every meeting there'd be fewer people listed as "online" in my video conferencing contact list. With what was happening, performance reviews and promotions weren't exactly anyone's priority. These facts meant I had plenty of time to concentrate on Observer tasks, and this was doubly true when my immediate boss stopped responding to emails.

Kat wasn't around much, either, as she was forced to work double shifts as an EMT due to events-related injuries and violence; she was even sleeping in her ambulance some nights, so for most of that period I was alone.

I'd been ordering from local food places for all of my meals, most of them just minutes away from my apartment, via food delivery web sites. I usually ordered from an eclectic fusion taco place and one of those small-chain caffeine-and-croissant type cafes, the kind that had better food than coffee. The pile of empty containers would generally pile up for at least a week before I'd bother taking them down, which was the only time I generally bothered to leave the apartment, and I never left my building at all during that stretch. I wore the same outfit every day for the entire period: black t-shirt and black jeans, if I bothered to get dressed at all.

One night that month I placed my usual order: two *banh mi* tacos with tofu and hot sauce. I didn't receive the usual confirmation text, which was surprising, as nearly every dinner for the previous three weeks was from there, and they always seemed to be open, day or night. I called the location, letting it ring a dozen or so times. No one picked up. I checked the number. Tried again. Nothing. This forced me into a trilemma: a) find another place, even though almost all the ones that were still delivering were atrocious, of which there were very few left due to delivery person resignations, anyway, b) go hungry, or c) tear myself away from Observer-mode and actually go outside of the apartment. I hesitated on this last one, actually considering going hungry, but my stomach refused to go along with the plan. I threw on my long, black peacoat and combat boots and stormed down the steps, getting a minor leg cramp from going too hard, too fast.

When I stepped outside, it was dusk: a deep indigo sending potent serenity-waves through my entire body, the air crisp. Winds were kicking up, pinwheeling the dry leaves across the cement, and pulling them from tree branch and windshield alike. I jogged in the direction of the taco-fusion spot, skipping over sidewalk tile lines, becalmed and almost joyous to be outside in the blue despite

 Leaves *and* Circles

vague leg-cramp echo. When I arrived at the front of the one-floor joint, it was empty and the lights were off, but the metal gate was up and food was still on the counter; they'd clearly left in a hurry. I pulled the aluminum door handle, but it was locked, which I didn't expect for that moment, but then I'd guessed it had an auto-lock mechanism. I stared at that taco, tilting my head to the side, dog-like, trying to determine what kind it was. I turned my phone's flashlight on to get a better look, but could only make out its crispy paratha tortilla. My mouth watered. I actually considered breaking the glass to grab the taco, but at the time, that still seemed nuts.

I stopped at a nearby bodega, where one very nervous man behind bulletproof fiberglass was sitting, a crowbar across his lap, one hand gripping its hilt. I'd never been in that bodega before, and he stared at me intently, unsure yet if I was a threat or not. I gave him one of those curt, forced corner-only smiles to try to reassure him, but he kept staring, completely silent. I plunked down assorted bags of pretzels, Kind bars, and a bottle of sparkling water, then plopped down a ten and said, "Thanks," which got him to relax his shoulders a bit, happy that I wasn't waiting for change and wasn't trying to drag him outside and throw him in a trunk. He loosened his grip on the crowbar. I started to walk out, showing my forced corner-smile again before I turned, and he started to speak. I was still in Observer mode at that point, barely cognizant of, and certainly nowhere near accepting what was happening around me. To me, this was a strange, unwanted interruption of my work, and I was eager to get back to my apartment ASAP so I could continue it just as before.

"This is my last night here. I'm only waiting for my wife to get off of work. Then we are taking a bus south to New Jersey," he stated with more calmness than I expected. "You should leave too. It's not safe here anymore. Not for anyone." I smiled again, for real this time, and nodded. I walked out, a slight feeling of disquiet bubbling around in my head and abdomen. Was he right? Should

I call Kat and get out? Knowing what I knew, we probably should have left already, but I was so into the work I was doing, I never even considered leaving myself until that moment; I was probably plugged too far in for far too long, but hearing him speak in his calm, grave way shook me out of it, eliciting in me a sudden sense of urgency, like some glass shattering and echoing in a silent garage. I decided to talk to Kat about it that night.

I trotted back to my back to my building and stopped to check my mailbox, which was surprisingly empty given that I hadn't checked it in at least a week. Apparently mail delivery had been cut down to one day, which you'd think I would have known, as work absenteeism was through the roof, according to news reports. This small, mostly inconsequential fact, in addition to bodega man's warning lead me to decide that we *definitely* needed to get out ASAP. I called Kat, and told her to grab a rental and come get me with just a hint of that aforementioned urgency, but I think she already knew what was coming.

Between the two of us, Kat was the driver; I'd never learned to, as I'd been straphanging ever since I was little kid. She rented one of the last cars available at a Hertz near her apartment, and then sped up to my doorstep on a deserted Bowery. I hopped in passenger-side. We were planning to take a ride out to Philadelphia, thinking maybe we could stay at a hotel for a bit while we figured out a new apartment or AirBnB situation. I'd been there a couple of times in the past, so I was at least familiar with the area, and it seemed a reasonable destination in any case: close, cheap, relatively safe (?) I'd packed only a few things, thinking that we'd just buy what we needed out there, and got us a hotel room online with surprising ease, one near the Liberty Bell on the East side. Kat had never visited that area, so I figured we could make a tourist trip out of it, try to at least enjoy ourselves away from all the insanity over here; we could wait it out, unplug, and decompress, which were all things I desperately needed to do, I realized. She already had a trunk full of useful items for the trip that she said she'd tell me about on the

     Leaves *and* Circles

way. We barreled through the mostly-empty side streets instead of the (we assumed) crowded avenues, Kat being an expert on these types of zig-zaggy drives from EMT work, and headed towards the Holland Tunnel.

As we approached the tunnel proper, we spotted it: traffic consisting of long lines of cars without any passengers, as people had apparently having given up on trying to escape via automobile. We didn't even get down the sloped street entrance to the tunnel before we were forced to turn around and head back to the rental place; it was our very own China One-Ten jam, with no forward motion from Manhattan to who knows where. I should have checked traffic reports, but after bodega man's ominous admonition, I'd briefly lost my planning-fu, shaken-up feeling taking its toll.

On the way back, we had to pass by the bodega again. I peered out at it through the passenger-side window, my head leaning against the seat, face mashing into the seatbelt, and stared toward it, knowing it was coming up. Its segmented metal gate was down and locked, and I got the feeling Mr. Bodega wouldn't ever be back. I shuddered, wondering if he'd made it out.

The Williamsburg Bridge was packed on the Manhattan-bound side, but empty on the Brooklyn-bound one, so we hurtled across unopposed; apparently Kat had earlier reached Manhattan by going over the bridge the wrong way. It looked like plenty of people had the same idea we had, and that's when I noticed the line of cars was actually going from Brooklyn all the way back down Delancey as far as I could see; I pondered if any of those people knew that traffic wouldn't be moving again with the tin graveyard that was now the entrance to the tunnel. A lone motorcycle, some kind of Japanese model with a sidecar passed by us, never even turning to look. The driver was all in black leather and shiny black helmet, no face exposed. I noticed a small terrier with a helmet and goggles in the sidecar, looking deadly serious for a dog; I hoped at that moment that at least they would figure a way out. Especially goggle-dog.

We drove through streets dotted with orphaned cars until we arrived at the rental place; its lights were all off, giving it a bit of an abandoned motel in the backroad-south vibe. The car garage doors were open, and it was pitch black inside the garage itself. A quick phone-flashlight scan confirmed that it was completely devoid of vehicles, which upped the eerie-motel feel. The front door, glass with the company logo on it, was unlocked, too, and there were fresh skid marks from the curb outside the door curving out into the street

     Leaves *and* Circles

leading away from the lot. I guessed that they were permanently closed, as most other places already were. So many people had taken cars and not returned them that they probably opted to just cut their losses, and their only remaining staff member probably just left with the last car. I wondered where all the rental agents wound up; I doubt rental car companies have a fleet of secret rescue helicopters just laying around for low-level employees trapped in disaster areas. In retrospect, I'm not even sure why we bothered trying to return it at all; it was plainly obvious that no one was going to still be there considering what was happening, but I think we were still only halfway to acceptance of the practical reality of what was happening. We took the car to Kat's apartment, parking it in an empty stretch just a few paces from the door, and went up, my jitters starting to kick in. Her father wasn't there, no surprise, and she shrugged. That fact was considered and dismissed quickly, barely even rising to the level of being perfunctory; we had much bigger things to worry about now.

The apartment building was largely unremarkable, not particularly appealing looking compared to its local competition. Plainly designed, off-white, but well-maintained outside. Inside was a different story, clean and functional, but sparse. It had a feel like a movie set version of a generic office that was trying to be an apartment. Floors were some sort of multi-colored speckle design, the kind you might see on subway cars that were trying to cover up wads of gum tossed by the thoughtless or those engaged in a kind of petty rebellion. Walls had pictures of farm scenes and flowers and vases, the kind of thing someone who just wanted to check off "has art on walls" for a rental ad might pick up at a five-dollar street hawker selling used books and scratched copies of *Miles* on vinyl. There was an elevator, too, a shade of pistachio green with thick, extruding buttons composed of plastic but made to look like swirled wood. All the other floors looked the same, minus the art. Doors were generally blue, the blue that's right in the middle of the blue area of a color wheel. *Duller Homes and Gardens.*

The apartment itself didn't have much to remark on either, mirroring the genericness of the rest of the place. One bedroom with plain white walls (no one cared much about decorating) and a standard kitchen with light beige linoleum tiles looking both neutral and slightly dingy. The rest of the apartment had some kind of light gray carpet, fairly worn, made out of cheap nylon that probably had been there since the seventies, smelling freshly cleaned but still dirty looking. Four windows sat along the south face, the kind that open from top and bottom, double height with narrow sills, with two of them leading out to a slightly peeled white fire escape. A cow print sofa, squat, with room for three, sitting not far from the steel front door, which was itself equipped with two locks, a flimsy chain only there to make people feel better, and a smallish round peephole, uncovered. We entered and I locked the door behind us, including the chain, and concluded that it did not make me feel better. This was home, for now.

Kat unpacked the trunk and brought its contents up, since our would-be vacation had morphed into a bunker-cation. At some point earlier on in the events, she'd purchased supplies for our nascent indoor hideout: wooden two-by-fours and two inch plywood sheets; a small metal hammer with a black rubber grip; three types of nails: concrete, slating, plasterboard. We'd have to learn to think ahead, plan ahead, stay ahead of the game, and it was clear Kat was already there. Search and scavenge was the way we'd have to make a living, I realized, with one-day deliveries from Instacart and Amazon probably not in our futures anymore. I felt wistful about that for a moment, things like that feeling so much a part of the background of the modern world, and now they'd receded along with so much else. We boarded up the windows with the plywood, blocked up the door with her cow print sofa, and armed ourselves with wooden baseball bats that looked fresh off a sporting goods store rack. That was how we started.

Adaptable, hard-nosed, always prepared, and always ready to react when things went pear-shaped, as the British say: that was Kat. EMT training had her always thinking in procedures and checklists, ready to perform the sequence of discrete, executable steps that define processes for things like stabilizing a victim with a gunshot to the upper right quadrant or how to splint a tibia peeking from just below the knee. Three steps ahead. Did we have food, bottled water, flashlights, glowsticks, weapons, and medical supplies? She was on it, checklist written in a small, black school notebook with ring bindings, obviously already mentally preparing for the power to die. Apparently she'd been thinking about all this for a while, probably during her EMT runs, but she'd never mentioned any of it to me. I'm glad she did.

It's somewhat strange to say when so many things were going wrong so fast, but I felt elated. While I was in massive infovore mode, devouring every piece of news and every pertinent post I could find—and I should add, the amount of consumable information was legion, so I was inhaling events-related information like an nineteen-eighties Wall Street analyst on a coke bender—Kat was thinking about how we might ride this thing out (assuming it was rideable at all.) For me, I think I was so taken in by the high induced by being a conduit, a connector, a human meat computer with digital cocaine coursing through my veins, that I wasn't thinking about actually having to *survive*. I was alternately staring, transfixed at a snowglobe full of mysterious happenings made of leaves and murder, and being a node in our ad-hoc information network; Kat was busy making TODO lists and packing the trunk. It might have been blind luck that I'd made it as far as I did; it wasn't my adroit planning skills, that's for sure. After that, I promised I'd never stop paying attention again, and I didn't. Except once. Once. Just once, and that's why she's not here now.

Fuck.

Maybe I should scratch that last part out.

That first night in the apartment, I gazed out over the sweep of Prospect Park from a front window, opening it to the perfectly crisp air outside. It was crystal clear out at mid-twilight, a shade of cobalt sky fading smoothly to scarlet which faded to black, all in sinuous ribbons; a porcelain moon, looking unnaturally close and therefore large, hanging silently in a star-speckled sky. The whole expanse of the park was autumn incarnate, variegated bands of forest green, gold, saffron, crimson and cherry, down to a walnut and deep ember, dry wind gently disturbing the woods. Serenity washed over me, eyes closing, overtaking my senses, but I was brought out of it after a moment by just a tinge of something, of foreboding, hovering at the edge of consciousness. I narrowed my eyes, disquieted.

Mid-to-late October, year one

The rest of that October was spent holed up in the apartment, planning, fortifying, and observing from our little *Fortress Prospect Heights*. We carved out small rectangular slits in the boards on the windows with a blade from a multi-tool, some sort of souped-up Swiss Army knife Kat always had with her that seemed like it would be in violation of some EMS worker regulation. The slits allowed us to see outside so we could monitor the goings-on, which caused me to think just then about what a startling step backwards it was, a step backwards into a world where the limits of your vision determined your immediate knowledge of the world.

Doing all that preparation was fun for me. It felt like an adventure,

 Leaves *and* Circles

hunkering down, getting ready for whatever might happen, focusing on the what and the how, and ignoring, for the moment, the why. I was channeling all the focus previously used for computation and data processing purposes into our new preparation tasks. I think those early days were good for us, stress-wise. Heads in the details, distracting ourselves from the bigger picture. It was especially good for me.

Visibility was middling up there, with us only able to glimpse what was in our direct line of sight, either from the apartment windows or (later on) other apartments and the roof, and that wasn't all that much due to the increasingly frequent fogs, anyway. Some streaming cams did still load (though *Earthcam* was dead), like the ones designed to watch city traffic, but those cams, if they weren't clouded up or fogged over, mostly looked down on nothing but car-choked roads, rows of uselessness that told us virtually nothing.

A few were pointed in the direction of other things that could have been useful in theory, but in reality they showed almost exactly what we could see just looking out our window: trees and buildings and haloed streetlamps, looking like somebody's faux-gaslamp London fantasy-scape, only grainier. It was quiet, too. So quiet. Near-complete silence hovered over the neighborhood, except for the hum of streetlights or the occasional distant (I assumed) gunshot popping. We saw just one actual person, the very first night, booking it down Prospect Park West so quickly that we barely got a glimpse except to say it was a probably middle-aged guy of indeterminate heritage in a canvas-y, olive-green coat, probably scared out of his mind.

Later that month, we heard the final sound we'd hear from another recognizably human person: a single, lone scream, jarring, tinny, and bell-clear in the near-silence. Visibility was zero through our window wicket, so we couldn't have seen her if she was hanging off the sill. The Wordless must have abandoned all efforts to be stealthy, dropping all pretenses about keeping their work under the radar, we decided. Probably since those metaphorical radar operators were far from their control rooms at that point. Then, explosions. One after another, shattering the silence, reminding me of war footage video set in a civilian area, people gathered tightly in some dusty, makeshift apartment shelter away from the windows, speaking with an indeterminate Balkan accent in grave tones about a never-ending conflict. Low, booming, sending small tremors through the room, feeling close but not too close. Enough to get your pulse up, but not enough to send you bounding for the bathtub. The booms continued for hours, eventually growing more distant, clearly things blowing up further away, then finally stopping, leaving a post-bombing imprint, like the air itself was still ringing.

We started out in fairly good shape, supply-wise. Kat had stockpiled enough food and bottled water to last nearly three weeks in her estimation, maybe more if we were careful. Medium-sized, colorful aluminum cans filled with dried peanuts, cashews, almonds, walnuts, with flavors like honey roasted and jalapeno; dried raisins and cranberries stuffed into resealable plastic zipper-bags, no added sugar; whole-grain bread, well-known brands, the kind with preservatives in them in the hope that they'd last a bit longer; quinoa and kale chips, sriracha, various frozen vegetables and half a dozen colorful bits of fresh garden-food. Kat got the feeling this might be the last time we'd get to see fresh produce, so she bought a pile of the top quality, spare-no-expense, locally-grown, rooftop-everything extravaganza stuff, planning for us to eat it all first. We opted not to cook on the stove, instead deciding to go raw or use the microwave on the off-chance that we wound up causing a fire, figuring no help would be coming anymore, nine-one-one only playing an unhelpful "stay in your homes" message after one ring.

After getting settled in, we started our research. We decided to start recording everything we'd learn in the coming days in the hopes that it would help us get through what was happening. Events, entities, and analysis would be neatly cataloged using a collection of legal pads in off-white and yellow in various rule widths, and a health supply of ball-point pens and number-two pencils. We both guessed that it was only a matter of time until the power went out, so we needed to go retro or risk losing our work. I'd already been storing Internet media related to the events as part of my work as an Observer, things like photos (mostly from outside sources, but some are my own, taken on a point-and-shoot Kat had) and screen captures of social media postings on a hard drive for later use, and I hope that it will be accessible for anyone who finds this work.

Internet connectivity continued to be available, but there wasn't much to see concerning the crisis anymore, with the twenty-four hour coverage giving way to scattered forum posts, blogs, and pastebins, none of which had information useful for us. News web sites must have been run by skeleton crews, as they went to HTML-only mode and provided only limited information about intake centers for internal refugees, which were all far from New York, located mostly in the southern US and west coast. We emailed everyone we could think of that might be able to give us fresh news, but we weren't getting replies, all my former caffeine-fueled collaborators having gone dark. Messaging apps were up, but no one was online. Radio and TV were playing only emergency broadcast messages and out-of-date information about local refugee centers we knew for a fact were already gone, no help at all. Social networks were in read-only mode, presumably finally overwhelmed with posts, and no one around to help expand server capacity.

No one was in charge here anymore, it seemed, with people too busy trying to get themselves out of the city or otherwise help themselves, perhaps holing up the way we were. I wondered if the mayor had made it, or if any government officials had for that matter. Was there still a city, a state government at all? How far did this thing actually go? One of the last updates I could find was about adjacent states finally closing their borders with New York, as their crisis centers were completely overwhelmed with refugees coming in via every possible method of transport you could imagine. Many people simply walked, most of them carrying nothing but their phones and the clothes on their backs to the various American Calais that had popped up all over the eastern seaboard.

All the news about other parts of the country and the rest of the world slowed to a trickle, then stopped altogether. The Wordless, if they were in fact nation- or worldwide, must have learned from their experience here, which may have allowed them to overwhelm other cities faster and with less resistance; it occurred to me that we may have been a testing ground. Photos and videos from other places were scant compared to the numbers taken or recorded here. Circles, crowds of terrified people, fires, streets illuminated only with flashlights and phones. Boston, St. Louis, Washington DC, Seattle, Los Angeles. The volume of uploads were not what you'd expect if this thing were truly everywhere, which is what led me to assume that the Wordless were eliminating potential threats before anyone could mount an effective defense in those places, allowing them to accelerate their timeline. Start fires early, overwhelm emergency services, take out power, and prevent vigilante groups from forming. I can't know that for sure, but the inference seemed reasonable to me. The whole of New York, and possibly even America, it seemed, was in need of a Sanctuary City.

All new information that was appearing, which wasn't much,

seemed scattershot, haphazard. There was no coherent narrative anymore, just a collection of sporadically posted accounts of individual experiences.

It felt then like old-world was receding little by little, the filter starting to pass over, fractionally, erratically, indelibly altering it and our place in it. We were at the precipice of a new stage, but didn't, couldn't yet realize the extent of it.

CH12
JET FUEL CAN'T MELT STEEL PUMPKINS

November, year one

No new posts anywhere online, and even emergency broadcasts had stopped playing. Pleas for help or a place to stay no longer popped up on Craigslist, and no new refugee house listings showed up on AirBnB. Independent forums and mailing lists set up to help refugees had no messages newer than a week or so. News web sites returned only old stories, still static HTML. I went to a popular image sharing website, one that previously would have had new uploads every few seconds and reloaded it, then again, then again, probably reloading it every few minutes for at least two hours, staring straight at my screen until my eyestalks starting throbbing in tandem with the load of each image on the page, hoping to see a new post, but none appeared.

The lights were still on, though. Strange feeling. It was as if the basic trappings of old-world were still there, but none of it actually *did* anything. A Potemkin village of modern infrastructure and technology, built to make you believe that it had a reason for existing, that it still served an actual purpose. The phones were on, but no one was reachable. The Internet worked but no one posted. It was a world of perfectly functional doors leading only to solid brick walls. The filter was truly upon us.

We spent a lot of time just staring out the windows. The apartment was situated a few blocks north of Prospect Park, with its faux-colonial lamps still burning their soft cream yellow. Spotlights the colors of the American flag shone on the great stone arch out front of the park in its stately *Beaux-Arts* triumphal style. The great water fountain, the one that'd always manage to spray anything walking within half a block, was off. From there, we had a clear view of the park during the day, and a decent one at night, assuming no fog, thanks to thanks to the piles of charred wood and ash that were formerly buildings laying between us and the park, along with a line of half-naked trees out front. I guess even mass arson can have a silver lining.

It wasn't long before we started seeing them.

The very first of the Wordless that we were able to see looked much like the photos of the ones that were captured, dressed in robes of forest green, muddy or light brown, crimson or blood red, or a soft muted, gold. They moved ploddingly, heads bowed slightly, always in groups of five or thirteen. During the first incident I witnessed in the park on dog day, I was unable to see any faces, any but that portly parks department worker, the one transfixed by a wooden circle hanging on a tree, but now we were able to get a good look at them. It dawned on me, thinking about the parks worker again, and it seemed so obvious in retrospect: people who weren't directly involved with the abductions had to be giving cover to the Wordless and their activities; nothing else made sense. Aside from their stealth capabilities, they didn't have any magic or anything; they had help. It was clear to me then that the city parks department, at the very least, was involved.

Who else was?

Emergency services seemed unlikely, given the amount of heroics they showed right until the very end, but it's possible. What I'm more certain of is that they either had some well-placed people in their pocket or scared enough of them to follow orders without any public leaks. *I wonder if Snowden is still alive, hunkering down in a disused gulag in Siberia by now.* There's no way they could have kept all their activities under wraps so completely in a jam-packed, camera-happy, UrbEx-obsessed city like ours without any assistance from someone on the inside, someone with access to logistics, organization, and planning information. They also had to have something else that allowed them to work with so little interference, something more powerful, something we couldn't see, couldn't grasp. Officials and the security services were able to, across the five boroughs, infiltrate gangs and would-be (or wannabe) terrorist organizations, stop organized crime syndicates, and surveil just about anyone they liked any time they liked, but weren't able to come up with a solid piece of evidence on a kidnapping cult operating city-wide, twenty-four seven that likely had members numbering in the thousands? I just didn't buy it; there had to be more to it. I mentioned these thoughts to Kat, and she mulled them for a bit, pensive medium-distance stare while her cores spun on it. She nodded in agreement, curling her lip sideways while new possibilities bubbled up.

People inside other city agencies must have been involved, covering for them, and probably helping them hide the proverbial—and actual—bodies. After what I saw in the park, it didn't seem a stretch to think other parks were being used in a similar fashion, as possible giant open-air meat lockers. The order to close the parks happened very early on, with the official reason being that they offered too many easy places for Wordless to hide and launch attacks from, which was a compelling and completely plausible rationale, especially with all the disappearances and intermittent reports of throaty babble talk and whispering coming from inside. Even those tiny one-square affairs, which were everywhere, were off limits, which never made sense to me. With no one allowed near the parks, Wordless could have been operating out of every one of them

Leaves *and* Circles

in the city with impunity. If someone with ties to the group were involved in convincing the mayor to give that order, that would have explained a few things. More than a few things. Most importantly, did the people helping them—whether or voluntarily or through coercion—have *any* idea what they were helping to bring about?

The chain of logic led to crazy places: millions of people disappearing, even with surreptitious help from plants and collaborators in city agencies? This idea would have made sense in the earliest days, and having insider access probably facilitated their plans, but they must have had something else, too, something powerful and unseen, to be able to work at that scale. It also didn't explain how the Wordless managed to avoid having their pictures taken in a city where everyone has a camera in their pocket. And where did all the bodies go?

CH13
TAXONOMIES START ONE ENTRY AT A TIME

We decided that we'd categorize the Wordless into distinct subtypes. Unlike in old-world, where we knew very little about them and were forced to consider them an undifferentiated mass, here we were able to spend significant time observing their behaviors and learning their patterns.

The Forlorn: that's what we called the first ones we observed. This subtype moved in groups of five and thirteen, with each group walking the same extended circuit. There was nothing particularly remarkable about them, physically; they weren't hideous, disfigured, or covered in scratches or scabs, and they didn't look particularly threatening. They were people of every complexion and heritage, every size and shape. Their movements, gait, style of carrying themselves, and especially their expressions, however, were identical. The edges of their mouths were turned down ever so slightly, eyes on the ground, countenances reminding me of people experiencing the particular sadness induced by promises left unfulfilled. They moved in plodding circles around the park, through the park, near the park, then back out of the park. Again and again. Endless. Some groups kept their loose, hanging sleeves connected together out in front of their bodies, others carried those wooden circles in two hands, bobbing up and down in tandem with the motion of their legs. Circles of purple and green in different shades and textures. Spraypaint. Crayon. Marker. I had the feeling at the time that someone was trying out different materials and colors trying to get just the right ones, but were never quite sure if they actually did.

For that initial period, all we saw were *Forlorn,* counting a total of three hundred and twenty unique individuals from our perch. Day and night they made their rounds, silently, never tripping, never faltering, never deviating. Not once did we see any of them appear to sit, eat, drink, or tire. They simply continued their circuit, looking bereft, their indefatigability and steadfastness accentuating the transience of the season by contrast.

Worries about the looming winter quickly bubbled to the top of our conversations. It was already November, and temperatures were dropping steadily, which meant we needed to go out sooner than later, at the very least to other apartments in the building in order to collect more food, clothing, blankets, and water. The taps still worked, so we filled every bottle we had, but we knew we'd need more. I wondered how they managed to stay operational without anyone, presumably, running the water services. It made me realize that I knew very little about how the city actually worked, and I deigned to look it all up later.

Early November was when we made our first trip out, and we needed to psych ourselves up to do so (when I say out, I just mean into the building itself; we weren't yet ready to go *out* out yet.) The first time we attempted it, we stood forehead to forehead and took some deep breaths, fists balled, shaking ourselves like a couple of people about to run out into the cold underdressed. We knew we needed to do this, and we knew we needed to learn **how** to do this. After several minutes of pumping ourselves up that way, we moved the bulky sofa out of the way, gripped our bats tightly, and gently opened the four-inch steel door, thankfully with no classic haunted-house squeak. We both sprang out, weapons gripped tight in front of us, crouching low like a couple of wannabe ninjas, and started looking every which way, scanning for threats. The building was silent, still. We waited several minutes, barely taking a breath. Still silence. Lip-chewing and squinting. Waiting. Waiting for anything. Nothing. We exhaled.

With the initial tension past, we decided that we should check for open doors before resorting to anything risker, like sneaking in through windows via fire escapes, or, if all else failed, trying to kick some doors in, our own apocalypse version of a police procedural. As luck would have it a few were actually open, no tree-log battering ram needed. I wondered if the people who'd lived there had gotten out during one of the exoduses, or if they were abducted, with us now picking through their residuum. That thought left me cold. We were still holding out some hope that we might come across someone else to team up with, pool resources, keep guard, perhaps get some bit of information about what was happening elsewhere that we didn't have.

We got what we needed on that first run. A gaggle of containers to fill with water.

Beer bottles. Milk cartons. Green San Pellegrinos, plastic. We mused about how we'd carry it all if we needed to move quickly, noise probably making a car a non-starter, we reasoned. The racket from trundling supermarket shopping carts was out, too. Maybe one of those two-wheeled shopping wagons you'd see pushed around in every Key Food? Seemed awfully handy now, an item I probably never consciously thought about until then, it going from barely noticeable to possibly incredibly helpful in the item usefulness rankings. I made a note to find some of those. For the moment, we resigned ourselves to packing some large backpacks and just hoofing it. One of the people living there must have been an alpinist or wannabe; equipment backpacks, some of those grippy climbing tools, a large art book about Everest, and a blue and yellow insulated sleeping bag were all in evidence. We swiped it all and brought it back to the apartment, the return trip uneventful. That netted us roughly a week's worth of food, which bought us some time to start stockpiling more. This was good. A successful haul served as both a

Leaves *and* Circles

salve and motivation to keep going; it convinced us that surviving this way was possible. We could do this.

We spent the next couple of weeks after that building up our stores in a similar fashion. First through the open doors, then unlocked windows. Fire escapes were all in decent repair, with just the barest of peeling white paint or the occasional ding, and many windows were in fact unlocked (though pushing them up from the outside is harder than it looks.) Of all the apartments in that building, only a handful would have required us to make any real noise, which we appreciated. We were still extremely wary of drawing any attention to ourselves, knowing what the Wordless were capable of. In total, we managed to gather nearly two more months' worth of usable food and water during those first runs, so we decided not to risk anything further for a bit. We opted to settle in for a while.

That gave me time to spend dwelling on an obvious question: were we completely alone?

CH14
ROME WASN'T BUILT IN HALF A MONTH, EITHER

Mid-November, year one

It was growing colder, but not nearly as much as you might expect for that time of year.

The mercury was hovering around fifty for most of the month, with nights dipping to forty or so. Chilly, but perfectly bearable indoors, especially snug inside an insulated sleeping bag. The steam heat in the building wasn't on, as there was no one there to operate it, and we considered it a bad risk to try to get it working. It was getting darker earlier by that time, so trips to the adjacent building that we had roof-to-roof access to, a nondescript brown brick with a still-standing, dark green scaffolding out front, had to be kept short, but this wasn't much of a problem. Access via open windows (most doors were locked there) was via the fire escape, which made it straightforward. The building, also dead silent and completely deserted, put up no other obstacles. Its hall lights were on, burning away as if nothing happened, life as an apartment building the same no matter what is happening to its inhabitants. The lights buzzed slightly, pale yellow rays shining on still-clean, white-and-brown mottled floors interspersed with the occasional furry, off-white rug. They used to burn all night while people slept in the apartments around them. Now they burned for nothing. Something about that unnerved me.

I came back to the question of just how many people were left here. In New York, that is. Were we really all alone in a city that that formerly housed millions? Could there be others doing what we were doing, picking through the ruined carcasses of shattered neighborhoods? Sea worms picking at a rotting whale carcass: small, unnoticed, just the barest disturbance on it all. Gathering, eating, sorting, going through our days, going through the garbage, living off the remnants.

We hadn't seen a single person in our trips to adjacent buildings, and our window monitoring sessions hadn't revealed any either. I felt queasy, like a half-hour past some bad whitefish being passed off as tuna at a no-brand sushi joint.

I also wondered about other things: Did these Wordless ever go indoors? Did they actually not eat, drink, wash, get cold, get hot, sleep? In our estimation, aside from the growing filth accumulating on their ratty, autumnal robes, the Forlorn didn't seem changed at all, appearance-wise. They hadn't gained any weight, nor lost any. We never saw any of them shiver or cough, despite the growing chill, and never saw them deviate from their predefined routes. All day and night, round the park, in, out, and then back again. In all our hours watching them, we weren't able to detect any deviation. We discussed it at length, every note reviewed, every time and event cross-checked. No anomalies. The robotic quality was unsettling; more than once we wondered if we were even looking at humans anymore, or if we had become part of the semi-arboreal sequel to *Westworld*. They certainly *looked* like real people. They didn't even look unhealthy. They looked much as they would have before everything started, just people walking down the street or doing shots in a bar. Financial analyst. Barista. Aspiring YouTube star, I bet; robotic and dirty, but still just people.

Later into November, days started growing shorter, and the humidity kicked up, making the environment more London soup than Brooklyn bagel. A willowy, cotton-white mist had snaked slowly through the streets for nearly a week, and the weeks after that were much the same. It was a world of wet leaves and stone, of ever-present dampness, of never-drying puddles, and of robes wandering constantly through the park. Puzzling, eerie, monotonous, and sometimes boring, but not yet alarming in and of itself, at least relative to what we'd been through just a few months before.

CH15
NEHENEM

Noise, causing us to both sit up, tensed. A sound like a rat trying to escape from the bottom of a metal bin full of aluminum cans, causing us to ask each other, purely non-verbally, if it could have been in the apartment. We stayed motionless, eyes darting, trying to decide. We tossed off the sleeping bag and pulled up the curtain, just slightly, enough to peek. It was one of them: robed, ragged in forest green, caked with mud and vaguely discernible detritus: bits of leaves and grass; the odd broken twig piece; a bit of tannish twine and uncategorizable bits of garbage.

He, or maybe she, scrabbled around in the garbage, a person-sized raccoon searching for an unknown quarry. Quickly, hands in and out, up and down. *"Washing bears"* are what raccoons are called in German, and that characterization seemed fitting for this one. Objects were strewn everywhere: bottles were smashed; egg cartons tossed; bits of plastic thrown aside, adorning the leaf-covered street. The first bin we watched it search evidently didn't have the desired object, judging by its reaction, so that bin was left in favor of another, and another, and another. This Wordless, unlike any we'd seen previously, moved with some measure of agility, but not quite grace. It wasn't robotic at all, though, not like the Forlorn: it showed emotion in its face, a look of perpetual dissatisfaction. Searching, searching, then stopping, scanning for more areas and containers to investigate, head bobbing and darting in every direction, sniffing the air.

It was a young woman, mid-twenties probably; face caked with grime, looking like some BBC docu-drama version of a feral orphan child just rescued after five long years in the jungles of Colombia. Eyes green, wild, obsessed, animated, scanning every which way. Something else, too: her sclera seemed receded, partially covered with an enlarged hazel iris, and pupils that took up nearly half the eye's size besides, seeming in constant motion along with the head. The scrounger finally left after going through what was probably every garbage can and plastic bag in the area, cacophony following in the wake of her tiny, scrabbling frame. She dropped down on all fours, doglike, then scurried down the trash-covered asphalt, kicking aside plastic bottles and a milk carton, causing them to roll and skitter. We didn't see her again after that.

While she performed her puzzling search, the Forlorn processions continued uninterrupted, as they seemed oblivious toward their compatriot's actions or obstreperousness. Even when objects apparently deemed uninteresting by the scavenger were being thrown in their direction, they simply weaved around or winced after getting whacked in the face with a bottle of Snapple; this was the first hint of anything resembling a human reaction I'd seen in the Forlorn since our observations began, but it didn't have more than a momentary effect. They seemed unruffled, unmoved.

I, on the other hand, was a different story.

     Leaves *and* Circles

CH16
THE STUBBORNNESS OF TIDES

December, year one

Leaves by t ha t t ime ha d stopped changing, that was another thing we'd noticed. No more greens to yellows to browns. Golds stayed gold, and russets stayed russet. That was one of two new datapoints, the other being the strange, dissatisfied, nervous little creature; our washing bear. What we realized then was that the colors hadn't changed at all from when we first started taking notes. We scribbled a few lines about it on one of the first observations, but hadn't bothered to update that section since, as that fact didn't seem particularly pertinent at the time. Now we noticed that they'd stopped falling off the trees, too. There were already plenty on the ground from October, but no more had fallen since. Nature, or part of it anyway, seemed suspended now. Alive, maybe even healthy, but in a stasis of a sort. The season itself was in a kind of hibernation.

Pumpkins, so emblematic of the season, many of which had been out for well over a month, didn't look changed at all, either. Other things, too, like the silverbells with their autumn-induced yellow cast on the outskirts of the park seemed to be in a state of decay, but were now frozen in that state, never decaying any further. I wondered if other organic matter would behave similarly, a fact that, if true, could actually work to our advantage. By the look of our last bits of lonely-looking produce on the bottom shelf of the refrigerator, now quite brown, I doubted it. I wondered if this phenomenon extended to natural processes going the other way, like grass growth and spring leaf blooms. I also wondered just how long this new decay-freeze state would last. We'd previously played with the idea of finding supplies to build an indoor garden to grow fresh vegetables, but we went back and forth about whether it would be worth all the effort if my worries turned out to be correct. There wasn't a shortage of food, yet—the houses and apartments we'd visited so far tended to have at least some edible, if not particularly healthy fare—but Kat warned about our reliance on laxatives rather than plant-based roughage, and my insides were already strongly agreeing with her. An unpleasant fact of life in new-world.

Days in that first December grew brusquely short, and most were thick with wormy white mists that seemed to be constantly disappearing and reappearing, bringing with them the scent of petrichor. A muted, sullen dawn would hang on until well after eleven. Days, too, were hardly much brighter than dawns, and twilight started arriving by four, four-thirty, switching to blue-hour color more quickly than in the past. We'd already hit all the accessible apartments and houses on the block by then—any place with roof-to-roof connections or that appeared to have open doors were cleaned out—and both of us were adamantly opposed to stepping on the actual ground outside until we had a compelling reason, like an army regiment barreling down the block in Humvees to rescue us. No acrobatics or feats of mountaineering were attempted, though, as risking injury wasn't something we were particularly keen on, hospitals being what they were, or weren't. I wished I had one of those action movie zipline gun things.

It was unseasonably warm for early December, but we felt a subtly nagging worry that the weather could shift at any time, leaving us in the lurch. Neither of us liked the idea of getting snowed in, even with all the food we had left, and there was no way we'd be spending time and energy shoveling, making a racket and leaving ourselves open to possible attack, especially after the long,

    Leaves *and* Circles

frigid winters of the past decade, when the season seemed to stretch on until April or May. The snows of that period—hard snows, not powdery Macy's window stuff—piled up high, causing even city snow removal services to buckle under the strain at times, despite heroic efforts and mounds of overtime pay.

It was clear to us that we needed to make a decision: move elsewhere immediately or start hunkering down. *"Shelter in place."* We performed a more thorough, wide-ranging scan of the area from the roof (binoculars would have been mighty helpful at that point, but we hadn't yet discovered any), trying to gauge what the Wordless activity was like on the surrounding blocks, trying to learn if leaving would actually be feasible; we were especially interested in whether they had started traveling on the streets further from the park. I wondered how anyone ever managed before the age of meteorological computer models and real-time weather updates automatically squirting into your phone. We had no idea how to deal with this particular problem, and realized we were probably stuck with guesses and last-minute panic-planning. We were not happy.

Aside from the area immediately around the park, where the Forlorn continued their endless circuit, none of the other robes were in evidence, which we took to be a good thing, or at least the lack of a bad one. From our vantage point on the roof, all we could see were matted leaves; strewn rock fragments; some wet, torn, graying paper that was probably once a receipt; various bottles; cigarette butts, smoked down to the filter, circling slowly in a large puddle by a curb; shards of clear glass; abandoned cars; some bombed out buildings; humming streetlamps; and stillness. We proved to ourselves, as much as that was possible given the limitations, that we could relocate. This wasn't actually helping, though; it was almost like we were waiting for something interesting to happen to force us to make a decision, but nothing ever did.

Wearying monotony over those early December days replaced the not-forthcoming sign as our impetus to make a decision. We decided to try our luck north, up near the Williamsburg bridge, which we hoped would help us keep our options open by giving us a possible escape route. There were several sturdy buildings by the Peter Luger steakhouse that could probably work for us from what I remembered, and Google Maps Street View backed me up. Not having any kind of first-hand information was obviously extremely limiting, as we had no idea about the state of the area or what the Wordless presence was like. We both shrugged and went with it. We made some jokes about the fact that we probably had our pick of every apartment in the city, with no worries about security deposits or open houses, or the imminent threat of an eye-popping rent hike just as we were getting comfortable. Empty apartments of every size and location were ours for the taking, but there were different priorities for choosing one now. Lowish rent, great *Ga Nuong*, and subway access gave way to fortifiability, access to plentiful food stores, and a lofty vantage point for good views of the area.

Our decision was made. We took our first step *outside* outside in over a month, and the first since we'd started seeing Wordless near the park after holing up in the apartment. We were apprehensive then, skittish, two cats after hearing a noise in a hall, tails flicking nervously and bending at the tips. It didn't feel very city-like at that moment, though that area never really did. These arboreal-urban hoods always had a liminal quality, occasionally situated in the perception somewhere between Salem and Gramercy, but never quite like that. The new feeling was of a nature in reverse, with the flora growing *out* of the asphalt and brick itself, rather than from the soil. Which wasn't true in any kind of physical sense, but it had that *je ne sais quoi.*

After some ginger creeping on our pawpads away from the apartment area, hopefully to a minimum safe distance away from the park, we decided to go up Bedford, one of the many previous battlegrounds for the changing face of the borough. We passed row upon row of attractively rough dwarf-height apartments, ones that

     Leaves *and* Circles

always appeared to have been run through some kind of nineteen-seventies filter grain, and non-brownstones that always looked like brownstones from far away due to the signature urban castle steps wedged in by sturdy railings.

We left early that day, probably ten-thirty, sullen cement half-light holding on as we walked through endless, densely spaced, oblong leaf-confetti streams the color of Halloween that seemed to decorate every surface. I felt warmth bubbling around my insides, pleased with every squishing leaf mini-mat despite the wetness, which actually felt marginally less oppressive that day. That could have been my mood, though, literfall underfoot gratifying me like some are gratified by bubble wrap popping between thumbs and forefingers. I'm not sure why it did so at that moment, the way it used to; maybe it was the difference in scenery, maybe it was the break from the stultifying damp, or maybe it was our receding proximity from the park.

We kept ourselves low to the ground, one knee down, heads swiveling back and forth, scanning for threats. We darted from car to car, careful to try to not scrape our rubber sneaker soles, which were now looking impressively worn due to constant use, on the damp pavement, using the intermittent mist cycle to our advantage. Not that it mattered, with the streets appearing devoid of all life, and the only sounds our pleasing squishes and carefully controlled breaths.

We arrived at Broadway, heading west near the bridge, and it was sparsely covered: a brand-new black Lexus, covered in condensation; some other cars barely visible through their leaf-blankets; random litter; bits of burnt wood from an unknown source; the usual leaf carpeting, a deep, sodden brown. Our trip was mercifully uneventful.

Next stop: the bank, which we had high hopes for.

The bank was in tatters, unusable. Doors were off their hinges, windows cracked, and the inside even worse: functional, lacquered brown desks, large, abdomen-height multifunction office machines, and pink-and-white deposit slips were strewn haphazardly across the black-and-white checker-carpeted interior. It looked burnt out inside, which meant structural integrity could be a problem, too. I'd hoped that we could have holed up in the vault or

something, but that was out now. Our next option was a multi-story just across the street, one of those SoHo "Iron District" style buildings painted matte black. Older, sturdy looking, not yet weather-beaten, with few signs of damage. Hearty, it seemed to me. Trying to climb it would have been futile due to a lack of handholds and fire escape, so we decided instead to risk breaking a window, our first foray into making actual noise on purpose, breaking our long-standing rule.

We took some long, deep, drawn-out breaths, trying to psych ourselves up again, knowing what our next action could lead to. We were tensed, ready to book it post-haste to the nearest open door across the street in one of the rickety multi-stories to find a hiding spot, preferably on a top floor. A round, blue, solid metal recycling can, a bit scuffed and so heavy it took the two of us to lift it, did the trick after several good swings, the glass shattering completely into a zillion minuscule, awkwardly-shaped pieces like crushed ice, landing all over the sidewalk. We hopped over the base under the window, landing with a soft thump on the polished, variegated black, white, and gray concrete floor.

We ran, teeth gritting, over to the door-person's sleek, solid black steel desk with a vinyl sign-in book atop it, and ducked down and waited, breathing shallow, controlled breaths for a good five minutes, listening intently for the slightest sound, but there were none. Nothing. We started our investigation.

Inside, everything was in fairly good shape, considering. There were several apartments, well furnished with high-quality beds, high thread-count cotton sheets, warm-looking blankets, and top-notch furniture. Stylish. Modern. Luxurious, but not in-your-face. We traveled fairly light, not wanting to risk getting caught out, so we opted for a sleeping bag, flashlights, D batteries, plastic bottles of water, a couple days' worth of food, and our phones and bats. Getting the place sealed up was the first priority, especially the missing window. Elevators were still operational, so we took the wide, black, ridged anti-slip steps to the basement and called the elevator, stopping the doors from closing with a wheeled yellow mop bucket, still smelling pleasantly of a cucumber cleaner. We did a quick scan of the basement, and on the way back upstairs, I felt a quivering sensation that seemed to originate from nowhere in particular other than in the back of my body, causing me to jerk my neck to look involuntarily. My subconscious bubbled up messages to my consciousness about someone or something being there, but not *there* in the building, stalking us. Something beckoning us over. It sent my heart racing, feeling like it was slamming against the bones in my chest, rattling my bone-cage like a fleshy rock ball against so many calcium bars. My calves felt taut and twisted, giving me both the urge to go towards it and run away as fast and as far as possible, forgetting all we were doing. There was *nothing* there, though, and if there was, Kat didn't seem to notice. I breathed out, relaxing slightly, but I still felt wary, semi-sure there was *something* there I didn't yet see.

The stairways in the new building were wide, so we blocked them up with couches and some solid, polished steel bed frames and thick, pillow-top mattresses. Exhausting work, and not exactly quiet, which was something that still worried us despite our luck and lack of Wordless presence so far. When we were done, we headed into our new apartment, the one with the door closest to the steps. It was a corner residence, with windows facing both south and east; vaguely-distressed pine wood floors made of solid six inch slats; tasteful, rich dark chestnut Bennett furniture with subtle, beveled bordering along the edges, walls painted with some kind of abstract piece that looked like long, stretched out black commas, bare except for a lone photo of a lone lifeguard station on a yellow-sanded beach, the whole thing put through some kind of cool aquamarine Instagram filter. "Lifeguard station at the end of the world, but at least we can surf" vibe. I was glad to see blackout curtains in the bedroom, as that would mean one less thing to worry about

     Leaves *and* Circles

while we slept; the idea of being spotted prone was a perpetual, if presently distant, worry. The other rooms had some unremarkable plain-white drapes, weirdly out-of-place considering the luxury furniture collection. Once we were settled, we talked through our options for the next day, and reminded ourselves to block up the front window we'd smashed in with a tarp, if only to avoid filling the place with blown-in garbage and rain. Maybe we could find one in the basement, though I felt a flicking twinge of unease about going back down there, phantom neck-jerk feeling reminding me of the recent incident that I only *I* seemed to have experienced. The real first order of business for the next day was to search the other apartments in the building.

The doors were all locked tight, so we spent some time kicking them in, newly emboldened after our glass-breaking feat the previous day. Fairly slow-going work, with the sky starting to show hints of periwinkle by the time we'd made any real progress. In the end it probably wasn't worth the trouble, especially considering how my shins felt after our third door, stippling pressure traveling down from knee to ankle. Only one apartment had much food, anyway, and it was nearly all spoiled except for some stale saltine crackers, which were just borderline edible. Kat did, however, find a drone, which was something we'd wanted for a while: a quadcopter, still in the box. Neither of us had used one prior to this, and I knew they were noisy, but Kat was almost giddy to try one out. We finally might have a usable scouting tool, which was almost as exciting as unspoiled food. A world with no newsfeeds, cable, social networks, streaming cams, or even neighbors to ask questions of was a world of unceasing isolation, puzzlement, and worry, and the drone could help with that. We deigned to test it out as soon as we got the chance.

The steakhouse seemed like a good next choice that day—we wouldn't be getting any chuck round or tenderloin, but they might still have canned goods we could use. What I really wanted was some pasta, rigatoni or fusilli preferably, but that seemed a longshot at a steakhouse. We jogged straight across the street, despite leg-ache, as there was little cover available for us to use, just a handful of leaf-cars and the Lexus. Considering the fact that nothing had so far shown up to investigate our door-smashing party, I felt a bit more at ease, not that we'd ever seen any of them further than the curb around the park, what we so far perceived as their event horizon, looking outwards. The steakhouse still looked almost stately in its faux-Colonial pub kind of way, with its gold-lettered sign on a black background made to resemble a cornice. The windows were smashed in, its pale wooden muntins twisted into painful looking shapes. It was a bust, too, not a scrap of usable food on the entire floor, kitchen strewn with putrefied steaks and racks of ribs. Luckily, the steel cellar door was still intact, though getting its lock off required some solid teeing-off, generating yet more noise and inching up our wariness needle. We were definitely not yet comfortable with our recent rule change.

We switched on our rugged black flashlights, heavy, police-style devices with beams that could cook a retina. We took a deep breath and descended a set of hollow-sounding metallic steps of indeterminate material down into the dark. There was some usable food there, so we spent time gathering it all and loading it up into our packs. Then we hit a nearby grocery, really a glorified bodega with the word "organic" in the name to try to reach higher-end clientele, sporting a pistachio green and orange sign, but it was completely cleaned out, not even a used scratch-off ticket accenting the bare floor. What we really needed was a hardware or housewares store, something with a bolt cutter or similar so we could get into some of the places that were locked up tight.

We spent some hours exploring the area that day, getting our bearings, learning the ins and outs of the new area we'd be calling home. We'd both been there before plenty of times, but not so much that we knew where all the local spots were straight from memory. Luckily, Google Maps was still saving the day, and it suddenly

          Leaves *and* Circles

seemed like a great idea to print the city out in case the power finally gave. No apartment in our new building had a printer, and we hadn't taken the other one with us. Too heavy. You never realize how useful old, seemingly obsolete tech is going to be until you really, really need it. It was already getting too dark to risk staying outside, despite our continuing luck, with indigo rapidly fading to black, so we decided to wait until morning before continuing on.

It wasn't so damp the day after the steakhouse run, our dry-ish reprieve managing to hold on a bit longer, keeping a buoy up below our tentative optimism. Maps gave us the location of a hardware store nearby, which we crept over to through the permanent traffic jam that was now the east side of Broadway, under the elevated train tracks. The El itself looked decrepit and sallow, its pale gray-olive and off-white steel girders, rivets, and striped black-and-white support beams peeling and weather-worn. The air was hazy, a thin, rusty, red-tinged gray just hovering in place, looking like the air itself had a lining of oxidation, and the avenue was a complete mess, shattered bits of glass of various sizes sprinkled on every surface past the line of vehicles. Cars littered the street: sedans, mini-trucks, vans, hatchbacks, and station wagons on every inch of the asphalt, most heading in one direction on the two-way, battered shops on both sides. McDonald's, windows spiderwebbed, advertising Tenders (made with TLC); a generic bodega, "Broadway Candy and Grocery," gates pulled down; a ninety-nine cent pizza place with its Italian-flag colored sign canting down onto the sidewalk; a Bank of America, looking like it had just been hit by a hurricane; a store called "Sneaker," which I can only guess specialized in rubber-bottomed footwear, its insides gutted, bare walls all that remained; and a smattering of others all in various states of disrepair.

Rattling sounds, some distance ahead of us. *Chikka chikka chikka, chikka chikka chikka.* We bounced down to a crouch, heads craning obliquely, low to the ground so we could peer under the lines of vehicular wreckage. We couldn't clearly see whatever the

source of the noise was, not with all the junk in the way now, and the haze wasn't helping, but we were able to make out some movement. More rattling and the clanking of unidentified metallic objects. Then we heard other sounds, more disquieting: gibbering, babbling, like someone swallowing a swamp full of glass shards, punctuated by growls of frustration and what sounded like whimpered pleas resembling a toy dog begging for a piece of its owner's meal; an animalistic tongue that registered as corruption. That was our first time out on the street actually near, what we assumed, was one of them in the flesh, and we were both extremely wary, unsure of how it might react to us. It was small, no more than five-one, five-two, picking through the trunks of cars, which was actually a great idea we later borrowed. (Thanks, pleading Gibberer.)

We sat there, each down on one knee, facing each other and occasionally stealing glances in its direction. We were some four blocks from the creature, our breaths slow and deep, trying to keep our nerve. In through the nose, out through the mouth. Apprehensive, but focused. We watched it fumble with the contents of a trunk for several minutes, interpolated from several brief looks in its direction, then watched it move on to another, but we were

117

Leaves and Circles

still too far away to make the thing out in any detail. It appeared to finally complete its monotonous task, then turned around and started heading down the avenue in the opposite direction. Exhale.

The hardware store wasn't even locked. Just one of its windows was smashed, apparently from the inside, its glass entrails littering the sidewalk out front, which itself had chunks of soiled-brown, off-white concrete extruding, looking like someone had taken a sledgehammer to the parts of it they didn't like. The sign read "Broadway General Hardware," painted in faded gold across a dirt- and rain-smeared rectangular window. Shelves, a rough dark brown, some listing sideways, still held up by just a few awkwardly bent screws, were mostly bare. It smelled vaguely of wet, powdery clay with a hint of mildew, not overpowering, the level that makes you curl your nose rather than gag, a vague hint in the back your throat urging you not to stick around for too long. We couldn't find a wire cutter, but tossed a few other items in a thick green laundry bag reading "Lau's" in white lettering that we'd found in one of the new apartments: a small, flathead screwdriver; some sort of crescent wrench with an adjustable jaw; and more wood, mostly one-inch thick plywood boards.

We looked through the dirt-smeared, intact window before starting our exit, seeing something that caused us to stop short and see-saw back on our heels. The thing from down the avenue, now obviously a Wordless, was right outside in his long, filthy, but surprisingly undamaged red cowl, hood twisted up in the back, bottom edge bunched up against the street, looking far too long for his slight body. He was a teenager, no older than seventeen, and lanky, with greasy black hair possessing that weeks-later buzz cut look, brown irises nearly covering the whole of his eyes, black pupils widening at the sight of us. There was nothing terribly unusual about him aside from the eyes and the impressive amount of dirt on his face, hands, and under his nails; he was absolutely filthy, but definitely human. Non-existent hygiene habits and living on the street were clearly taking their toll on him, and them, I supposed. Fingernails were short, though, which seemed odd.

It didn't take a moment before he lunged, forearms-first, right through the glass, causing it to shatter into large fragments, obviously not tempered, himself crashing down onto the tan, hardwood floor and taking half the counter with him. We were bowled over, shoulders slamming down onto the floor. In a moment, his light but unnaturally solid body was on top of us both, blood pooling in an oval around the wounds, then leaking onto us in alternating short and long drips, a physiological Morse code from a clean horizontal gash across the length of his exposed abdomen and scattered cuts across his forearms. Panic meter went to ten, amygdala hitting overdrive along with my heart rate.

He snatched Kat up by her calves, flipping her over, then started shaking her as if she were a bag of coins turned upside down, her limbs yo-yoing in the open area in front of the register, over the piles of blood-streaked glass fragments. She was trying to scream, but it was only coming out as a sputtering warble, like someone trying to talk with a bubble caught in their throat. I swung my wooden bat in a wide arc right towards his ribs and he winced, clearly feeling pain, confirming he wasn't just an automaton. In response, he backhanded me so hard I was dropped to the floor flat on my back, stunned, vision flashing with multi-colored stars, head ping-ponging off the floor. My assault seemed to have been enough to get him to release Kat, thankfully not onto the glass. She beelined out the door, smashing every car window in sight with her bat, trying to lure it out after her. Smart move.

Sedan, station wagon, mini-truck. Shattered glass from side windows blanketed every surface, adding to the impressive amount already decorating the asphalt. I halfway got my bearings, chest throbbing with hand-shaped pain, hopped to my feet, and staggered out the door towards Kat, who was bounding west back down the avenue, weaving around spaces between ruined autos. He turned to

     Leaves *and* **Circles**

us after a brief moment of apparent confusion, his head sweeping left to right, then dropped down on all fours, loping and hopping from car roof to car roof, thuds echoing, his slight frame not causing a dent. Though dazed, I tried my best to follow Kat, still staggering, eyes trying to focus like a camera lens that can't quite adjust to the light level, trying desperately to catch up with her. Red-cowled Gibberer with giant-like strength was now screeching roughly, a sound resembling wooden boards being cut with an electric saw, reverberating from every metallic surface around us, prompting thoughts of aural funhouse mirrors.

Down Broadway, from quite a ways, we heard rough, echoing screams in reply, like primates calling to each other in a cave of steel and concrete, signaling for help. Hearts in throats, stomachs on floor (or at least mine was.) Knowing Kat, she was probably calm, self-taught relaxation breathing techniques and EMT training paying off. That was first time they engaged in anything that seemed to require active coordination, which was a horrifying thought that I was barely able to process. Then again, maybe it was purely instinctual, one animal simply reacting to another, in turn signaling the rest, a troop of hooded robo-chimps. I continued running, calves on fire, chest heavy, knees nearly buckling, rushing towards the bridge, weaving uncontrollably from side to side from the terror of pursuit. I was shaking, frantic, causing me to drop our laundry bag and everything we'd just gathered next to a graffiti-covered elevated train girder. He was still coming, springing on all fours, a human turned canine, but not particularly quick anymore; he seemed to be slowing down, leaps coming less often. We were well ahead of him then, but my nerves were in tatters, body wracked, conscious control functions completely out of the loop.

Looking back to see where he was, we were able to espy a long trail of blood streaking on the glass-carpeted asphalt behind him. He was wild-eyed, furious, needful, but winded. He was huffing, big breaths, starting to bend down to one knee; we kept going, fueled by fear and the force of will. We reached an underpass just south of the bridge, and by that time he was well out of view. We finally stopped, completely exhausted, but not banged up too badly: I had a back-of-hand shaped bruise on my chest, which smarted, and we were both wired from the adrenaline, but were otherwise unharmed, Kat's face revealing the relief we were both feeling. We balled ourselves up tightly, hands on top of our heads, breathing as quietly as we could manage, crouching behind a green metallic dumpster next to a simple forest-green wooden barrier dividing us from some sort of rough-looking maintenance site.

We had no idea if the Covetous—we now had a name for this subtype of Wordless, though we hadn't decided on it during that exact moment—was still following. We'd put several blocks of distance between him and us, but couldn't see a thing from that non-vantage point. We couldn't see much of anything there, and it was almost twilight, so we needed to decide on our next move right away: either try for home, risk crossing the bridge, or just sleep in the dumpster, which we seriously considered. The bridge seemed a decent choice; it was closer, we could hop from car to car, maybe find a truck to hide in or maybe even find our way back to my old apartment, and in the worst-case scenario we could jump in the water, we supposed. We knew that would be an incredibly risky move, but compared to facing Mr. Gibbles again, we might have done it, fear potentially overriding completely sound logic.

We were stopped in our tracks almost as soon as we got our bearings and actually looked at the Williamsburg Bridge. Before, it was a glorious product of human ingenuity and engineering that was designed to get vehicles from borough to borough, helped power commerce, and thrilled bicyclists and joggers.

It wasn't any of those things now, instead replaced by some sort of outlandish alien structure. It. Glowed. Green. Electric Neon Green. Cold light, with an almost cartoonish roundness to the edges, pulsing, but not visibly, at a frequency beyond conscious perception.

 Leaves *and* Circles

A massive, bridge-shaped club decoration, mute and eerie, glowing from girder, to arch, to cable, its former faded amaranth replaced wholesale. We also both felt something from it: a pull, a faint desire to approach it growing stronger the longer we looked, immediately reminding me of that feeling I had back in the basement. Hairs were standing up, the urge unceasing, but it didn't feel scary at all. Muscles began to relax, as waves of serenity washed over me. It was inviting, beckoning, but also sickening in the way certain kinds of addictive stimuli can sometimes be. We turned and ran again, forcing ourselves to not look back at it, though something made me want to. I tried to stay in control, tried to will the outside world to stay outside where it belonged, and not approach us with its dog-people and hypno-bridges.

We sped up the stairs and hurtled into the new apartment, slamming the door behind us, no longer thinking about our old rule, and with nothing to show for the day except bruises, the burn of lactic acid in every muscle from the waist down, and lingering abject terror. The combination of the attack, the likely attraction of who-knows-how-many other Covetous, and the inviting-slash-sickening replacement bridge had us anxious, twitchy, waiting for another shoe to drop. Our tentative optimism and relative placidity was shattered that hour, putting us back in full alert-survival mode.

We blocked the door to the apartment with the bed rather than sleeping in it, and huddled in the sleeping bag against the back wall of the (mercifully clean) walk-in bedroom closet with the door closed. I don't think we slept more than three, maybe four hours total that night. Just too wired, still sure more would be running up the steps to smash in our door and drag us out. That was the first time we had a serious encounter where we were actually afraid that something might go wrong, seriously wrong.

I tried to look down at the bruise on my chest, thoughtlessly, in the pitch-dark closet. We didn't even crack a glowstick in there, so afraid that it could be a beacon, that maybe they could now somehow see through curtains, stone, steel. It was irrational, or at least I think it was, but we were terrified, not thinking straight. We lay there, unmoving, pins and needles notwithstanding, trying not to make a sound, though that was probably ridiculous, too.

When we finally gave up trying to sleep, it was three AM. I crept out of the closet, snaking along the floor on my back, chest throbbing badly, and flattened my back up against the wall, just next to the window curtain, which I moved aside slightly, almost a suggestion. Pitch black except to the west, where I could make out the green glow, slightly distorted, fuzzy through the haze. I jerked my head back away from the window, believing I could feel a hint of its pull in me again. I crawled back into the closet, and we sat there wordlessly, in a strange twist, for hours. Things felt truly dangerous to me for the first time since it started, no more outside observer peering into that globe. It was too real now.

CH18
SORRY, THE GRILL'S OFF

We didn't utter more than a few words until well after noon because of the previous day's events, and there was something unmistakably different about Kat; she was somewhere else for a moment, then back again, completely un-Kat-like. She didn't seem just Kat-silent, but silent-silent, which bothered me, causing me to halfway grimace when she was looking away, though I tried to avoid dwelling on the issue; we had so many other things to worry about all of a sudden, adjustable-jaw wrench going from that laundry bag right into our plans. We were shaken, the afterimage of adrenaline and primal fear still imprinted on our bodies, just an edge now; vague, but still present. Kat peered out the window when she was with me again, pushing the blackout curtain aside, and then quickly yanking it back. She shot me a worried look that said there wouldn't be any kind of scavenging that day.

Outside, the streets were filled with Covetous checking every nook and cranny, every container, every car trunk in sight. One of them would topple a garbage basket sitting on a corner and rifle through its damp contents, and then another would repeat the procedure on the same can. Then another one. Then another. There was some comfort in that, at least; it was clear enough that they didn't have any ability to communicate beyond the most primitive alerts. There were probably a dozen of them in their variously colored cowls; filthy and disheveled, brushing away leaves, splashing through puddles, sifting through the junk. There wasn't too much mist that day, so we had a clear view of them. Hours and hours we watched through the slightest bend in the curtain, flat on stomachs until half our torsos fell asleep, with me having to hover my chest-bruise slightly off the ground to avoid wincing. We only nibbled on the food we had—maybe three days' worth were left—even though we were starving after the previous day, a runner's hunger, urgent and crampy. It would just have to wait, as we didn't know just how long they'd be spending out there looking for whatever it is that they look for, and presumably, us.

The following day was much the same, with them having shifted their search down the street a short ways, doggedness undiminished by perpetual failure. Faces were difficult to discern, but we were sure it was the same ones from the previous day. Well, mostly sure. They'd searched all night, scrabbling noises working to periodically wake us up, which all but confirmed the fact that they didn't need sleep. A less than comforting thought: a preternaturally strong, gibbering band of obsessives that seemed impervious to the weather, didn't need to eat, and operated relentlessly—that were probably hunting us. Then we saw him: the first one, the one that pancaked us through the glass, his face unmistakable. His robe was gone, and his filthy, almost hairless naked form was covered in dried streaks and smatters of blood, though he seemed unfazed by all of it. From up there, the wounds looked nearly healed, too. Add to the previous list "superhuman regeneration capabilities." Now we were really worried.

Trying to take them on physically was going to have to be a measure of absolute last resort (as if we needed further persuading in that regard); stealth, stamina, and smarts would have be our tools, much like it had been for humanity's brief history on the planet. We did have some things on our side, though: they weren't exceptionally fast; they didn't appear to have any inclination to climb; they tired more easily than we did, which seemed strangely at odds with their lack of need for sleep; their coordination skills were unimpressive;

     Leaves *and* Circles

they were very patient, but we were more so—they could ultimately be waited out, or at least we hoped.

I woke gently on day three of that period I'll call *"The First Ordeal,"* with one eye refusing to open until a preset time threshold passed. It was delightfully warm that morning, body curled around body inside the bag. It wasn't silent the way it usually was in those first moments; she'd apparently found a pair of cheap over-the-ear headphones—some pre-millennium ones you might see in a sneaker ad—and was listening to a droning, ambient electronica, no vocals. Soft, gentle pulses with long, polyphonic pads, bottom end filtered out, reminding me of old-world subway proximity listening.

A list came to me just then: *"Facts about the post-events world."* No sequels or reboots of movies would be made anymore. No more Yelp reviews of the latest mashup pastry joint would be written. The student loan crisis was solved. Cleopatra was now closer to New York being emptied out than she was to the building of the Pyramids. *Any music with vocals we listened to now was being sung by a person who is probably dead.* Her eyes were still closed, not realizing I was awake yet, so I decided to close mine again and block out reality for a while longer.

Later on day three of *TFO* they were off the streets, confirmed by checking the windows on each building face repeatedly for an hour. None in sight, no indications of movement. We just had to hope they'd decided to find a neighborhood in a different ZIP code, hopefully one far east of us, somewhere we were unlikely to be headed any time soon. Floral Park: that would do, I thought.

Kat thought that it might be a good time to test out the drone she'd found to scout ahead, to see if it was "safe," or the equivalent, as that word became quite relative and nuanced in new-world. She got it up and running quickly, using her phone to control it; I was amazed that she managed to still get something off app stores considering the state of things. I opened up a window on the south side of the apartment and she fired it up. The noise was incredible, but it glided out with ease, and she commanded it to fly east. The noise, the only thing you could hear out there, really, was audible for several blocks.

I watched in amazement as she brought up the streaming cam the app offered. Cars, apartment buildings, trash, and shops flew by. Our scouting problem might finally be solved, and I felt almost jubilant for a moment, suppressing my misgivings. Then it happened. After what turned out to be less than ten minutes out there, ten minutes of pure recon joy, dozens of robed-clad Covetous showed up, bounding down the streets like rabbits, right toward the whirring racket. They had objects in their hands: rocks, chunks of metal, and other indiscernible but heavy-ish looking items. Then they began to toss them at our drone, mostly missing. Then one landed a direct hit, and the video went out instantly. Status: connection lost.

I knew that was the likely outcome. I really did. That didn't stop the despondency from rolling over me, causing me to slump down cross-legged and stare out the window for an indeterminate period. Where are you, little drone? Why did it have to come to this for you? And us. I pushed thoughts of that aside, and Kat only showed a hint of knowing disappointment. We had to move on.

Food was next the priority, more urgent than usual. We ate the last of what we had, even with rationing, so we needed to head back out and gather. We'd cleaned out the steakhouse already, but there was an open taco spot back on Broadway, not far from our assault-scene-slash-hardware store. The building we were in had no roof access, which meant no soaring views of the surrounding neighborhood, so we were forced to chance going back out into the streets with less information than we would have liked. You'd think a building that pricy looking would have that as standard, but apparently top-shelf rent didn't always guarantee top-shelf views. How did they do maintenance up there? With still no ability to scout ahead, options were limited, forcing us to improvise, as usual. We opened a window, tossed out some empty glass bottles and some plain looking coffee mugs, and then watched them shatter on the leafy blacktop below. Nothing stirred. We did it again. Still nothing. I three-quarters expected the Covetous to come barreling towards the noise the way they did with the drone, rocks and steel in hand, but none showed. Exhale again.

We slinked through the streets over to Zocalo as gingerly as too raw, post-recent-panic people could manage. The brick-red, aluminum sign with yellow text and a cartoony cactus read "Delicious Mexican Food" and "Free delivery," the latter making me glum for a moment, but the feeling passed.

Inside, the place was an absolute wreck, with nearly everything overturned, smashed, or otherwise damaged in some way, a shambles. Classic curved wood-backed booths, normally screwed down, and cheap, one-legged pale wood tables were upturned throughout. Tortillas were moldy and rock hard. Cheese looked almost alive. Produce was rotten. Beans putrid. We found a box filled with stout, clear jars containing those spicy pickled carrots, surprisingly authentic fare for an unremarkable-looking faux-Tex-Mex joint; perhaps they thought they'd give the real thing a shot for once, try to get the gourmand-novelty crowd excited. There were a dozen or so jars in a box along with some sealed up containers of thick red salsa, which to our surprise seemed like it might be the real deal rather than just chunky tomato paste. Pickled and dried foods were always a good find, and catching a break after the previous few days felt wonderful, brightening our spirits and causing a spontaneous mini-dance in the rubble, bruised and shaken as we were, or I was. Everything tasted fine, maybe even delicious at that particular moment. We stuffed our goodies into some plastic bags from behind the counter and headed back towards the apartment, trying to beat the incipient drizzle that seemed like it might turn into a downpour. We'd caught a break, and it felt good.

It's comforting to think that even during a cataclysm, you can still get good Mexican in Brooklyn.

CH19
NOSTOS

The next few middling gray days after *TFO* were spent padding through the drizzles and hitting up poorly stocked independent fast-food joints and stubby brick walkups nearby, the kinds with the doors flush with the sidewalk that you'd expect to see only in the permanent quaint of places like Philly. Ultra-relaxed fit Colonial filtered through mid-Progressive-era utilitarianism, mostly red-bricked with plain one-color steel doors and black iron bars on the windows, possessing a low-slung gritty charm, a remnant of a rougher time, along with a few of those one-floor jobs whose owners still hadn't been asked to sell the air rights. Low quality bubble-letter graffiti with uninspiring tag names adorned the front walls and rooftop decks; no *Gaia or Faith47* masterpieces there.

We went back and forth about our next move. We could stay where we were now that it had gotten quiet again, but we had to worry about Covetous returning. We also had to deal with the fact that many places were actually locked up in the area, which meant that we'd have to make noise in order to get them open, which caused us to start worrying all over again

because of the chase and drone incidents. The places we were able to get into were very light on food, too; people around there either ate most of their meals out, or were living paycheck to paycheck and couldn't stock up. The effects of the collapse of the middle class were apparently inescapable, even in new-world.

Another other choice was to pick up sticks and move; maybe Greenpoint would be better stocked, or Clinton Hill pantries would be full up. We had no better idea about what those hoods would be like than we did about the one we were in, and there was the chance they'd be worse, which made this choice risky. The last option was to give the old apartment another shot, the two of us reconsidering our decision to leave in the first place; commandeerer's remorse. We left it originally because we were scared, and now we were thinking about going back because we were scared. Well, I was scared, anyway; Kat seemed to have something else going on: an appearance of being rattled alternating with a kind of vacant nonchalance, the effects of the past day's events possibly still lingering. I wasn't sure which yet, but it discomfited me, making bendy-straw knots out of my insides, urging me to leave immediately.

In the end, we decided to go back to the old apartment. Or rather, I did and Kat complied without discussion, her usual terseness reinforced by post-bridge affect. I enumerated the pros of leaving (we knew the area better, Covetous seemed infrequent near the old place, maybe we could gather new intel from the park), thinking that maybe it would jumpstart her, Kat previously always in the mood to talk plans and tactics, but instead she stared back blankly, head looking leaden, nodding softly when I was done. Her reactions, or non-reactions, were beginning to worry me even more. Something was clearly wrong.

That was the real reason I wanted to leave, despite my list of apparent justifications: to get back to the familiar. I'd hoped that taking her back to a place that hadn't *intrinsically* changed, for a certain definition of *intrinsically,* that a place she knew well (even if any emotional attachment to it was recent and short-lived), would start patching up the rents in brain tissue I pictured were rapidly forming. I reasoned that we'd spent time there together: plus. It was mostly empty in the past, it'd be mostly empty now: another plus. It was probably (hopefully) still in good shape, and aside from the relocated sofa, it was still in the same arrangement: plus again. But what I wanted most of all was for us to be away from that bridge.

Besides, maybe things actually had changed over by the park.

I thought about the Forlorn then, in their groups of five and thirteen, moving as they do in their endlessly repeating epicycles, synchronized to some unseen and unheard frequency, wondering if they'd still be there, or if they'd be any different, if my suggestion that there'd be new things to learn would turn out to have any truth to it.

Before finalizing the decision, I revisited the idea of leaving the borough altogether, just to be thorough. Crossing the bridges was almost certainly not worth considering after what we'd just witnessed; wouldn't they all likely be like the Williamsburg? There were other possibilities, of course. What about just walking to Queens? That was a no, for now. Its borders are contiguous with Brooklyn, which meant getting there was doable (no need to cross bridges or water), but I doubted the state of things would be any different over there, likely making it a waste of energy. I mentally filed it away for possible future consideration.

What about trying for a boat? Aside from the fact that neither of us knew how to pilot one, we had other issues: where we would go, not knowing what, if anything was now in the water, and the distinct likelihood that there weren't any seaworthy ones left after the previous outrush of people. And what would happen if we got stuck out in the water, or worse? Life is very different when you don't have anyone you can call for help. Besides, we both knew the

          Leaves *and* Circles

area better than almost everywhere else other than Manhattan. The idea seemed an even worse one now that Kat wasn't quite Kat all the time; what if she jumped out of the boat, trying to answer the siren call of that bridge? It's hard to grasp just how much we take for granted the presence of other people and urban infrastructure until it isn't there. When something goes wrong, you are really, truly on your own, in a shore-lined, skyscraper-decorated *Touching the Void*. The whole thought exercise was academic in any case: the biggest issue with boating, as I noted previously, is the now non-existent surface tension of the waters in the rivers and oceans around the borough, which would mean a watery grave almost instantly. That was the last time I spent any time on that possibility. We headed back to the old apartment.

Brooklyn suddenly felt very small.

Late December, year one

The mists had been minimal to non-existent in the days since *The First Ordeal,* but the temperatures finally started dropping, as we assumed they eventually would. They were below freezing according to the flat, magnetic strip thermometer we took everywhere. Clothes were no problem, though: we found warm coats and gloves—paired sets of some high-end brand with insulating material inside, and smooth, synthetic, two-toned black and blue exteriors with round clusters of material on them—inside a tony two-story before we left. The place we found them in had a copy of a Magritte (the one with the apple, which I thought looked appealingly edible for something made out of laminated poster material, a kind of art for food's sake), a pile of workout equipment, healthy eating books, some wildly over-sugared peanut butter and chocolate granola (which seemed out of place given the other items), and more brand-new gaming consoles and tablets than you'd know what to do with. We never left food if we could help it, but sugarbombs were always a letdown; cramping up when you need to run from filthy nutjobs with super-strength is something to be avoided. We were losing the light, so decided to camp there for the night.

The bedroom was medium-sized, cozy, with walls the color of coffee and a carpet, still looking somehow freshly cleaned. The bed was very comfortable, one of those Savoir models, feeling appropriately old and new at the same time, and the nightstands and dressers were a sleek lacquered maple, high end. The window, a floor to ceiling type with a single wooden crossbar muntin, sat facing the street, view partially obscured, strangely enough, by tall maple trees, which still sported a good amount of crimson leaves, somehow perfect. As we started to settle in, it seemed like the day had jumped right into deep indigo dusk with nothing in between, leaving me feeling slightly bewildered for a moment. Kat must have been exhausted, because she was already asleep under the light gray covers on the bed. I started to turn around, but heard something that made me pause: a moderate gust blowing through the storybook trees behind me, at first pleasant, then shifting to what could only be described as a dozen whispers, normal whispers spiraling into a mess of garbled guttering speech, somehow modulated by the rattling leaf bodies, then into a gentle breeze again, a smooth declension. I half-turned around, staring down obliquely at the wall but also at nothing, tensed, waiting for what would happen next. Nothing did, though. At least not right away.

When I awoke it was still deep into dusk, with a hue of blue tickling the coffee carpet. The curtain, some kind of thick white linen, was open, though I distinctly remember having closed it. Kat was snoring gently beside me, facing away from the window. I considered for a brief moment that she might have gotten up to open it, but that seemed unlikely. I supposed I'd forgotten to close it after all. I swung my legs of the edge of the bed, picking up my wooden bat and two-handing it as I approached the window. I

     Leaves *and* Circles

popped my head back in surprise, taken aback at what I saw. Out in the front was a Wordless, dressed in a deep brown so filthy it was nearly black under the streetlamps. I felt angry at that one, furious, skin temperature rapidly rising. I had the sudden urge to go out and cave in its chest in with my bat. I ran down the steps to the front door, swinging it open, slamming it against the wall inside, two-footing a jump over the threshold and right over the welcome mat down onto the concrete path out front. Rearing back my bat, powering it up, I jogged toward him with a grimace, teeth bared, more furious now than I was inside. He kept staring straight ahead, looking at nothing inside the mass of leaves with his deep-set brown eyes. I swung at him, landing a blow solidly across his solar plexus, exactly where I imagined. I heard the bones crack, and he grunted, falling down onto the sidewalk tile with a thud, but not putting his arms up in defense. I smiled broadly, all teeth, proud of myself then, wondering if I could smash every bone in his world-wrecking body. I bore down on him, still smiling maniacally, finally exacting justice and feeling the righteousness of my new cause flowing through every vein and nerve. Then I collapsed next to him, a horrible shooting pain in my kidney.

My face slammed down onto the sidewalk, right next to the head of the unmoving Wordless, whose eyes and mouth were open wide, slack. My nose pancaked with a sickening crunch, and my forehead ping-ponged right off the coarse sidewalk, leaving me wobbly, half-there. I rolled over onto my back, groaning, a creaky garble in my throat, now laying in the same snow-angel position as my victim, too woozy to move, head lolling back and forth. In a moment there was one standing over me, balling two fists together, getting ready to pile-drive them down onto my chest. Then there was another, then another, then there were five, eight, thirteen, then too many to count. Now they were all pounding on me with two fists and grim, stoic faces, over and over, shattering my body, leaving my head and face untouched so I could watch my body be smashed. Pain signals flew in too fast for my mind to even begin to keep up, now just a solid mass, one giant fog of pain, alternating wracking and swarming. Warm liquid was leaking, then pouring from my mouth and nose. I started to cough, choking on it. I could hear every bone, tendon, and connective tissue fraying and cracking in my ears, blending then being drowned out by the sound of blood throbbing like distant war drums, but then too close, in my ear canal. It was just a spiral of fists, hoods, and faces, swirling.

I woke up, snapping into a sitting position, to the rapid beating of my heart. The sheet on the bed behind me was caked in a William-shaped sweat silhouette. Kat was still snoring, and the white curtain was still drawn. My fists were clenching, and my abdominal muscles felt permanently frozen in place, utterly taut. I looked hard at the curtain, trying to convince myself it was dark behind it, and that only glowing streetlights and trees were out there, lizard-brain disagreeing with that, trying to force me to believe otherwise.

I picked the bat up and slinked over to the window, sliding my back against the wall, refusing to open the curtain. I fell asleep there, weapon at my feet.

When I woke, for real this time, Kat was organizing her bag on the bed, looking at me briefly but saying nothing, her micro-expression reader likely telling her I had a rough night. Or maybe it wasn't working at all; our previously impressive ability to communicate mostly non-verbally was much shakier now, and she was talking even less than before, causing me to bend my fingernails back and forth between my front teeth at the thought of it. She went back to work packing, and I tried to focus instead on our upcoming trip, struggling to suppress my residual anxiety, forcing a brain background process to convince the rest of my mind that it was a nightmare; that also caused me to forget about leaf-wind gutter-whispers, at least temporarily, so I couldn't mention it to Kat.

We headed out, taking a slightly different route back to the old apartment, with me thinking perhaps that we could scope out

     Leaves *and* Circles

something that was worthwhile: maybe a new class of Wordless or a store with some prime supplies we could grab without much effort before it got dark. Actually, I'm rationalizing. I wanted to see something different, especially after what happened the previous night. I was shaken, but also bored; it was clear that Kat didn't care one way or the other. Bored. Bored of scavenging, bored of hiding, bored of just surviving. Bored of the deepening silence, both out there and in here, between us. Post-trauma and post-nightmare shakiness was subsiding, and I thought that doing something different, that putting some new input to the system might help with the rest of it, like pain in one part of the body distracting you from pain in another. I felt a flashback twinge of that first set of fists coming down on my chest, my body tensing unconsciously, lips curling.

I realized I'd been somewhere else; Kat was nowhere in sight. My head started darting back and forth, and I questioned if she'd even come out with me in the first place, doubting my own memory, as nightmare and reality increasingly seemed to be blending together now. I went back into the house, finding everything as we'd left it, but no Kat. I ran outside, clearing the threshold in one leap like in my dream and skidding out onto the welcome mat like it was a skateboard. Against our renewed policy of near-silence, I started calling her. I ran up and down the block, past overturned garbage cans, silent cars, and more undifferentiable leaves.

I stopped then, realizing I was standing on the spot from my dream, the one where I'd killed one and they'd killed me, and I felt strangely neutral for that moment, the thought of that altogether less distressing than losing Kat. I ran back towards the bridge.

I approached the area close to the up-ramp, which looked as deserted as when we left it. I passed some oversized graffiti of headless people being beamed up and down through some sort of colored tubes, and a mural of a woman in a black and white striped shirt looking into the middle distance with a sense of loneliness, her spray-painted expression seeming more human than the ones in the robes ones around me.

I hopped over some dark gray cement plant pots, brushing aside mini trees inside that somehow looked like Christmas. I scoured the area, careful to avoid looking at the bridge, using my hand as a visor as I searched. No sign of her. I worried that she might actually be on the bridge itself, and I had no idea what that could mean.

I kept calling her, still unconcerned about the attention I might attract, holding my bat so tight in the middle I thought it might snap. Nothing. My growing anger at that moment seemed to be blocking out any of the bridge's magnetic pull, which I was thankful for in retrospect. I looked up at it, full of fury, taking it all in.

The enormity of it amazed me, even through my exasperation. I studied it more closely, more intensely, this time. Here was clearly the bridge I'd gone over for most of my life, but now imbued with properties wholly unrecognizable. Electric green, cold, alien. A thing that seemed to have always been there, that belonged there, but that now also didn't. I started to walk up to the ramp, but my brain started screaming at me to turn around, the exact opposite of what the bridge would be asking of me had I not been almost shaking with rage.

My desire to find Kat started battling with my instinct to turn around and get away. I called for her, again, and again, then again for good measure. Louder, then even louder until I was almost hoarse. My anger was starting to give way to desperation, and the bridge's pull started coming on, first starting at the edge of my perception, then moving right to the median. I felt then that if I continued to stare, I might never come back. I turned face and ran back, pushing aside the faux-mini-Christmas trees, and headed down to the end of the block, breathing heavily, nerves wracked as fear replaced anger.

I stopped short, then dove into a nearby alleyway strewn with damp cardboard boxes haphazardly stacked up in front of a dumpster. Then there it was: gibbering coming from multiple directions. I

     Leaves *and* Circles

figured there must have been at least five of them. That was a very bad place to get caught out, knowing their predilection for patient dumpster diving and general thoroughness. I held my breath through gritted teeth, jumping up on top of the rusty green receptacle with a metallic thud, then hopped right into the low roof above it, pulling myself over the flat rectangular edge.

I was likely only a dozen or so feet off the ground, and could clearly see the street down below. I flattened myself out on the semi-slick, dull off-white roof, which was strangely, but helpfully, devoid of any sloping. It was around two in the afternoon, hints of an early twilight starting to hover in the distance, just a line of charcoal black next to the flat grayish-white.

The gibbering continued, along with the now-familiar sounds of objects of all kinds being tossed haphazardly onto concrete and asphalt alike. Clinking, breaking, rolling, and thumping from all sides continued for the next several hours, which I pictured were followed by looks of fleeting disappointment, though I couldn't actually see any from where I was.

Then it got louder, and close. There was one in the dumpster just below me.

I started to hold my breath and pull myself away from the edge as quietly as possible, pressing my lips tightly together as if to silence myself further, like that was even possible, snap-grimacing automatically in reaction to each breaking bottle. Scrabbling, clinking, crashing. It continued for hours, and I needed to use massive willpower just to keep my shuddering under control. I bit the sides of my mouth, trying to stay focused, keep my breathing slow and even, and keep my body rigid. Acute discomfort from holding in urine.

It was well into night before that one left, and I'm pretty sure I could have easily counted the number of breaths I took in that time, culminating with a long, circular, even one. The sides of my mouth ached, and I felt stiff, an ossified exoskeleton sitting on top of my endoskeleton. I was famished, too, having avoided touching my supplies the entire time. The suggestion of electric green could be seen in my peripheral, and even that was enough to make me feel the urge to look at it, but I didn't. I knew I needed to get indoors quickly, to rest, to heal, and to avoid the temptation of the bridge. Luckily, our appropriated luxury pad was very near.

I scurried over to it without incident in the near-dark, a relief after what I'd experienced that day, most of the lights on that street seemingly not on for some reason, perhaps finally having burned their bulbs out. When I got upstairs, I slept on the floor of the closet covered in soft blankets since the sleeping bag was still inside Kat's pack, which was presumably still with her.

After a night of mostly fitful sleep, I woke to a day of deep gray, still exhausted and raw, but I was determined to find Kat ASAP; I didn't have the luxury of time. If she wasn't at the bridge, where else could she be? Anywhere. She could have easily been attacked or even captured if the Wordless were so inclined, but I didn't have any evidence of that, and I refused to allow myself to consider that possibility too much. I had to focus, and base my assumptions around the idea that she was safe somewhere out there, just lost. Was there anything else around there that was familiar to her? I suddenly wished texting or IM was still working. Phone calls all went directly to voicemail, and I'd already left her half a dozen. We should have set up a shared forum on a server somewhere, something that we could control, but I don't think it even crossed my mind that we'd ever get separated. Stupid.

There was something I had to go on, though. Kat had introduced me to a classmate she'd become friendly with, probably the only person she spoke to regularly outside school besides me, a woman named Ilayda that everyone called Val because she hated her real name. I didn't know that much about her, but I'd been to her

   Leaves *and* Circles

apartment once to pick Kat up from a study session for some test that included items like "Simple Squamous," probably anatomy. Val was studying something historical, but I couldn't remember the exact subject. She lived in some low-slung salmon apartment building, probably three stories, having a look that vaguely reminded me of a southwest pueblo filtered through a pre-war. Out behind it was a small, out-of-place structure that looked like a wooden clubhouse, fairly dilapidated, but stable according to Val, built on top of a garage. It was somewhere near Broadway, I was sure of that.

That was familiar. Maybe she'd go there. I hoped.

I scoured the streets, taking great care to listen for sounds of Covetous while ducking inside graffiti-covered doorways or inside empty alleyways I knew they wouldn't bother with, some of our observational knowledge finally paying off. It was quiet, the only sounds being those of the changing walk signs (a satisfying clunk from the remaining previous-gen ones) and the pitter of light rain on car hoods, which I preferred to the usual cloud of silence just then. I passed a run-down building that looked like it might have once been a factory, sporting a noticeably faded sign, with walls

speckled brick-red and a dull white revealing multiple paintings; square panes of glass falling right out onto the sills; some iron bars and a green wooden double door leading strangely to nothing, making me wonder about what it was once designed for. A door to nowhere, strangely fitting.

The building was locked up tight, with window bars on the ground floor and the doors seeming locked from the inside. The fire escape looked fairly precarious, and unlikely to be worth risking a climb. Otherwise, it could have made a good hideout for us.

There was no sign of her or them.

I sighed, cursing the rapidly approaching dusk, a deep bluish black, which I hadn't noticed, the dark seemingly creeping up faster than I could perceive it. The rain had stopped, and the streets were disquietingly silent then. I wished it would start again.

I wandered back across Broadway, having systematically checked the streets on the south side, and I'd found nothing.

It jumped right out at me.

Almost directly off the corner on the north side on a street with no street sign was the clubhouse and its salmon sibling. I beelined directly for the building.

I found myself surprised, and I was surprised *at* my surprise at what I found. The entrance to the building was narrow, hemmed in on both sides by some kind of black iron railing, strangely un-rusted, and crisscrossed with a thin metal wire adorned with aluminum cans and glass bottles. Someone had thought to build an alarm system. *A person, an actual person besides the two of us might still be here.* The possibility of this momentarily blotted out my gnawing consternation about Kat. I'd hoped it was Val.

The windows in the front were all covered over with thick wooden boards, and the front door was completely impassable, technically

     Leaves *and* Circles

open, but stuffed with filthy mattresses and some kind of wooden furniture cut up and used to cover every gap.

I went to the back and found the off-white fire escape behind a fence of barbed wire. The back windows looked relatively clean, which suggested someone had been living there recently. I climbed up the fire escape, whispering each of their names alternately, hoping to alert either of them that I shouldn't be whacked over the head as I came up. There was no reply.

I peered through the glass. The inside was bare wood, looking naturally distressed, with just a brown three-legged stool and a trestle table in the corner, and no Val or Kat in immediate view. The window opened without any resistance. Inside was empty, no food at all, and nothing but major appliances and a few plastic buckets smelling faintly of excrement overpowered by cloying fake lemon scent in evidence. The front door of the apartment was nailed shut with wooden planks and a heavily scratched oak armoire, looking generations old. I searched the handful of rooms, all of which looked recently lived in, but there was no Kat and no Val.

I climbed back down, peering through the other windows, but they appeared to not have been opened in a while. The insides were empty, too, floors caked with a fine layer of dust and no footprints evident. It was feeling like a failure; I wanted to scream. Then I looked towards the "clubhouse."

The clubhouse was an odd structure, something I'd never seen anywhere before, and it looked particularly, but appealingly, out of place in Brooklyn. It had that "what if we put that here" look you'd sometimes see, like a subterranean tattoo shop or hair salon on a strange twist of a street. It was a dark gray, looking perpetually rain-sodden, covered in brownish-gray vines and pink, string-like items of an indiscernible nature looking like they were made to match the nearby apartment building. The rusty red door sported a large, ragged hole in the front, with some smaller rents near the bottom and a blue stencil of an unidentifiable face with a hat leading out onto a narrow overhang, a slightly different shade, a dull cherry. There was an intact window in front, stained with white splotches and clearly revealing the openings in the roof above where rain was leaking in.

I pulled myself onto the ledge above the garage and pushed open the door, which gave no resistance. Inside was Kat sitting in the sleeping bag in a corner surrounded by drawings of landscapes on white construction paper in what must have been chalk, some of them runny from the rain, making the place look like the aftermath of a sodden *Holi* festival. I made a mental note to ask her about the art later, which I'd hoped was recent, and hoped was Val's.

She was sitting up, straight black hair matted to her face from the rain, and a bemused look on her face. She was calm, looking somewhat distant in that moment, like she didn't notice me just then.

Then she started to speak.

"I don't remember leaving the house," she stated, with a slight quiver in her voice, a little rough from not having spoken in a while.

Leaves *and* Circles

She coughed it free, and I handed her a plastic bottle, which she sipped slowly, still diligent as ever.

"The last thing I remember," she said, "was being near the bridge. I don't know why I was there, but I couldn't stop walking towards it." I nodded, as that confirmed what I'd guessed.

"Then I came back to myself, I was able to think again..briefly. I turned and ran, but I felt confused. I couldn't remember how to get back to the apartment. I felt like I only had some of my memories, and they were all jumbled up. This was the only place I could remember that I knew you'd know." That was comforting at least; some of her memory was holding on, if only episodically and in fragments. I took her hand and gave her some jerky, which she ripped off pleasingly. She'd lost her food, water, and phone.

I started to sigh, but stopped myself, blowing it into my cheeks and smiling instead, just glad to see her in one piece, but conflicted about how to handle what was happening. She couldn't remember much at all about what had happened, and wasn't able to offer up anything useful, medically speaking, other than a suggestion to keep an eye on her, which I'd already planned to do. She mostly just shrugged and shook her head, looking almost disappointed with herself, which was made me finish my previously interrupted sigh. She chuckled, half-expecting it. She knew none of it was her fault, but she had the look of someone who blamed herself anyway. Blamed herself for looking at that light, for losing her things, for leaving me alone. I took her hand and we started to get up, but then stopped simultaneously.

Outside, guttering. Gibbering. Needful sounds. Too familiar already, and too unwanted. We ducked behind the door, away from the tear in the roof and out of sight of those outside. Then the noises. Glass smashing, cans rolled over. They were searching the area, just as expected. Could it have been the same five from my last incident? I wondered if there was any chance that they'd actually followed me, but that seemed unlikely; maybe it was something they did unconsciously, picking up trails and going towards them, something deep in their programming they weren't even aware of. A strange thing to think, considering that we weren't even sure if they *were* self-aware.

We pushed the door enough to give us some room to sleep, as we knew they'd probably be there awhile, performing their search, and it was pitch black out already. A slight mist could be felt coming through the rip in the ceiling, so we pulled the sleeping bag up more closely and turned over. Despite the discomforts and the threat from outside, I felt contentment. We were back.

When I awoke, it was still dark, a flickering streetlight from down the block the only visible light outside. The rain had picked up significantly, hitting cars and rain gutters with a continuous dull metallic thrum loud enough to drown out any commotion from our obstreperous friends outside. The backlit display read eleven AM, but it might as well have been midnight. This was a new development, and I wondered how long it would last. Kat was still fast asleep, her signature soft snore letting me know she was still there in the dark. She was probably exhausted from her ordeal, and there was no reason to push our luck; better in the clubhouse sheltering from the rain and hiding than risking her collapsing outside where they had the advantage.

I forced myself to go back to sleep, rationalizing that I could probably use it, though I wasn't tired at all.

When I awoke again, it was silent, the barest hint of gray light revealing that the extended night session had ended, which felt slightly reassuring, but I was still left with an ominous feeling tracing the lining of my abdomen and around to my back.

She was awake, now, too. We peered out of the window, both looking in different directions, craning our heads to see if there were any Wordless left, still scrounging or searching for us. Their telltale sounds were gone, meaning they probably were too, as I'd expected, so we gingerly climbed out onto the ledge and made our way down. Before heading out, we gave Val's apartment one last look, just in case she'd come back while we were asleep. No sign of her. We agreed that once we'd gotten settled back in and gotten our supplies in order that we should search for her more thoroughly, though we didn't have a clue where to start beyond her apartment. Kat remembered that she'd never gotten Val's number; they communicated solely through Snapchat. The dangers of relying on centralized, proprietary systems. Finding her would be challenging, to say the least. Regardless, the possibility of finding another survivor cheered us both up, perhaps making us even beam a little.

We left the clubhouse and wended our way back to the old apartment, with the trip thankfully uneventful that time. I kept a vigilant during the way back, with no daydreams or silent soliloquies, which I think she found amusing. The fact that she was still in good spirits after what'd just happened to her was encouraging to me.

Not far from the apartment, I stopped on the sidewalk, with Kat stopping automatically with me, but not turning to look at me. I stared down the tunnel of trees over the concrete tiles, eyes fixed on the crosswalk sign, presently on orange, pointlessly telling us not to go, then towards the adjacent streetlight, looking red but blurred with condensation, then back to the crosswalk light. My head canted slightly, tilting in wonder: the world was working, or some part of it was, seeming so strange, so incongruous still. Systems for traffic talking to people who weren't there and to cars that would never move. Then the streetlight blinked to green, and I obeyed, with Kat following in silence.

The park came into view under the streetlamps as we made our approach, looking unchanged at first glance, Forlorn processions continuing on as if we'd never left. We crouched low behind a sky blue mini-van, starting our survey of the area. A vehicle seemed so tempting at times, but after seeing the condition of most of the roads—and after the incident with the drone—we decided against it; the thought of bringing down a neighborhood of them upon us turned my blood to icewater. No, we'd just have to stick to our low-noise meatwheels. We thankfully managed to snag a couple of fresh pairs of high boots with a furry lining at Magritte-house (the former residents of the last spot were probably skiers in addition to fitness enthusiasts.) Warm. Good footwear is a must when you're trudging through wet leaves on top concrete and through puddle-ponds for hours every day, the condition of our discarded pairs of sneakers a testament to that.

We noticed something new, something of interest. One of them, standing alone in his dusty brown cowl, almost black with filth like the one from the previous day's dream, was patrolling the park entrance, in and out, never traveling past the outer lip of the fountain, patriotic light-show still shining above it. His head was held straighter, only slightly bowed. Eyes, heavily lidded, face ashen, lips closed. Grim, focused. Definitely aware of his surroundings, head slowly sweeping left-to-right like some druidic radar dish.

There was no fog that day, so we were able to see another one of them down the road, this one in red, going in and out of a side entrance, back and forth through invisible revolving doors. His eyes seemed unchanged, unlike the others, possessing no hint of iris enlargement. He had a different look overall, a spark buzzing behind his expert poker mask, cold, but not inhuman. Clearly he wasn't part of the Forlorn processions. He was part of a new subtype, one that we named Watchers.

CH20
ARTICLE THIRTY-NINE WOULDN'T HAVE APPLIED, ANYWAY

The Watcher patrols were roughly five minutes in, five minutes out, staggered so they weren't all in or out of the park at once, to my mind, information we gleaned from watching them for a good half hour. We tiptoed back into the building and up the stairs back into the apartment, which was exactly as we'd left it, thankfully. We blocked up the door again, put down our things, and went into conference mode. Kat was present again, eyes narrowed slightly, a look of concern on her face, waiting to see if I was going to say it first. "They're not like the others. There's something there. Something behind those eyes. Intelligence." Kat stated what we

were both thinking, a reassuring sign from her, suggesting perhaps that her brain was straightening itself out.

Pushing aside the curtain, Kat ripped off pieces of teriyaki beef jerky and watched intently. The processions and Watcher patrols continued, gears rotating in a mechanical clock, unbroken and well-oiled. It was then that we figured out why the leaves weren't falling out of the trees anymore, after spending way too much time staring at them and not noticing: the leaves were fused to their respective branches, appearing to have lost any differentiation between their stems and the actual branch itself. The way they were connected together was subtle, just a slight overgrowth of brown where the stem met the branch, like some kind of hardened putty, difficult to discern without close scrutiny. Why they didn't change color was still a mystery.

I was still staring at the fused leaves with some fascination when Kat tapped me on the shoulder, presenting me with a beat up, but unexpectedly clean red cowl that she'd apparently grabbed at some point after our babbling hardware-store friend had managed to lose it, though I suspected the bloodstains that I knew were there just

          Leaves *and* Circles

blended into the fabric. "One of us should try sneaking in there with this on," she proposed. I was dumbfounded. Was she joking? Had this world destroyed her will? Had post-bridge affect given way to suicidal urges? She half-smiled at me, somehow sure it would work, offering only a part of a turned-up lip to try to convince me. I thought she'd lost her mind. She slipped it on over her clothes, head bent, hood pulled low over her brow. "Convincing?" I had to admit that it was, though she'd surely be the cleanest-looking one. I wondered if the Forlorn would even notice, or were able to (Watchers were a different story; they worried me immediately.) I was extremely skeptical of the plan, but I knew dissuading her would be about as easy as trying to strike up a conversation with the Wordless, a quality in her that was, due to the fact that she tended to be right most of the time, simultaneously respect-inducing and incredibly frustrating. The memory problems and recent ordeal made it even riskier.

She hadn't lost her mind, though. This was Kat being Kat, taking calculated risks to advance our understanding or position. Intellectually, I understood that. She was lucid; the plan made sense; we could learn a great deal from direct, close up observations, which could lead to us gaining new advantages; and I was of course extremely curious. The tightness in my abdomen and spiraling feeling of worry, on the other hand, didn't care about the plan's possible utility, especially after nearly losing her twice. My mouth was open, body refusing to sync up to mind, and I shook my head nearly the entire time. I struggled with it; wasn't this crazy?

She went outside straight away to test it, not waiting for any protest or debate. Her first move was to see if the Forlorn would react to her from a presumably safe distance. She stood on the park side of the great arch, head bent downwards, trying to mimic their body language. The Watcher patrolling the closest visible entrance had just finished its outside segment, so Kat had several minutes to try to attract attention. She rolled some lime-green glass beer bottles like bowling balls towards them, with impressively good aim, some sort of fictional Old West bartender serving drinks to thirsty gunslingers in her saloon. The Forlorn didn't react. She clapped. Nothing. She smashed a bottle into a zillion pieces. They didn't miss a step. The Forlorn were unshakeable, all-cult-business, all the time. Then they entered the park via their entrance and disappeared from view, unperturbed. A successful first test.

The north entrance Watcher was next. Kat stood frozen, head still bowed. He stared straight in her direction, presumably *at* her, rarely blinking, stone-faced. He made no attempt to approach, but also didn't continue his patrol. He just stood, statue-like, impassive. Once his five were up, though, he about-faced and left. My misgivings weren't going anywhere, but so far, so good.

The knot in my stomach tightened further. She walked straight into the park, head practically horizontal with the ground, overly long cowl dragging on the moist concrete. She gave me a quick look back and a brief "don't worry" smile, and then carefully continued inside, past leafy overhang, gradually disappearing out of view. Long inhale.

 Leaves *and* Circles

I was glued to the window for the next several hours. It occurred to me that we'd been looking right past the Soldiers' and Sailors' Arch, along with statues of Slocum and Warren. Stone monuments to what was now a **previous** civilization. How does one ever imagine oneself as being able to look at one's **own** civilization, one's **own** society as the **previous** one? *The dead one.* Even those who watched their countries destroyed by war could still look to the continued existence of the rest of world and derive some sort of comfort, some sort of feeling of continuity from it, a connection to humanity and civilization. As far as we knew, we were all that was left, the last people with living memory of the previous era. I hoped that was just despair talking and that it really was just New York. I needed to focus.

Anything using the wired Internet was mercifully still working, but not 3G/4G or phone, and SMS seemed borked. I wished it were the other way around so she could signal me that she was safe. Maybe we could set up a mesh network or find a flare gun somewhere. Hm. I also reminded myself that I hadn't checked pastebin-type posts that I'd made a while ago, so preoccupied with everything else that was happening. I'd set up a shared (world editable) bin as an ad-hoc communication mechanism, but I doubted there would be any new replies, as previous attempts hadn't garnered any in a long while. We were grasping at straws, but straws were all we had to work with.

I was lost in thought for a while dwelling on all that, eyes going oblique and blurring with bokeh, so Kat had made it back inside the apartment without me noticing. She could tell I was somewhere else, so she left me to it. When I de-reveried, I shook my head quickly, surprised, and relieved, to see her. She smiled, both of us moving to sit against the far wall away from the windows, and she filled me in on what she'd seen. We finally had a view from the inside.

CH21
THE FRACTAL QUALITY OF CERTAIN QUESTIONS

New York has always had a hidden silence, the kind that someone who never lived here or only spent time in the parts that were constantly in motion might never encounter or notice. Even in a city of millions, there were times and spaces where everything outside a moment disappeared, that one parcel of urban space you stood on temporarily separated from everything else. A floating island of experience, sometimes lasting only an instant. A copy of one particular area's state transferred to someplace outside time, experienced then destroyed, with its observer then brought back to the original entry point.

New York didn't have those anymore.

I thought about that after Kat filled me in one what she saw in the park, where she spent several hours observing them and taking mental notes. I ruminated on the inversion of that formerly hidden, and in some ways almost sacred, experience.

You could never tell from outside, but the park was full of them. Them, and their wooden circles hanging from the trees—their trees, now, I supposed— painted purple or green, or simply not painted at all, and all perfectly round, similar to the ones I saw that first day, and even more similar to the ones I'd seen a million times online.

There were more Forlorn, performing their eternal procession inside as well as out, and Watchers that came and went from every entrance and major subsection in the park. She'd also discovered a new type; one that apparently spent its time chopping logs into perfect cylinders, carving said logs into circles, painting them, and hanging them up. All of the Wordless worked under the park lights, they worked in the dark. It didn't seem to matter much to their eyes, the ones with their oversized irises, though she noted that the pupils seemed smaller. "Octopus eyes." Did that help them? I wondered, though they were definitely more ant than cephalopod. The Watchers, too, were able to carry out their patrols, even though their eyes seemed unchanged, cold as they were, which I thought was curious.

She noticed that they'd finally settled on their colors, after many months of apparent indecision: some sort of ochre paint made from something they dug up from under the ground, and a deep green made from grass and pine needles. No more spray-paint or *Crayola* hues.

Many of the Carvers, as we were calling them, left the park to hang their circles elsewhere. She followed one of them for several blocks outside the park until he stopped at an unadorned oak, she thought it was, to hang a circle from. Other circles were hung up on the doors of houses, and still others simply left on the street, with no detectable pattern to the arrangement. It was our first time seeing any of them leave the immediate area outside the park aside from the Covetous, which was concerning, as they might wind up interfering with our scavenging trips if they behaved toward us the way the Covetous did. I flicked my thumbnail in my teeth.

We were in new territory again, every few months bringing yet another shift, another set of new phenomena, and it only left us with more unanswered questions. Could they communicate with each other? She said she never heard any of them speak a word or utter anything more than a grunt when lifting a heavy log, and they never seemed to notice each other, much less gesture, yet were able to stay in perfect formation and follow their routes at all times, like it was all predetermined for them.

Did any them have any free will? Who decides on the division of labor? Was there someone in charge? The Watchers seemed an obvious candidate, but they seemed too oblivious for that, if you could characterize them that way. Was there another entity involved, one more difficult to discern, perhaps residing somewhere else and issuing orders remotely? How would that work, anyway?

     Leaves *and* Circles

Aside from their robes, carving knives, and circles, none seemed to have any possessions.

No food was in evidence, either, backing up the idea that they had no need for it, though we supposed they could just be eating grass and bark or something. She also didn't find any latrines or obvious waste areas, but that wasn't proof of anything. Had their "human" biological processes just stopped or been replaced by new ones? Was there something else, something we couldn't perceive, that sustained them? Did they have any memory, or even interest, in the previous world or what became of it? For this last one I still think the answer is no. The Forlorn didn't seem like they were wishing for an old world, but a promised new one. Carvers were building, hopeful that their labors would pay off someday. Coveters seemed to seek something, but it's unlikely to have been something from the old-world, as that was already all around them for the taking. In not one observation did we ever actually see them actually *take* anything, for all their searching and fussing. Instead, they'd discard everything they'd find, seemingly perpetually dissatisfied with their discoveries. The Watchers appeared to be waiting for something. Was I reading too much into the admittedly simple though cryptic behaviors they displayed? Was I just humanizing them, trying to connect them to something that was actually comprehensible?

I don't have evidence to back any of that up, so this amounts to little more than (wild) speculation. I'm not sure even a perfect understanding of their motives, assuming I had a way to ascertain them, would help me in any concrete, day-to-day way anyway, but I felt the need to consider it all anyway, so consider I did, and do: human motives. Though new ones are added and some fade with the rise and fall of cultures, others remain constant: the desire for power, the longing for salvation. What I read in the various faces and behaviors of these beings is longing, desire, patience, impatience, eagerness to please, and broken trust. For whatever of their will has been taken away, emotions—though now limited in number, scope, and incidence—seem to remain somewhere behind those icy countenances. Something more than emotion sustains a person, allows them to go on without eating, sleeping, or even bothering to stop moving, of course. Those hidden things that drive them are surely the more powerful forces, but does that mean nothing is left of their old selves? Couldn't there be something of the person behind those strange new eyes? Sadly, this doesn't seem open to discovery, as none of them have shown much of anything beyond their "programming." Even the Covetous, the ones that appeared to be the least single-minded, if the most brutish among them, simply return to their endless scrounging and scrabbling once they've lost interest in you. The Watcher did stare at Kat, but maybe that's just part of their programming, too, with them designed as sentinels, albeit simplistic and seemingly ineffective ones. Maybe I was wrong about it all, and what they displayed was simply a side effect of how they'd been changed. Maybe I really was humanizing them, or struggling with a kind of emotional apophenia, seeing emotions in faces where there was none. I couldn't know either way, but I never stopped thinking about it.

CH22
THANKS, HERBERT STEIN

We continued our robe camo tests. It felt like we were getting a handle on how they'd react, or fail to react, to us garbed in standard cultist uniform, which meant we finally had gained a way to scout: Kat would don the robe and canvass the street up and down, checking for Wordless presence, making sure it seemed safe for us to move, then report back so we could make a decision about what to do next. Most streets were deserted as usual, nothing but the familiar arboreal adornments, cars, and trash, so we had little trouble getting around. On the off-chance that a Carver or Covetous was present on one, we'd opt to take another route, bypassing them or sheltering nearby until they decided seek their fortunes elsewhere. Scouting in that way took some of the perceived risk out of scavenging, putting us at ease, and allowing us to stockpile a solid amount for winter without much trouble, which I wanted to believe was due to our incredible tactical planning and skill rather than blind luck or other unknown. The tradeoff involved with the new method was that runs would be much slower, but we were satisfied with that for the moment.

We felt good after our newest discoveries, bordering on optimistic, having gathered enough supplies to likely last us until March, maybe April. The water was still on, and so was the power, having lasted far longer than we would have expected, prompting a joke about the possible existence of *Maintainers*. We filled a good number of bottles and larger garbage cans: green for water, blue for water, and silver for water, with water, which we stored in an adjacent apartment, enough to last us a while, even with washing. Heat wasn't yet a problem since it was still unseasonably warm, and we'd found a good-sized electric space heater, oil-based rather than one of the fire-hazard ones that reminded me of hot dog grills, in any case.

Candles, glowsticks, and flashlight batteries were items we had more trouble with, finding fewer of them than we would have preferred. Batteries were a problem in particular, since many of the ones we found were showing the telltale brownish-red crust of corrosion due to the ever-present humidity, or so I assumed. Again I wished I knew back then what I know now so I could have ordered boxes of every kind of solar charger on the market, another item that revealed its true usefulness only now that we badly needed it, though I mused about how well they would have worked in the perpetual gray half-light. We also found a gas-powered generator in the basement of a two-story not far from the apartment, but again was the noise risk, the motors being incredibly loud as I'd recalled from the Sandy days, and it weighed a ton besides. Covetous would likely waste no time interrupting their treasure hunts and swarming toward it if any were in earshot, and we didn't know how our new carving friends would react, either. I was still traumatized from the drone incident, clearly. I also wondered if gasoline would be a problem; it was plentiful with all the cars around, but I remembered reading an article about it going bad due to evaporation or oxidation or something. We opted to leave it alone just then, but knew where to find it if we changed our minds.

The end of the year started approaching fast. I began to feel like we were getting things under control, us able to impose our will on things again, rather than simply have them imposed on us all the time. The memory and physiological afterimage of the tribulations from Williamsburg, too, were starting to recede, at least somewhat, allowing feelings other than perpetual half-panic to seep in. I felt that we were learning to adapt better, and maybe that we'd come to some sort of unspoken détente with the Wordless (I wanted to believe that, anyway.) Their patterns appeared to remain unchanged with nothing to perturb them, providing a measure of comfort, though below our newfound positive feelings was a vague worry, inchoate, a blurry background noise stuffed in a mind-crevice, distant in perception-space; it's difficult to ever feel completely at ease in new-world, but I was trying not to think about it too much. Covetous were nowhere to be seen, the last sighting being back in WB before we fled back to the first apartment. We had an estimable amount of food, bats, thermometer, digital watch, tools, plenty of water, warm clothes, a sleeping bag, and light sources. Too few dependable batteries, but overall in good shape. We felt ready for winter, assuming it was really coming. I wanted to stay positive.

With the lights on and the Internet working (though it existed now as more of a snapshot of a previous digital existence than a *communication* network at that point), we were still able to experience some of the pleasures of old-world. We could read endless books. We could look at photos of nearly anything. We could still enjoy cat gifs. We had enough video to last several lifetimes. We'd also been printing out anything useful we could find about any subject that we thought might wind up being useful from Wikipedia and Google Maps. There was a bittersweet element to it all, but by and large I think we found it heartening, and even a little nostalgic, though not for the usual reasons. Nostalgia, though typically associated with unreachability due to chronological distance, I think in our case was due to being catapulted across a delineation: old-world/new-world Rubicon. There was a bright line between "then" and "now," and this was our way of looking back across it.

Between our supplies and ability to endlessly amuse ourselves, we felt that we could adjust to the odd vicissitudes of new-world, having recalibrated our expectations down just enough so that it didn't seem like everything was on its head, though it clearly all was. The hedonic treadmill was now peculiar and on turtle speed, but at least it was still rolling. We could find a way to live like this.

Then the lights dimmed, flickered, and went out.

CH23
SO DARK ALL OVER BROOKLYN

Still late December, year one

We knew we'd miss everything from before, or what we had left of it, but not this much. Well, not everything: subway cars with no seats left, cardboardy bodega coffee, skyrocketing rents, we wouldn't miss those. Everything else, though. We were just getting used to the new reality, convincing ourselves that we could find a way to live with it, live in it. Then it went and changed again. I was wrong before; there wasn't just one Rubicon, there were multiple, each bringing changes worse than the previous, and we'd just crossed another.

We enjoyed looking at what the world used to look like before all this. We enjoyed the connection to it. We enjoyed reading about a time before we were perhaps the last two people, huddled in the dark, hoping to not be found by beings whose true motives were as inexplicable as their actions were predictable.

Just as we began our previous adjustment, we were forced to begin again. Our pleasures would have to become more basic: books, board games, and conversation, though that last one was becoming increasingly fragmentary due to Kat's condition. It's not that all this depressed us, per se. We could adjust to the more limited options, as people do. Hedonic adaptation. It was the fact that this meant that one of our *last real connections to old-world was now gone, and it probably wasn't ever coming back.* We hadn't, until that point, really allowed that idea to sink in.

We sat silently for days, barely a word beyond the very basics, with the only sounds being human breath and the occasional wind gust, whipping through branches and fuse-leaves and bits of urban detritus. Every time we'd look away and then look back, it was closer, the horrors and depredations of new-world. We felt severed, everything getting too real, putting us too close to the substrate of existence.

January, year two

First of January, our first new year in new-world, and it seemed to welcome us in a way. We woke sometime around eight in the morning to the sounds of wind furiously blowing and rattling the windows, a sound that made me grimace, worrying if they could shatter from our own katabatic in the heart of Brooklyn. I wondered what wind-speed the typical apartment window was rated for. I read the thermometer hanging on a window frame, and it displayed negative fifteen degrees Fahrenheit. After spending the previous months in relative, seemingly unnatural warmth, this was somewhat of a shock, even if we were prepared, in supplies terms, for it. Snow was coming down in buckets, barrels, with probably a foot down by the time we looked outside. Visibility was approaching zero, but we were able to briefly make out some Forlorn continuing their rounds, little flecks of cloth and color through the undulating wall of whiteness, seemingly unmoved by the fact that we were currently in the Arctic.

We'd been through blackouts before, first in two thousand three, then Sandy. During that one, the temperatures were nearly freezing, especially at night, and we had no heat, which theoretically could have prepared us for this. That, however, was nothing like this. We layered up and zipped ourselves in, a human cocoon of cloth and zippers, taking turns doing status checks at the window. Whiteout, temperatures still dropping. Negative twenty, twenty-five, thirty. More layers. Still warm inside the bag. Outside the bag was challenging, even layered up. Eventually we stopped getting up altogether, resigning ourselves to the fact that it'd probably be bad for a while. We fell asleep in the afternoon, and didn't wake up until well after four AM.

Black world, pristine white if not for the lights having gone out. No moon, no stars. We might as well have been in a lightless cavern filled with albino shrimp or at the bottom of the sea. I switched on a keychain flashlight just so we could look at each other, then slipped back into the bag. Anything else was pointless, as it was still far, far too cold to be outside of it for long. We were situated at the apartment's front wall where the sofa used to be, as far from the window—about twenty feet—as we could get (the hallway was far too drafty to make that a possibility.) We whispered even though no one would hear us up there through those walls, with the wind whipping outside like some comically overdone B-movie sound effect, except real, just because it seemed appropriate. I was worried about how this would go on. New-world rules weren't exactly available at the latest cultist administration office for perusal at our leisure, and there wasn't a death-cult equivalent to 311. No more minute-by-minute updates or talking head debates over US vs. Euro weather models to obsess over now, just two sets of eyes and a cheap thermometer to figure things out. I wondered if survivors in Texas or Hawaii were faring better, though the humorous pessimist in me imagined the latter probably had the Wordless somehow catalyzing Kilauea, making the place a tropical Pompeii. Negative twenty.

We finally got some light back around seven the next morning. A flat, middling gray, the color of freshly poured cement, but enough to see by without flashlights. Cars were covered over at least twice their height, streets invisible, some trees bowered a third of the way up, causing an unexpected sense of *hiraeth* for some period during America's early days, of log cabins and frontier living, though in an oblique way I suppose we were already doing that. Six, maybe seven

     Leaves *and* Circles

feet of snow in total, I estimated. After one of the mildest spells for this time of year in memory, this. "Climate change," Kat tried to joke with a wink. It was a flat sea of unending white with colorful cloths cutting a neat sidewalk-colored stripe through it. We were probably going to be stuck inside, at least for a while.

CH24
WE DON'T EVEN GET A PENGUIN

Still brutally cold. Outside was still a flat white landscape broken up in the middle by the tops of lampposts, trees, and a line of colored robes tunneling through the snow with their bodies, only occasionally visible. It was the taiga in Brooklyn, parts of Russia leaking over the Atlantic into Brighton Beach, then spreading out across the rest of the borough. The snow remained solid for a good month, packed so hard that we couldn't get the door to the building open, though we only halfway tried, doubting it was worth the expenditure of energy. Between the mounds of snow and temperatures rarely breaking zero, we were homebound. Sleeping-bag-bound, really. Activities were talking, eating, sleeping, huddling for warmth, watching our breaths in the frigid air of the apartment, and occasionally reading until our fingers got too cold. There was a nice stack of National Geographic magazines that we liked looking through, and as was common, they had plenty of cheerless stories about the latest species put on the *Red List*. Fitting. *Black Soft-Shell Turtle. Guam Rail. Scimitar Oryx.* I joked quietly to myself about our swift journey from LC to EW status. I imagined early settlers again, glad we were several stories off the ground rather than in a cabin buried under the snow.

February, year two

February brought another shift, again the weather. Temperatures shot up to around forty-five, not bothering with any in between, with some areas, like ladder rests on street lamps starting to thin out, looking wet. We didn't go back out immediately, though, waiting until mid-month before attempting that, to allow the streets to clear a bit more. It warmed further in subsequent days, accelerating the snowmelt, but bringing back the fog at times, which was thick, like a mat of white pillow stuffing hovering in place, feeling almost semi-solid. Humidity soaked through everything, and peeling off clothes felt like removing old bandages, making those stories about shut-ins getting fused to their couches no longer seem so outlandish. My skin was working to convince me that supersaturation was possible at ground level.

We were eager to get out of the apartment, though, despite the risks, with both of us a little manic by that point, chittering nervously about the plan for our first day back out, stir crazy from being in that same room for so long, mopey feelings of severance subsumed by curiosity. When we finally got a clear day, we rushed out to find bicycles, or even better, tricycles with ample basket room, an idea that probably should have occurred to us earlier. Bike usage had been widespread in New York for a while, a growing environmental consciousness combined with the sexiness of *eco-chic* in that post-millennial cultural moment playing no small role, everything from one-speed trick bikes that people would use to practice on the fountain rails across from the court buildings in Civic Center to foldable, powered ones that were favored by delivery people, always in the legal gray. I wondered about the range on those things and what it would take to charge them. Did they run on gasoline or did they need wall power? They could be very handy for us. After a short search, we found a couple of three-wheeled adult trikes with rear baskets, also commonly used for deliveries, chained out in front of "Kami," some kind of Asian fusion spot with a plain green and white sign and wrecked inside. Big improvement. Trikes were in passable shape, though they needed oiling and were definitely showing some rust. We grabbed them and walked them carefully,

Kat leading us back toward the park entrance. She was there still with me, with no recurrence of post-bridge drift during our recent hibernation, and I allowed myself to feel tentatively optimistic. I had to, really; there wasn't much else to hold on to at that point.

She surprised me on the way back to the apartment, stopping right near the park entrance instead of heading right back to the building. I kept myself low behind a black SUV, out of sight, one foot near a pedal, ready to jump on the bike to speed away if needed, some kind of over-the-top *Bollywood* action star move. She pedaled right up to the gate, obviously confident that she'd still be left unmolested, and she was right. The Forlorn simply routed around her like water around a rock in a stream, uncaring, nature being nature. The north gate Watcher, however, looked straight at her—I was sure again it was *at* her—then through her, then at her, then through her, cycling between the two for his allotted five. I was then sweating under my layers, which I probably had too many of, but Kat remained as unruffled as ever. When his punch-in time came up, he went back to work as itinerant rent-a-cloak. Anxiety decremented. Still, that disquieted me; it really seemed like the cognitive wheels were starting to spin up. Maybe it was just my nerve-fueled imagination.

Kat looked back, very pleased with herself as usual, wry smile cracking. I was pleased too, though tinged with doubts. She was right again, which meant that we probably could venture a bit further out now, us having theoretically validated the efficacy of our cult camo, which was clearly the entire point of the exercise. She ghosted the bike back towards me, and we conferred about what to do next while my consternation turned to reluctant approval at her latest stunt. She grinned, playfully smug, fully aware of it. I needed a cloak for myself, we decided. Considering the unwaveringly consistent behavior of the Forlorn, maybe we could just mug one while they lay there, limp, allowing us to strip them naked and run off. Of course, doing so could also be the trigger that sent them all into a bloodthirsty frenzy leading to us being buried somewhere outside *The Ravine* in the park, cutting short our brief existence in new-world. It's not like all of their pre-first-Rubicon behaviors never happened or were forgotten in the layers of strangeness and unreality; we knew what they were capable of, and the more recent memory of the drone incident again wasn't helping.

We opted for another plan instead: we'd set up an improvised tripwire out of twine to try to trip one of the solo Carvers out on one of their decorating "runs," out of sight of the park. In the confusion, we'd snatch the cowl and make a run for it, hopefully able to get away before they regained their bearings. Seemed safer than trying to mug one right next to the park, anyway. We turned down a side street and set our trap; our two-person elite tripping team versus Friar Nut. It only took a few minutes for one to show up, as they're nothing if not completely predictable, bundle of circles bouncing in arms.

The trap went off flawlessly. Just as expected, she fell face first into the melting white, wincing and grunting as he tried to right herself, wobbling from side to side, and falling back down several times. We grabbed her ratty, oversized, deep green cloak and booked it west. I only looked back once, and saw her still sitting there in the thinning layer of damp snow, naked but not shivering, head cocked to the side with a look of a puzzled dog, guileless, almost sweet. We glided to a halt on our heels in the middle of the street where I threw on the robe, then ducked behind some garbage bins near the lower entrance to a stately brownstone, right next to the oversized steps. We waited, listening intently in case she'd decided to chase us, or worse, if our action triggered some sort of warning system that brought others out, hunting us like the Covetous did in WB. We looked back and forth at each other, than peered out just above a step to get a glimpse of the street. Slow, controlled breaths. Worry meter unsure of which way to go. There were no other sounds other than winds through tree branches, rustling the fused leaves. We started to relax.

Once we were satisfied that we weren't being pursued, we looped back around to grab our transport. During our second exit we saw the nude Carver re-entering the park, apparently having figured out verticality again, and The Watcher on "break" didn't even glance at her. Kat's mouth twisted into a ball, nose crinkling, and my lips pursed. The robes weren't the whole story when it came to identification, that was immediately made clear, and we did not like it.

CH25
MORE BRIDGES TO NOWHERE

March, year two

We didn't venture far for the first few weeks after our first foray into banditry, and when we did, we kept runs short. Roads were slick (though improving), so we were careful on the trikes, and we gave the chains a good oiling to keep the squeak to a minimum. We used our knowledge of their traveling patterns to avoid being seen, always wary that something could trigger a hostile reaction, especially from Covetous, who tended to attack on sight. We were getting better at this.

Keeping away from the Wordless and being able to move more quickly, wheeled as were, we felt a kind of separation, like an invisible boundary was up between us and them; we were the pair enjoying *fatteh* in Homs from one of the few remaining street food vendors still getting deliveries, blocks away from the area cordoned off due to the presence of cluster bombs, danger out of mind for a brief moment. A *VICE* documentary clip transmuted into west Brooklyn, filtered through trash, burned-out shells of buildings, wet leaves, and robes. Amid all the ruin, all the inexplicable everything we'd found the ability to forget. The ability to live, if only for a little while.

When we rode, this world subsided, pushed back to the places it used to reside in experience-space.

By mid-March the snow was liquid; temperatures settled around

fifty, and mists were back along with the unrelenting wet, a bit of a mixed bag. Puddles and large ponds were everywhere from the snowmelt, with leaf boats and stem canoes performing slow drifts and bobs in little archipelagos-in-reverse. We continued to keep our rides on the meandering side, not wanting to skid out, and we kept well clear of the park. Parks in general, really.

We frequently witnessed Carvers, the only ones that seemed to be venturing far beyond the park, doing their sylvan Martha Stewart-ing while out on our runs, generally only seeing other types of Wordless when going in or out of Fortress Prospect Heights. Even those few times Carvers could have spotted us, they were completely oblivious to our presence, which I was thankful for. At times it felt like we had unrestricted access to the area, allowing us to explore and gather unopposed. It'd been months since we'd last seen a Covetous, which was both notable and relieving, though we were always on the lookout for them, wary of their possible reappearance.

Kat convinced me one day that month that I needed to see it all for myself, up close: them in their habitat, the heart of it, to really understand them. I didn't want to. I didn't. I was happy with the status quo we'd settled in to, the détente it felt like we'd reached, even if we were the only side involved in drawing up the agreement: we were *living,* unmolested, in separate non-overlapping magisteria of existence. Things were better, relatively, than they'd been in a long time. I didn't want to rattle it, to touch it, fearing I'd somehow

171

cause it all to move out of place, to topple over like so many wobbly Jenga bricks; our safety always felt fragile, and I was afraid that introducing any new distortions into the system would ruin it, but she insisted that it was important. I finally agreed, reluctantly, and we headed in through the north entrance.

I looked ahead, down the two lanes of the north road, wide enough for half a dozen cars across, snaking into the park. The lanes were abutted on each side by mostly half-bare trees, leaves of olive green-yellow, rich honey-gold brown, and amber, somehow looking both dead and alive, sinister. The sky was a solid whitish gray, betraying no hint of sun or even the barest hint of delineation between clouds. Just a bare blanket, unbroken, with the clouds themselves seeming to drift down to the tops of the trees below. The park seemed somehow bigger now, larger than it should have, dwarfing us both. I felt squashed, tiny, almost insignificant inside it. A group of Forlorn began plodding toward us, heads bowed, funereal, seeming to grow in size along with my fear, feeling like they could recognize me and smell the terror right through my cowl. Kat and I scuttled behind some sort of watch-post building, filthy and soaked, looking something like a cylindrical one-person prison room with latticed windows and a topped with a ridged alphorn-like roof the color of red currant. I crouched behind it, knee squishing down on the damp grass, nervous, but Kat stood calmly, one mouth-corner curling up with a knowing confidence. I looked up at her, looking for any hint of concern, but she seemed unperturbed, the look of someone dealing with the theoretically alarming suppressed by a learned familiarity.

We crept through the park, slowly and with great care to avoid the Wordless and minimize left-and-branch-crunch underfoot, watching, taking pictures but few notes. We observed the Forlorn and the occasional Watcher performing part of their circuits, circles on arches, puddles and their leaf-boats, more groups of five, thirteen, and sometimes eight across a vale with a fog-topped trees. We saw Carvers performing their expected wood shop ritual, and then disappear out of view. There were parts of the place, matted with leaf-carpeting and decorated with silent trees overhead, that unsettled me. I looked down at the grounds, damp, earthy, leaf-

          Leaves *and* Circles

covered—all things you'd recognize—and there was something about it, something that seemed wrong. Something besides all that was already so *obviously* wrong. The contours of the ground in places seemed odd, almost bumpy, uneven in unexpected ways, but I wasn't sure that was it. There was something else, something difficult to articulate, elusive. I was deep underwater, blurry puzzle pieces streaming past me in a deep sea current, graspable only for a moment, then slipping through the ends of my fingers, struggling to close against the density of the water.

There was a scent mixing with the wet leaves and bark, petrichor and the smells of greenery, something I couldn't quite place, but that left me queasy, peristalsis and stomach-swirl turning my insides every which way, but subtly. I felt like it was a question that we would have to revisit at some point. Things felt more wrong with each step.

We passed the occasional fire pit, several feet deep, bottom covered over with damp off-white ash with any other contents hard to discern. I tried not to think too hard, at least then, at what it might have been before.

After walking awhile, we came to a stone arch shaped like a rounded half-almond, with a short tunnel leading to an ascending leaf-strewn path, stopping at a circle drawn onto what seemed to be a natural canvas, lightly cocoa-colored and weather-worn just inside the tunnel. There was a Watcher at the other end, mostly silhouetted, half-turned, unmoving. I started to drift, perception warping sideways and crisscrossing, ribbons of my visual field

Leaves *and* Circles

tearing across in both directions, everything going out of focus and out of phase.

I felt strange, drifting further. I got that feeling again, the one where it seemed like I was in that same familiar house but where everything was rearranged, fitting but not quite fitting, everything seeming just slightly out of place. Objects familiar but unfamiliar, switched around, occasionally replaced or just altered in minute ways: a coffee cup, once white, now green, or an oak table now pushed against a window instead of the middle of the room. I knew

the place, and it surely knew me, but we were somehow strangers, old friends who'd been away from each other and knew the faces, but who'd changed enough to feel uneasy, not quite sure what to say next. I drifted back, rubber-band tether to new-world perception un-stretching, snapping me back into the now.

I turned to Kat, who was staring up at a painted circle, electric green but with no feel of beckoning to it, looking somehow wistful, like its color evoked in her just an echo of the desire to be back at that bridge, flowers painted on stone making her wish for the real thing. Not enough to make her waddle towards it, just enough to keep her transfixed.

My stomach dipped slightly seeing her like that, just a suggestion, lip curling limply with dejection, feeling helpless. I rubbed my forehead with two fingers, trying to will her to snap out of it. A few moments later she did, and I sighed, relieved. She looked at me, smiling weakly again, almost nonplussed at my visage, unaware of her episode as usual. The Watcher was still standing there at the end of the tunnel, head bowed sidewards towards the tunnel wall but looking vaguely in our direction, askew but just barely, and catching me by surprise. Had he been there the entire time, watching me watch Kat stare at the circle? I bit half of my lower lip, twisting it, curling my ankle awkwardly in discomfort. I started to pull at Kat, and she came with me, smoothly transitioning into a moderate walk, unruffled and not missing a beat. I breathed out a stuttered sigh, only half-relieved then. I needed out of there. The wrongness became too much.

We exited the park, and I took a long, forceful breath through my teeth. We desperately needed to get away from the it, to go somewhere new, perhaps somewhere outside of our immediate

Leaves *and* Circles

scavenge zone, maybe find signs of survivors or figure out the fate of other parts of the city.

We decided, or I did, that we'd head to DUMBO, and simply forget about any neighborhoods adjacent to the park for a while. First I wanted to try to get a glimpse of Manhattan from the waterfront just south of the Brooklyn Bridge, an old-world area of aspiration and status defined by unobstructed views of its more storied sibling. It sits adjacent to the old tobacco warehouse with its cherry and mahogany brick and portals that always looked they should have housed Union soldiers arming themselves to fight Confederates rather than cigarette inspectors. I'd always found that amusing. We headed west through rain-slick streets and endless blurs of leaves, the trip blending together as if in fast-forward away from what I'd just seen.

We arrived on the cobblestone streets of DUMBO without incident, stones cracking from neglect, just as slate gray gave way to brighter slate gray. Everything, though open-air tomb-like in feel at times, still had that pleasing mix of quaint and stately, drenched in history, though it wasn't the kind of history that actually happened in reality. Some places are fueled by the history of your imagination more than what actually occurred, and I liked that. Especially now.

It was on the brisk side, with intermittent gusts blowing both us and the mists to and fro, seemingly from out of nowhere, making it difficult to look straight ahead at times. We should have looked for goggles. We entered the park by the river, then stood at the railing by the edge, the boundary between water and land, right beside the area where the Brooklyn Bridge should be, though we couldn't see it through the cottony soup. Maybe we were better off not looking for it, I thought to myself.

I was prepared for the possibilities. Maybe Manhattan was gone. Maybe there was a giant void in its place. Maybe it was filled with wooly mammoths, back from extinction. We'd witnessed plenty of strange things so far, things whose purpose or origin we were at a loss to explain, but none of it—aside from the bridges and their glow—seemed to defy our basic ability to grasp. I wondered if whatever happened to Manhattan, assuming something did, would be any different. All the things that had happened so far seemed possible, though of course exceedingly unlikely in old-world: a combination of mental illness, brainwashing, ideology, and drugs could cover the Wordless' behavior. Their unseen source of sustenance and seeming imperviousness to the elements were more difficult to grasp, but even they were amenable to some rational explanation: perhaps they were automatons, incredibly lifelike, placed here by some foreign power or resulting from an out-of-control secret program financed by our own government. Maybe they were genetically engineered to not need rest or food, or to draw sustenance from microscopic matter floating through the air. Hard to accept, but not necessarily hard to fathom. There was, I convinced myself, a way to rationally explain these things, to make them fit it into our understanding of the world.

I leaned over the railing, lost in thought, my mind running a background process willing the fog to clear to no avail. I looked to my right, expecting to read Kat's disappointment or resignation, but she was gone again. *Gone again.* Nascent panic. I scanned left, right, and then saw movement, just a blackish-blue blur from that vantage point, a few clicks up the block north. It was Kat's coat, presumably with Kat inside it.

She was walking towards the bridge.

I jetted, maybe rocketed towards her across the sodden stonework. I halfway knew what was happening, though I couldn't mentally put the pieces together at just that moment. I got closer, just feet behind her. She was moving slowly, stiffly, but with definite purpose, an awkward robot returning to its charging dock. In my peripheral vision I could just make it out: Cold. Electric. Green,

 Leaves *and* Circles

and just for a second, I could feel its pull, its beckoning, those same serenity waves briefly washing over. I knew then that the fog around the bridge must have cleared at some point, just enough to employ its neon siren. I forced myself not to look at it; Kat must have.

When I finally caught up to her, panting, but in control of myself, I grabbed hold of an arm, yanking her in an arc back towards me, and away from *it*. Her eyes were heavy, pupils and crystal-blue irises both dilated, but deadened, like some kind of Anime girl experiencing immediate post-peak opiate-nod. I was in full-bore panic, feeling like all my extremities were shaking, even though they weren't, cortisol coursing like a raging torrent, hard and buzzy, though my veins. She was the only person I had, my only friend, and now she wasn't Kat, and there was nothing I could do other than try to drag her back. I used every ounce of will to contain myself, keep myself there with her, keep myself from imploding and get her turned around away from that bridge.

I led her back to the park by the hand, her auto-following without question instead of turning back around, mind still located somewhere offsite. I sat us down on a wooden bench the color of corn, wet as always, though I didn't care, facing away from the bridge. I tried talking to her, shaking her gently, then harder. I let out a scratchy groan, frustrated, angry, panic subsiding in steps, articulated and choppy. She was entranced, not making a sound, still moving toward that bridge without moving at all.

I sat there waiting, with her sitting up, unmoving, a human statue, me periodically glancing over the water toward where Manhattan should be. We waited for two, maybe three hours, twilight creeping, fog never letting up, the forces of this new un-nature seemingly determined to prevent us from learning anything about anything, though crepuscular calm started permeating with a shade of blue, defying my mind's efforts to stay angry.

I tried to think about something else while I waited and watched her: the reason we went there in the first place, to see what became of Manhattan. I knew that any previous ideas about using a drone to espy Manhattan would come to naught, though the results of our last drone flight attempt should have been enough to have already dissuaded me. In that fog, it wouldn't have gotten more than twenty feet. Hopeless idea either way. Neither of us were going back near that bridge now, and swimming in those choppy, gust-churned waters seemed like guaranteed suicide. Not like she was in any condition to swim, or even walk. Not a boat in sight, either, just as I'd expected. Not that it mattered. During both of the exoduses, people were piling into boats desperately trying to get out; Ellis Island in reverse, huddled masses streaming straight in the other direction, yearning to breathe something other than smoke-choked air and the scents of meat-hook murder. There was a shortage of fuel, boats were overloaded. Many sank according to eyewitness reports I read, and others likely just drifted aimlessly out to sea until people starved or finally jumped overboard in a last-ditch attempt to swim to shore, a *Sophie's Choice* between starvation and possible abduction and evisceration.

I was resigned about the skyline, not even sure if I really even cared anymore. Not after what just happened. Why did I think going anywhere near that bridge would be a good idea? We could have easily done our surveying further down the coastline. We didn't need to see the glorious portals of the cigar factory, and we didn't need to see the trolley track, a gently curving reminder of a daintier age, and we didn't even need to see Manhattan. We didn't need any of it. *Nostalgia was once considered a medical condition, and now I understood why.*

I did manage to make out the bronze lady standing in the water when the fogs intermittently parted, still holding up her torch, making me think that I *should* feel nostalgic, even though I didn't, mind now fiercely rejecting any further suggestion of the sentiment. That was something, though, a real glimpse of a remnant of old-world, when things like Liberty and Rights and Freedom were perennially lip-serviced in presidential debates and daily thinkpieces. *Freedom.* What did that really mean now? The freedom to starve, like there was before. Now we had the freedom to be chased, the freedom to be hunted, the freedom to be sucked in by glowing hypno-bridges, the freedom to wonder just what exactly anything was anymore. Old-world had its chaotic, fractal quality, a Mandelbrot of overlapping everythings, shifting beliefs and fads, cycles and countercycles, old things made new and new things made old. A world of opacity through informational volume. A world of differences fought over using the fist, the pistol, the scimitar, or the Belfastian car bomb, but at times through various shades of democracy and ordered systems of liberty to avoid the brutal methods of the previous list. That all seemed so distant now, fallen far below the horizon of possibility. I came back to the thought again: now it was a world of opacity in the older way, the way of distant prehistory, when the limitations of your experience defined your understanding of the world, and that was, ever more clear to me, *essentially nothing.*

I sighed and sat closer to Kat, looking into her glassy, languid, slow-blinking eyes, waiting, hoping that she'd pull herself back from the bridge. Another few minutes and she did, just enough; she was still dazed, but had sufficient awareness to be able to understand me again. I, sighed, thankful but somber, then took her hand and lead her back home though sodden, silent streets, leaving our bikes behind, her mind probably reeling from its position in electric-green nether-space, optic nerve gradually feeding the look of cognizance back into her eyes.

CH26
NOT AN ONION IN SIGHT

I didn't want to be back at the apartment so soon, but I was grasping again at the familiar and well-understood, trying to keep myself anchored, especially after DUMBO. I felt shaken all over again, with months of confidence and calm shattered in just a single trip. And it was my fault.

Food had started to run down faster than we'd estimated it would, our exertion levels being higher than expected, and with some supplies not living up to their implied industrial food system process promises of lasting indefinitely, so we were back to making potentially risky trips outside. It was easier going after the acquisition of our new murder-druid-camo, though we were once again relegated to carrying backpacks on foot (I worried Kat might blank out mid-ride, her episodes as unpredictable as ever, so wheels were out), which upped calorie burn rates. Keeping stocked was always a conundrum: theoretically, there was food everywhere, but finding it, sorting through it (to make sure we didn't take something spoiled, which at that point, there was *far* too much of), packing it, and carrying it presented constant challenges. It was logistics, rather than supply, that presented us with real problems.

March, year two - April, year two, roughly

Watchers had changed, I noted with unease. When I saw them now, they'd stop and stare with a frozen calm, eyes fixed, seemingly unblinking, probing. I was convinced that they were trying to learn, trying to do what humans do, to rise above their programming. They were trying to put the pieces together, the pieces that confirmed to them that we weren't what we appeared to be, that we were deviant, *Other*. I felt a creeping fear that one day they would, that something would finally break through, that the human turned robot would turn human again, or something like it, back to an un-artificial intelligence that could recognize us for what we were. I felt vexed. A nagging suspicion that we couldn't keep all this up forever began to develop. We needed to adapt again before they did.

Then there was another shift.

We were in mid-stroll across a sleepy street northwest of the park a day in early March of year two, when we came across a young woman sitting on the stoop of what was left of an apartment building, weeping inconsolably into her dirt-streaked open palms. Her cloak was jet black, hood resting on her shoulders. Her face was caked with grime, her hair encrusted with so much mud, dark brown with streaked reds and bits of nature, that she might have once been blonde and you'd never have known.

She looked undeniably human, with no trace of Watcher iciness or Forlorn bereftitude; her countenance said something else, though I wasn't sure what just then. Could she be a survivor, like us? Was she one of them, but finally free of her programming or enslavement? We approached her slowly, inching up, then standing a few feet away, behind a ruined, undefinable chunk of building, concrete with steel corkscrew bars jutting out of it, watching silently for several minutes. "Hi?" Kat finally said, sounding like a question. The woman didn't respond or even indicate that she'd heard. More greetings, more attempts at questions. A bit louder. Nothing. We glanced around, wondering if any of the noise was attracting attention, but there was also nothing. We walked right up in front of her, uncharacteristically bold, but with fingers curled tightly around bat-hilts. Kat placed her hand softly on the woman's shoulder, perhaps to console her, and the woman looked up for a moment, head rising slowly to meet Kat's gaze, then dropping back down to resume her pitiful activity. Nothing was getting through, clearly, and the tears continued, now soft little burble-sobs accompanied by short inhales, her programming, I assumed, immediately causing her to forget our presence.

I shook my head. Kat tilted hers upwards toward the leaden sky, eyes widening, sighing with frustration. A few more blocks, another young woman, also weeping inconsolably. Every few blocks here there was another. Identical black robes. Filth. Different faces, pale, tan, brown, teenagers, women in their forties, twenties. All the same, none regarding us in the slightest. All they had was their grief. Their irremediable grief. *Weepers.*

I don't even remember the trip back home I was so busy trying to force myself to understand it, or wondering if there was anything to understand, mind practically refusing to analyze any of it, insisting that I just give in to frustration; there was a seeming pointlessness to it all. When we finally got back to the apartment, we slumped down on the disheveled cow-print couch, dejected, bats thunking onto the floor and ending with a roll.

For a brief moment, it seemed like we had the chance to really reach out, a window of possibility. To them. To humanity. A chance to create a connection with some semblance of intelligence outside of each other. No, instead, it was another facet of new-world, frustrating and baffling in equal measure.

I came up with my own explanation for their meaning, though, as usual, without any real proof. I had nothing else to go on. When I saw them, these Weepers, their visages said to me that they were victims of more broken promises, inducing in them a feeling of *weltschmerz* that eventually progressed too far; instead of torpidity, it manifested in them the familiar human face of unrelenting disappointment and spiritual anguish. Rather than continue their "duties" like the Forlorn did, diligently, steadfastly, with the belief that eventually their struggle would be rewarded, as the faithful must, they gave up. Believing that none of it was ever likely to come to fruition, they retreated into tears and solitude. Sad, pathetic, broken creatures, all their dreams into dust, ignored by the very forces they helped precipitate. *Forsaken.* It's strange to think about them, to contextualize them, to try to come to terms with them in a way that leaves you feeling like you still understand what you are. Is it anthropomorphizing when you talk about those humans in the Peoples Temple, or people with catastrophic brain damage, but with enough physiological and brain function to stay alive? Can you anthropomorphize other humans if those humans don't seem very human anymore?

The following few days were quiet, neither of us in any mood to talk after the Weeper incident, the reverberations of our own disappointment, that particular kind of disappointment that comes from feeling that you were so close to realizing some goal, only to have it yanked away at the last second, weighing on us, inducing an existential languor. Silent days started feeling more commonplace since the bridge even before the Weepers, so we spent our time alternating between our Wordless observations and attempts at reading. *Sex in History. Neuromancer. Still Life With Woodpecker.* I didn't have much attention span, though, my mind constantly wandering back to thoughts of the Weepers, feeling a kind of rueful melancholy for them. I also thought about our time in the park, that eeriness, that wrongness creeping back up on me, starting at my side then slowly inching up my back to the base of my neck, some sort of unseen hand running its finger there. I looked at the photos I'd take on the viewfinder of the point and shoot I'd used in the park, too, trying to make some kind of sense of it all, the circles, and the robes, and their inscrutable, monotonous patterns. I replayed the events from the beginning in my head, things I remembered from my time as an Observer, trying again to connect it all to what we were seeing now.

I thought more, and felt more, about the Wordless. Even though they had broken our world and shrunk the space of possibility to primitive levels, it was hard not to feel a twinge of pity for them. Maybe it was like the sympathetic feelings people experienced watching those robot dogs get kicked, a compassion for the insentient caused by the human mind's tendency to assign agency and emotion to things that seem sensate, forgetting for just a moment the horrors those things had precipitated.

I was starting to think—I *wanted* to think—that I was actually starting to see a vague direction to things. A shift towards something I couldn't yet articulate. Something foreboding. New classes of Wordless. Shorter stretches of daylight, even though they should be getting longer by now. The curious changes to the weather. The fogs and mists. The bridges. A sense of growing fear, adumbrating the edges of consciousness, starting to leak over, a chemical precursor to feelings of alarm. Until the day in DUMBO, we were bordering on optimistic, our recalibrated expectations nudging us from worry to concern to a tempered nonchalance. That was gone. I reminded myself again that we had to start planning our next move.

I turned to Kat, starting to talk, and I stopped pre-vocalization, only a curt breath making it. She was facing the front door, eyes empty, face impassive.

CH27
GO SOUTH, YOUNG PEOPLE

Kat was back with me again, no memory of the latest blanking episode, and no memory of the incident at the Brooklyn bridge. Her eyes were saying that her limbic system was becoming increasingly unreliable, her episodic memory turning into wall splatters. I started at her, despondent, and started floating, body in a far away sea instead of a desert, my only friend now vanishing one electric green bullet firing inside her medial temporal at a time. Then I was outside the apartment, floating over the park stretched out endlessly in all directions, Wordless standing silent and motionless below. I was hurtling backwards, about to slam down onto them, hopefully destroying them all. Maybe I was the one affected by the bridge, and maybe I'd disappeared into another dimension made of sun-illuminated ocean or a Prospect Park stretching thousands of miles, a whole place existing just below the waterline.

"William," she said with no sign of urgency. "William," again but with a hint of concern, her pitch bending up ever so slightly at the end, microtonal. I was lying down already, apparently. Not standing at all, not swimming, and not floating over an infinite wood. She was back again, for the moment anyway, looking puzzled, face wondering if there was something wrong with *me*. I felt better for a moment, but then worse, as it was clear that she didn't remember me asking her about what happened to her by the door. I pushed it out of my mind, forcing it into a psychic lockbox so that I could stay focused, trying to hide my sigh as a deep breath, but it only half-worked. We needed to regain our composure. Well, I did. Regain composure and focus again on replenishing supplies, restarting our observations, and going over our notes. Maybe some activity would shake something into place in her or cause a spontaneous reboot, forcing the bridge to loosen its grip. I didn't believe that, though. I looked at her, realizing what was really happening. I suddenly felt very alone.

We continued, and then concluded, our on-off discussion about what to do next, deciding that we'd head south, far away from the park what we assumed was the current core of their activities. I felt a new sense of urgency now, that leaking alarm catalyst filling up its psychic vessel. I wanted as far away from the bridges as possible, and as far away from everything we'd been through as we could get without leaving zones of familiarity altogether. There was a tension, a revulsion, just barely perceptible in the air now. We both agreed that we felt it, but neither could pinpoint a cause. Kat looked more lethargic than uncomfortable or alarmed, though, and I wondered if she was really feeling what I was feeling and hiding it well or just trying not to worry me. So not like her.

Kat eased her way into the sleeping bag, her light snoring buzzing gently in minutes. I sat by the part of the wall extruding next to the window, my arm resting on the sill, staring out into the dark, wondering what we'd face on the journey south. I breathed out slowly, evenly, through my teeth, a muted whistle flowing out with the air between them. As if in response, it happened again: a gentle crescendo of wind, building up through the unseen trees outside, turning guttural and harsh, but in a whisper, a subtle attenuation taking the edge off the throat sounds, then dipping back down and returning to a rustle. I shuddered hard, scalp prickling, thigh muscle involuntary going rigid, back teeth gritted together awkwardly, scraping slightly from side to side. I forced myself to focus, trying to think about the meaning of it rather than the growing tingle down my side or my tightening muscles. Maybe that was how they

          Leaves *and* Circles

communicated over longer distances, I thought. Or maybe it was just a side effect of this new world, having a meaning that was all but impenetrable. Or perhaps I was imagining it, fear-fueled waking nightmares periodically spiking up, starting in my amygdala, then moving to other areas, triggering hallucinations.

I sat there, waiting, thinking it might repeat. It didn't, but I was afraid, sweat beads pooling up on my forehead as the memory of the previous post-whisper nightmare started pressing towards the surface of impacted consciousness, pushing chemicals through my system that would force me to stay awake as if in response, having a bad bodega coffee-edge taste, but with turbo-charged espresso fuel. I breathed deeply, in and out, trying to bend my sympathetic nervous system back into shape while trying to avoid waking Kat. It took about an hour of that before I was able to fall asleep. I finally slumped over near the window, using the bottom part of the blackout curtain as a blanket.

When we woke the next day, Kat was lacing up her knee-high combat boots, looking present, having a hint of subdued excitement in her eyes. I was still working off last night's faux-coffee overdrive buzz, the edges of it tapering off like a feathered halo, amorphously body-shaped, around my person. I opted to leave out what happened in case I was in fact hallucinating, and even if I wasn't, Kat was still coping with residual bridge episodes and probably didn't need my issues on top of them.

Our plan was to head down Fourth Avenue into Bay Ridge, then turn down Eighty-Sixth street eastward. We'd hit Shell Road, then south into Coney Island. Plenty of food stands and densely built housing developments there that we could gather supplies from. It seemed as palatable a plan as any. I thought of crinkle-cut fries then, wondering if they'd taste good cooked over an open flame.

Before the events, we could have managed a trip like that in two, two and a half hours easy; now, it'd probably be most of a day due to our need to scout, avoid obstacles, and avoid falling into the occasional sinkhole that had formed in the rutted asphalt of unmaintained streets.

I was worried, though: worried that the cowls wouldn't work for much longer, worried that Watchers were wising up, worried about how Covetous would react to us now. We headed out just as the first hint of dull, limestone light pushed through the rolling blanket of *undulatus* clouds.

As we stepped out of the apartment, there was a distant rumble, deep and heavy, unnerving through the darkening sheet of gray. It was misting then, fine, tickling, bordering on pleasant, dialing back the ominousness of the day by a hair. We headed down Eighth Avenue, as we'd planned on taking it down a ways to stay clear of the park, but we were quickly forced to change plans. To our west, we could make out at least a dozen Wordless, some walking upright, others down on all fours, probably Covetous, heading toward us. It was a shocking scene for us, this being the first time we'd even seen different types walking together on streets outside the park. They were some distance from us, and their pace was moderate, but we were sure to get caught out if there were any more on the streets ahead of us. I considered turning us around, heading back up Eighth, and then taking a long detour east along Atlantic, but there even were more behind us. We were caught between them coming our way from multiple directions and the park, the very thing we were trying to get away from. We had no choice, anyway; a look back revealed even more Wordless picking up the rear, heading our way.

We turned towards the park, fast walking past the still-flickering gas lamps on the rows of empty houses that formed our own little unexpected stretch of old London right here in Brooklyn. I'd forgotten about that sub-area, a Sherlockian enclave abutting the park, and I was half-tempted to make us stay there and live out our days under the gas light that was at that moment incredibly alluring. A haunting link back to old-world, even if it was to an era

     Leaves *and* Circles

before our time. We couldn't, though. Not with all of them getting closer. Not right next to the Wordless ground zero.

We stepped onto Prospect Park West, which was strangely empty at that moment. I looked to Kat, hoping for an idea, but she simply shrugged and shook her head. I looked up and down the street, expecting to see a clade of Forlorn, but there were none, and no Watchers were up ahead at the next side entrance. We stopped; mist forming a fine sheen on our faces and clothes, me suddenly thankful we'd upgraded our gear.

I gazed into the park; just briefly, enough for a sea of variegated yellows and golds to come into view, instantly going bokeh, the rain seemingly blurring my perception as well as it would a camera lens at the moment. I was lost just then, somewhere distant but still there, with the peculiar feeling that Prospect Park, where we now stood, was the fixed point of New York, the central area around which everything else revolved. The center of gravity was now close to the physical center of the five boroughs, rather than the metaphorical former one that was Manhattan, particularly lower Manhattan or sometimes Midtown.

What was this place really like before? Did I even remember? The filter that had passed over everything had caused perception and memory to blur together, making me unsure of what was and what is, the changes in places being subtle enough to make me second-guess myself. Was this a painting that had been smudged, or more like an overlay onto an existing work? It *looked* like the latter, while sometimes *feeling* like the former. I felt unsettled.

It was strange, too, because that part of Brooklyn never felt quite central to anything before, as Brooklyn never seemed to have a center, always feeling more like a pastiche of neighborhoods, some of which smoothly flowed into other neighborhoods, while still others felt like islands unto themselves. Now there was a center, and my native New Yorker brain wasn't quite sure how to come to terms with that. *"If you don't like a neighborhood, wait ten minutes"* was the epigram, but what about when the whole thing shifted seemingly at once?

The bokeh switched to clear frame, and I came back, vision washing out and resaturating from gray to a pointillist multicolor back to the proper yellow that was actually there. Then my pulse started to rush, pittering, then pounding, raindrops beating on a metallic roof, hard, running together rather than differentiated.

There was another rumble, still distant, then getting closer, only the closer one wasn't in the clouds or the sky, but was under the ground, feeling like a continuation of the thunder above, somehow connected in a sort of continuous wave, but I knew they weren't. Aftershocks of some distant earthquake, I thought, causing us to list from side to side, forcing us to hold onto the stone wall encircling the park's perimeter. Windows rattled across the street in a stately multi-story home, one with conical gray cupolas, looking like it belonged somewhere in old London, too. Metal garbage cans shook, and I could hear their contents jostling about, hitting up against the sides of the cylinder. That went on for several minutes, on and off, leaving us continuing to grasp onto the wall, forced down to a knee. It finally subsided and I tried to stand up.

I raised my head, looking into the park towards the trees, then right, further down the street south. I began to swoon, and started to fall over towards Kat, trying to use her to stay upright. She held fast, solid sinewy arms keeping me from falling, though my knees had very nearly buckled by then, the acrid taste of bile creeping slowly up into my throat, demanding I empty the contents of my stomach onto the wet sidewalk.

Inside the park in front of me, behind the gray stone side wall, stood a sugar maple with leaves of anzac and old gold, medium thick-branched, but sturdy. Strapped up on smooth wooden bands on a pair of upward-facing horseshoe-shaped limbs was a latticed wooden gibbet, a bullet-shape human cage, hanging limply. Inside was a human shaped object clad in a plain, faded black canvas robe in the same style as the Wordless, covered in various bits of natural detritus, bits of leaves and stems, and the odd unidentifiable object.

A face was clearly there inside the robe, unobscured by the pulled-up hood, which dipped just slightly over the forehead. Its face was ashen, features rounded, bulbous. It was clearly a man, probably mid-fifties of ambiguously southern European ancestry, grave-faced with eyes shut, appearing to be in a deep slumber, appearing stiff, but altogether undecayed.

My knees went out, completely unable to support my weight and I went down, listing forward over the sidewalk, expelling the contents of my insides in shades of yellow and brown all over the sidewalk, making an odd soup with confetti leaf croutons. Kat was hovering over me, kneeling, a look of concern but not alarm on her face, her hand on my cheek. I started to roll over onto my back and she forced me to sit up against her, turning herself into a chair with her legs as chair legs next to mine, forcing me halfway up. I sputtered and coughed, trying to maintain some kind of grip on reality, trying to force my brain to unsee what it had just seen. We sat there like that for probably twenty minutes, mist cycling between ocean spray and humidifier sweep on our skin, my brain trying to turn the beads of water into comfort. I closed my eyes, my head back on Kat's chest, and then it all went black.

When I roused again, everything looked the same. I was still lying up against Kat, her hand petting my face. I looked up at her and she smiled weakly, a knowing EMT look saying that I'd be fine. She helped me up, snaking her arm around me in a horizontal bar, making me feel like an injured soldier from a Kubrick-era Vietnam movie. We went slowly, with me staggering and dragging a leg while she pulled and held me up, still solid and showing no signs of strain. Kat had one of those stiff, sinewy bodies, the kind that resemble taut, wizened twigs, and are deceptively strong.

We continued on down the leaf-strewn sidewalk, occasionally broken up by a long wood-bar bench or informational park sign graffitied with circles, innocent objects now appearing to be somehow linked with everything, and having a more malign cast. We crossed the street to the sounds of wind through leaves, and as we got further south, the sound of swaying gibbets. There were more of them hanging from stout branches or propped up against the park's outer wall, faces white, cocoa, deep brown, all the same unmoving, grim countenance. I forced myself to look down or away, not wanting to see anymore.

Kat kept looking back, but kept our pace steady, signaling to me that the Wordless we'd just seen weren't yet on the street behind us. We only got a few more blocks before I couldn't go on, though. I sat myself down, back up against a black, wrought-iron door encasing glass, overhung on each side by stern gray lion-heads, extruding from the transom, the door reading "Ark Hill," which meant nothing to me, but had a strange gravitas just then.

My legs were pounded rubber, unable to support my body weight, stomach empty and brain forcing hand forcing mouth to accept some plain jerky, arguing constantly with my legs about just giving up. Kat knelt down briefly, then started to cross the street towards a hanging cage. My head canted up, vocal cords trying to vibrate but failing, shoulders slumped. I continued to chew, watching Kat with a measure of languid resignation. She picked up a curvy, gnarled, leafless tree branch off the cement.

Kat approached a cage leaning up against the park wall, solid porcelain face encased in the same dull black robe, cautiously, with measured steps, keeping the stick in front of her with one hand and the bat ready in the other. She stared at it up close for a solid minute, trying to discern anything about it, but it had the impassiveness of the dead, which it clearly looked to be. It was a woman, probably early thirties, smooth-faced, eyebrow-less and with no other hints of hair. I kept glancing left, my neck just about the only part of my body I felt that I could consciously move, expecting with each

    Leaves *and* Circles

passing moment to see the dozens of Wordless pass a corner and emerge onto our street, but they hadn't. Not yet.

She slowly moved the tip of the stick, slightly crooked, through the wooden latticework. My near-empty insides started to tense, and the taste of bile started tickling up towards the back of my throat again. My body felt too weak to even shake anymore, so I just stared, mouth partially slack, eyelids heavy. She touched the woman's body somewhere in the midsection and immediately its eyelids flicked open, revealing a solid mass of unblinking eyes, looking like some sort of fuzzy neon sign the color of plastic lemons, pulsating and looking almost alive the way neon sometimes seemed to. Kat staggered back, falling down onto her haunches and scrambling to her feet, running to the middle of the street towards me, then stopping, turning to look south, now looking impassive.

I kept looking at her, the woman in the cage with her neon lemon eyes, feeling an incredible desire to leave immediately, panic immediately rising to eleven and causing me to double over again, retching the bits of undigested jerky mixed with clear fluid onto the sidewalk. Round, globular pain bubbles started radiating through my abdomen and chest, body having had enough expulsion of items and fluids for a single day, but the fear urged me on, and I started to crawl towards Kat, desperately wanting to snap her out of her trance.

I glanced up again the eyes in the nearest gibbet, looking somehow both dead and alive, and suffused with an urgent warning to leave immediately, somehow able to communicate this with a purely visual system. My stress response system started to urge flight, terror building, fighting against exhaustion, trying to burn my body itself for fuel to escape.

I swiveled my head back and forth, looking for more cages out of the need for confirmation, and I saw them. Pairs of eyes appearing up and down the block, one after another, on the park side, that same imposing yellow, what once would have been a color that practically screamed pulsing bass and synthesizers and all night drug binges was now screaming at me, one pair at a time, that I had to exit the area immediately, and that's exactly what I wanted to do.

Another set of eyes, then another, some from inside the treeline, others further down hanging from branches, until there were dozens, all with the same insistent warning: *leave now.* My again-empty insides started to churn, and I forced myself to look down, body heaving in a limited range, unable to reach a full-on wave, simply too spent. My mouth and throat were doubly sour, acrid, feeling torn to shreds. My muscles tightened, head started swirling again, spinning, the feeling you get trying to move counter-clockwise against vertigo, forcing your proprioception to get back into line with everything else, but only half-succeeding. I managed to get myself straight enough, physiologically, though sheer force of will, to continue to crawl.

I'd failed. I looked down into a street-lake in a depression in the damp asphalt with two leaves afloat in it, diagonal to each other, circling in slow clockwise Coriolis motion, looking somehow lost. The world was washed in reverb and slow-mo, and I had lost control of everything.

All this time it was Kat who'd been saving me, saving us, thinking of how to get us to the next day, the next week. Now things had been turned around and I was there, palms scraped, head-space swirling, unable to even stand, trying to save her. It was over, I thought.

It wasn't, though.

I dragged myself two-palmed on the wet, leafy asphalt to Kat's side and tugged her hand. She immediately snapped back and reached down for me, pulling me up to my feet, my ankles feeling like no more than sponges. We started to run, or something resembling it, south down the road, body switching to some kind of emergency fourth wind backup system, deep ravines of survival mode being delved.

When we were finally away from the park, as far as the last of my reserves would allow, which was about four blocks, Kat opened the door to some kind of blue hatchback and tossed us in with the sleeping bag. I fell asleep immediately, survival mode transferring into complete shutdown.

CH28
WE SHOULD HAVE LOOKED FOR VICODIN

When I came to, Kat popped open the back of the car, lifting it up in a pleasingly smooth motion towards the sky, letting in something like fresh air. I breathed in, trying to come to terms with what we'd witnessed. Kat handed me a plastic bottle and I drank slowly even though I felt drained of all liquid, trying to heed her unspoken warning about imbibing too quickly. I put various things into my mouth, chewing with great purpose and deliberation, trying to savor and drown out the lingering bitterness of my insides.

I swung my legs over the lip of the car, looking in the direction of the park but mercifully unable to see if from there. Kat was kneeling, futzing with something in her pack, looking up at me with a reassuring smile. "You were out for two days," she offered, almost amused, and I don't even think I felt surprised, but two days seemed a very long time ago at that moment. "I didn't see any more of them. The ones we saw back before the park. They never came this way," she added, knowing immediately that I needed reassuring on that point, her micro-expression reader seemingly back in working order.

I knew we'd be going slowly for a while in my condition, and braced for a trip that was going to be long, but should have been short. Bikes were even more out of the question now, between Kat's intermittent episodes and my likely inability to keep myself upright on one. The thought of attempting to balance on two wheels or even pedal with three made me laugh at myself.

"Do you remember what happened?" I queried, weakly, but with concern.

"I remember approaching the cage, putting the stick in. Then I don't remember anything until you pulled my hand, and I saw you down there below me. I do remember feeling very sick, though, like I needed to vomit, but I didn't. At least I don't think I did," she offered with a look that revealed the kind of puzzlement you get after waking up after twelve hours thinking you'd only slept a few minutes. I nodded.

The effects of yellow-eyes were somehow different on her, and I had a nagging suspicion it was due to the lingering effects of the bridge, somehow putting her only halfway between one effect and the other. I was glad about that in a way, maybe slightly relieved; at least she didn't have to remember what I did, nor did she lose her last couple of meals. I decided it was better that way. I also decided that it should be last time we'd try to poke one of them with a stick or any other pointy object, though I was rarely in a position to convince Kat of anything like that.

I sat there on the back of the car, still sipping, still chewing, trying to center myself. The wind kicked up through nearby trees, and I could almost feel the garbled whispers coming with them. They did. I looked away from Kat, trying to hide my crooked grimace, but she didn't even look up, not hearing it, which I was thankful for. It blew for a solid minute, and I almost decided that it sounded different each time, that perhaps those were messages being sent back and forth, and not always the same ones. It then tapered off into the soothing sound of familiar *decrescendo* leaf-flutter, and I felt more relaxed, automatic reactions to pleasant stimuli pushing out negatives. I was looking down, trying to force my face back into neutral before looking at Kat and continuing on. I think I succeeded, as Kat just looked up at me plaintively, seemingly unaware of my inner unease. I hoped she wasn't.

It was time to go. Kat picked me up again, acting as a bipedal crutch, and I hobbled with her down towards Sunset Park, trying and failing to suppress the lingering feeling of terror from those neon lemon eyes, screaming at me to leave but only telling Kat to stop. I swallowed hard, trying to refocus on getting out of there, telling myself that the further we got from the park, the better things would get, but I didn't really believe it.

The trip to Sunset was the longest sustained one we'd taken in a while, and it was quiet, bordering on unnerving, causing me to involuntarily grind my teeth when I stopped paying attention. Whatever effects the eyes had on Kat weren't showing themselves, or at least I didn't think they were, but they were still hanging on to the edges of my consciousness. I had a residual taste of bile and feeling of stomach emptiness, even though neither of those things matched reality at that moment, a kind of memory-induced sympathetic effect. At least it was starting to finally subside. I tried and failed not to worry about the effects on Kat, and maybe myself, but I thought I understood the latter at least. A subtle knot was building in my lower right quadrant, just enough to keep me in a state of unease, but not enough to stop me from pushing on. The quiet was something else, though.

The streets were quiet. The sky was quiet. She was quiet. We were always on the laconic side on runs, but rarely like this. I looked at her and she looked back, smiling at me with corners only, torpid and empty, like when her eyes were fixed on the apartment door. It was still the green, not the yellow, for her.

We plodded along, making very tepid progress towards Sunset, only getting about halfway down Fourth Avenue.

Then we stopped.

Down Fourth, we took it all in. Devastation. Burned out auto-repair shops offering While-U-Wait service. A tattered bodega sign printed in the ubiquitous french-fry yellow and bold red. A paint store that itself looked like a Pollock. A wall-sized ad from another era by the font, unreadable, something with a smiling man and a laptop selling a service dependent upon many layers of societal abstraction that no longer exist. Cars, silent, driverless, with phones and Slurpee containers still in their passenger seats. More shattered auto repairs. One abandoned two-story rowhouse, alternating whites and reds after another, still bleakly charming. A window with one of those waving white cats with the red ears in them, no longer waving.

Damp. Gusty. Cans and bits of miscellaneous garbage blown from sign store to gas station to burned out ultra-downmarket fast-food chain clone.

Several times over the course of the day we saw Covetous up ahead of us, performing their joyless treasure hunts, breaking the ceramic silence with crashes from tosses of new-world detritus. Rather than risk attracting attention, we'd hole up in a rowhouse or still-standing KFC in the middle of a parking lot, chicken long rotten and wing bones littering the branch-strewn, safety red tile floors, until they decided to take off. Covetous never seemed to bother searching indoors for their unknown quarry, I noticed, and I wondered why that was. Limitations of their programming, perhaps. Maybe no one got around to adding indoor pathfinding.

It was well into twilight, nearly dusk, magical indigo smoothly incrementing towards black, when we called it a day. It was obvious to me that the trip would go on longer than a single day, concerns for safety overriding any desire for speed. We did make some progress towards Bay Ridge, but the constant stuttering stop-starts hitting us with intermittent cortisol spikes were already wearing on us, or at least on me. Coupled with the effects of the previous incident, there was no way I could go on. We needed to stop.

We decided we spend the night in a stable-looking rowhouse (or I did, since Kat was back to more or less just following at this point, showing few signs of fatigue or any inclination towards decision-making), and headed towards it. As we approached, I stepped over a sewer grate, partially covered in the usual leaves and a plastic bendy straw when I heard something from inside it, somewhere deep below. Water flowing, whooshing, sound like a torrent, all white noise and liquid rumble, not far away, pushing through a long, metallic tube. I put my ear down to the grate, hoping to learn something beyond what I could while standing up, but it was the same. Kat noticed, squinting ever-so-slightly, but said nothing. The sound tapered off after several minutes, leaving me to wonder what it meant.

First it was the whisper grumbles, then the coincidental thunder-to-ground rumbling that was really just ground rumbling, then that. Kat looked at me, shrugging, not interested in speculation at that moment, but thoughts of those sounds stayed with me. We went up into the house, door already unlocked.

We set up in an empty attic, wood-floored and windowless, with loose piles of yellow-brown sawdust spread over the floor, no tools or hints of mold, and a retractable ladder that I pulled up. I liked it better that way, feeling like there was no route to us, everything

Leaves *and* Circles

retracted, with solid layers of material between our bodies and the world. That was probably wishful thinking, but I wanted to think it.

Kat was asleep in the bag before I could even bring up the sewer and the sounds, her ability to instantly switch off working seemingly better than ever, especially since the bridge. Would you too become a green bridge mind-slave to never need Ambien again? What an ad campaign that could have made.

Night settled over us quickly, a small hole in the wood above us displaying a deep nothing. I stared up into the blackness, laying on my back, trying to fit the pieces together, but failing. Forlorn; Watchers; Covetous; Weepers; Wordless starting to walk together; green trance-bridge; yellow repulsion-eyes; people cages; earthquake aftershocks; water sounds in the sewers; daylight and weather changes; decay-pause. So many different, seemingly disparate parts, nothing lining up, some pieces looking like pieces and others just shifting in my mind, formless, Rorschach-like. I fell asleep with a picture of a leaf in mind, that first one falling into the void of the sewers, but changing into a circle at the last second.

When I awoke it was black, but of course it was, since there were no lights or windows up there. Kat was still asleep, facing the side wall away from me. I stood up, switched on my keychain light, and tip-toed towards the attic entrance on the floor, putting two hands on its pull-up handle, some sort of cheap metal. I felt strangely good, no ache or muscle tightness at all, and no stomach discomfort. I thought I'd go down a flight and have a look outside, though there was probably nothing I'd be able to see.

I started to yank the handle, but it felt stuck, completely unmovable. I was worried. I'd probably need Kat's help to get it open, but I wasn't sure I wanted to wake her, and I also wasn't sure what time it was; my watch was dead. Maybe I'd gone through the last battery faster than expected, or maybe they were older than I'd thought. I grabbed my backpack, sitting cross-legged on the floor, and started fumbling inside for new ones. There weren't any.

How did I manage to lose them all? I had at least a dozen of the mini-packs. I shook my head, frustrated. I had to wake Kat, feeling dismayed. I crawled over to her, kneeling behind her. I put my hand on her shoulder and shook gently. She rolled in my direction and the ambient light of my flashlight beam glistened on her face, which was distinctly damp. She was crying silently, tears streaming down, her part of the bag completely soaked. She had no mouth.

I jerked upright, panting, heart pounding. Kat wasn't in her spot. My watch was working; it was ten AM. I tilted my head obliquely, and smirked, laughing at myself. Another nightmare, but I wasn't going to let this one linger for the rest of the day, I told myself. The tiny hole in the ceiling showed an amorphous shade of gray.

I looked toward the attic entrance, and it was open, as Kat had already gone down to survey the block to see what we'd be up against when we went out. I went down after her and found her sitting on a silver bar stool, the front room being a home bar decorated to look like some kind of Elvis-Vegas-tribute thing, complete with colorful tubular juke box and plastic guitar. It looked cheap, kitschy, and there were no actual bottles of anything; the former occupants probably had themselves an end of the world party or just absconded with it.

She was looking out the window intently, up towards the north where we'd recently come from. I sat down on a couch up against the wall, some kind of blue suede material under a painting of peanut butter and bananas on a counter, done in Warhol cartoon style. I put my feet up on a table shaped like a guitar case, or maybe it was an actual guitar case, and started on breakfast.

Peanut butter we didn't have, but we did have packaged peanuts, lightly salted and still strangely fresh. I chomped on those and some fairly stale, overly chewy raisins, washed down with tap water out of an old Gatorade bottle. Glass was always too heavy and dropping one meant losing your water. Not to mention the noise.

I was leaning back still, continuing to savor my peanuts, barely glancing at the window. Kat's eyes widened, a look of astonishment growing across her face. She ducked down, peering just over the windowsill. I tossed aside my breakfast, even though I was starving, and hopped up, kneeling down next to her. Something was up.

Heading down from the north on Fourth was a procession of at least a hundred Wordless, the largest group we'd ever seen together. There were Forlorn, clearly, Weepers, and I assume Watchers, standing solo on the edges, looking stern as always. They walked silently, passing the rubble of the world they'd created, unconcerned, grimly focused on their unhurried southward march. My stomach alternately swirled and dropped, but I was locked in place, staring, in disbelief at what was occurring. *Five hundred.* This solemn, silent march, parade, procession consisting of world destroying, mass-kidnapping murderers right on Fourth Avenue, beggared belief. The fact that it was happening, *could* happen, stretched my credulity, even after everything I'd seen and experienced so far. Our consensus reality consisted of the beliefs of just the two of us now, so I looked to Kat, making sure she registered what I did. Her eyes followed them as they went, and that was enough. How could anyone have *imagined* just one year ago that this was even the remotest shard of a possibility?

I lost count, the sea of them just too much to keep track of. It took roughly fifteen minutes for them to go out of sight, and I don't think I took more than a handful of breaths the entire time. We both sat there for a while longer, watching the north road, waiting to see if there'd be more, but there wasn't. I breathed out a long, even breath, tentatively, almost conditionally, relieved. Kat looked puzzled, which I took to be a good sign considering her other recent reactions to things. Better puzzlement than no reaction, especially to something like that. We decided to stay another day out of an abundance of caution, and probably shock. Our food stores were still in decent shape, so it wasn't a problem. I mulled just staying put, too, after what we'd just witnessed. Maybe we'd be safer where we were. Maybe going the same direction as they were, as we'd planned to do, would turn out to be a bad idea. On the other hand, we knew we'd be taking a risk no matter which way we went, and we felt that we'd been forced to switch things up far too often lately. We continued as planned.

The day after Procession Day was uneventful, dead silent under a dull grayish-blue cover of *opacus* clouds, looking sullen but holding back. Rowhouses gave way to two-level multi-families and low-slung red and brown brick apartment buildings common to the area. Sleepy neighborhoods turned even sleepier, and no Wordless march was in sight, much to my continued relief.

We finally approached Eighty-Sixth Street around one-thirty in the afternoon, another feeling of comforting familiarity, less mixed with the bad stuff, gently rolling over me. Things might be better further from the park, it seemed to me in a moment of fleeting cogitation, the kind that only lasts a minute but feels much longer. We stopped dead for a moment, then gingerly strafed into a one-floor auto-body shop with a missing door and peeling sideboards. I drew in a sharp breath and held it tight at the bottom of my throat.

They were everywhere.

We peeked out from the south-facing window past the Gulf gas station sign and saw dozens, maybe hundreds of them. Forlorn, doing their march. Watchers on their patrols. Carvers carrying their painted circles, in and out, in and out. It was the golf course. That strange, country-club novelty that always seemed so out of place was suddenly a buzzing hive of still-inexplicable cult robe activity. There was something new, too: *Diggers.* No shovels in sight, just rough bare hands making grapefruit-sized holes across the moist green-lawn, piling smallish mounds of damp, loamy dirt next to each hole, and eventually adding to a huge pile out in the middle of the street which looked like a mutant anthill.

We double-backed several blocks to change our route somewhat, but we'd have to be even more careful than we felt like being right then, post-Weeper dejection and post-procession terror-slash-astonishment vying with a new fear. There were too many things going wrong lately, and too much shaking it off. Every time we tried to catch our breath, something else seemed to go wrong, and repeated hits of anxiety, panic, fear, and stress were taking their toll. It felt like they were just *everywhere*. I felt frustrated, surrounded, trapped.

We headed southeast on Eighty-Fifth, passing an endless succession of drab single stories, some of which had Weepers on stoops acting out their incessant grief play in their jet black robes, heads in palms, sobbing. We stayed clear of them, just wanting to get away from Wordless altogether, a growing sense of being overwhelmed starting to take hold. I began to worry that the behavior of the Weepers could change for the worse towards us, which was dangerous, as they were generally stationary, and along side streets we used to avoid the main roads. If they became hostile, as the Covetous were, we'd be in serious trouble, as we'd lose our main travel routes. We might have to start crawling through backyards or hop from roof to roof, which, considering our physical conditions, filled me with absolute dread and an anticipatory, sympathetic body ache. Something was always changing, shifting in new-world, and the Wordless' behavior, especially, was the thing we had to be wary of. In light of the procession and the new beings in the gibbets, my worries felt all the more justified.

We kept on going. My unease ebbed and flowed every few minutes, a kind of undulating wave of comfort and discomfort from the familiarity of the place and the events of the past few days mixed with the sad eeriness of the sobbing Weepers. Kat was mostly distant, somewhere not there.

Along Eighty-Fifth we saw fake spider webs, tacky plastic flint corn, and skeletons, all hanging from fence posts or strung up on door-knockers, fake props of a real season that had seemingly metastasized and transformed into its own vivified entity, engulfing everything. More red brick. White wood. A house with Monroe, Superman, and Spider-Man, as well as a gaggle of other superstars of old-world, perfectly rendered in fiberglass on the lawn, on the roof, by the door. Expert work, but triggering no nostalgia this time. Instead I felt a kind of wistful confusion; these old-world statue-equivalents, faux-war heroes of our former ultra-commercial era, an era far more benign and desirable than anything new-world could offer, were friendlier and un-alien, their Hollywood crassness stripped away by contrast to our new horrors.

I unconsciously slipped back into cogitate-mode, spacing out right there in front of the statues, mouth probably hanging open and Kat too spaced herself to notice. How would a superhero fare in this environment, I wondered. Superhero myths work because there's a world in recognizable shape, but in need of repairs. Something with cracks, a seedy underbelly, a broken past but some kind of path to the future; fundamentally a place that could be saved. Here? Spider-Man would probably be an alcoholic.

Cogitate-mode wasn't switching off. I slipped back in time, sometime decades earlier, but the same time of day. Marigold sun streaked through cumulus clouds, with people sitting on their porches and cars driving by. Kat stood in front of me, admiring the statues, and the owner of the house smiled at her from under his thick salt-and-pepper mustache, pleased that someone was appreciating his creations.

I felt ecstatic, delighted, not afraid or upset in the least. I wanted to stay there in that imaginary old-world for as long as I could; I no longer wanted to snap out of it. I wanted to go get hot pizza and walk the streets without thinking about gibbets or green bridges or Kat slipping away. I took Kat's hand and we started to walk with no sense of purpose or determination, smiling. I refused to leave. I *wouldn't* leave.

Kat was now staring at me, holding my hand, head angled slightly,

     Leaves *and* Circles

puppy-like, a hint of mild concern, curiosity. Now *I* was the space cadet, blanked out, staring at nothing, but she didn't say a word. I was back in new-world, barely having touched the waking dream for any appreciable length of time, and I instantly felt the mood-drop of disappointment, shoulders slumping in tandem. I wanted to go back. Back. I didn't want new-world anymore. I wanted pizza and french fries and spumoni and milkshakes. I wanted fusion tacos. I wanted the sky. I wanted to just walk, walk without fearing for our lives every single time we stepped outside, every time we turned a corner, every time we approached a bunch of trees surrounded by a fence. I wanted a world with no autumn-colored cowls, no mass kidnappings, and no murder-houses. I wanted to go back, but we couldn't go back. We continued on.

Eighty-Fifth merged into New Utrecht, and we made the turn back on to Eighty-Sixth. I knew I wanted to pass by L&B Spumoni—the best square in the boroughs, with their sauce on top of the cheese, perfectly seasoned. Fresh, hot, always coming out of the oven one after another. Lines moving like lightning, always another tray before you could ask if one was coming out. Beautifully soft pillows of dough, sauce, and cheese. I'd have traded all my raisins for a single square, even ice cold.

It'd been a while since I'd missed something quite that much, felt an ache, a real pang for old-world outside before that particular day. The superheroes did nothing for me, but the thought of that slice sent me careering back twenty years into a sunlit day of sauce-doused obliviousness. I wanted back in that dream.

We made our way down Eighty-Sixth, almost sauntering on our way to the pizza place now that all the Wordless were well out of sight, stopping short on the cracked, heretofore white sidewalk when we found ourselves engulfed in a flood of colors. The circle colors, purple ochre and cold, neon green, like the bridge, surrounded us, washing over the both of us, turning our skin into an otherworldly tri-color mix. There was the white, too: plain, soft, almost gentle. It all felt strange, this time only because of the unexpectedness, the dissonance of the lights in that area, glowing as they were over fast food signs, traffic lights, and streets devoid of people. The green didn't have the same pull, not like the bridge; it seemed somehow weak and insipid, and neither the purple nor the white seemed to evoke anything at all. There was something else, too; the signs, the traffic lights: they all somehow looked *on,* though they clearly weren't—they couldn't have been—when viewed through the tri-color.

I jogged up the elevated train steps, hopped the turnstile, and went up to the platform to see if I could make something of the new phenomenon, perhaps find its source; it seemed to come from everywhere and nowhere in particular. I took in the sweep of tracks and sky in front of me, looking west, gazing at light-drenched signs, train traffic signals, and what seemed to be parts of the sky itself, trying to glean some meaning from it all. Then I just stared for a bit, bemused, head oblique, losing myself in thought and color. I looked west towards the sky, and saw streaks of wavy cloud and pinkish-orange light, evoking a feeling from old-world. Traces of

 Leaves *and* Circles

awe. *Hints of a fading sun.* I kept staring, watching it fade, then disappear, giving way to the sourceless tri-color, causing the awe to turn to wistfulness. After several moments, I turned and hurried back down to the sidewalk where Kat was standing, apparently unmoved. I wanted to tell her about what I'd seen, but I couldn't seem to speak right away. Kat kept staring, no hint of curiosity. We resumed our walk, faster after that. An unsettling feeling hung on, causing my insides to list left and right slightly until we reached L&B.

The pizza place delivered; there was edible food left. We found perfectly good cans of tomatoes in a crate under a partially collapsed piece of steel holding table, with no signs of spoilage, a great find. Before stopping to eat, I climbed up on the roof, something I'd always wanted to do when I was little, but there wasn't much to see up there aside from a plain, long, squat building, a Dunkin' Donuts, and elevated train tracks accreting a layer of rust.

I climbed back down, and Kat was already digging into the contents of the cans. We ate our fill, grabbed a few things, trying to balance potential nutrition with weight concerns, then continued on towards Coney Island. We felt pleasantly full, but the high from those oddly perfectly ripe-tasting tomatoes didn't last long. No parts of our bodies, hearts especially, were really in it that day. We were just drifting upright on two legs, shoulders slumping. We turned on to Shell Road, under the elevated line, with its look of deep corrosion and scattered bubble-letter graffiti wrapping the support beams.

Out of nowhere, we were bowled over, again, slammed flat on our backs by a Covetous that hadn't even entered the edges of our window of perception, our perception being somewhere else; I was still waiting in line for a square and Kat was probably still back at the bridge, hearing its silent siren call. Stunned. His tiny, solid body leapt on top of me, and he turned sidewards, sitting right on my chest, eyes wide, green irises covering every part of his eyes. He was short, maybe twenty, twenty-one, a hundred pounds soaking wet.

His grip was cast-iron, both arms around my back now, squeezing. His teeth, filthy, but not in bad shape otherwise, slammed right into my forearm. My vision swirled. I was trying to reel my mind in, snap it back to my body to react, but it wasn't coming fast enough, refusing to leave a decade when Wordless didn't even yet enter into the realms of imagination. Blood everywhere. It felt like a bone in my forearm was going to snap right in two, just a toothpick in a mouth containing a jaw that was much stronger than it looked, dog-like resemblance morphing immediately into tangible reality. Then a crack, loud and clean, but my arm still looked intact. He attempted to turn himself around, scraping his toe mounds on the rough asphalt, but his legs twisted over each other, confused vines of flesh receiving inverted signals from the brain. He fell backward in slow motion in my perception, arms reaching up to hold nothing in front of him.

My ears were ringing, head awash. Kat was now on top of him; bearing down on him, bat in two hands, screaming. Over and over and over. At that moment she was a berserker, a murder-dervish amped on amphetamines. I think it was the first I think I'd ever even seen her raise her hands. He was on his knees, turned away from her. Again, again. I was staring at the bat, too, wondering how it wasn't snapping under the strain, that fact seeming so notable at the moment, like the brutality was a show briefly off to the side. The back of his head finally caved in and he fell sideways, slumped onto the leaf-covered asphalt, bone, blood, brains splattered on every tire, hood, and roof.

I was wide-eyed, mouth agape, and Kat, Kat was an animal, huffing, mouth half-open, taking deep, ragged breaths, body wracked, hands shaking, earthquake aftershocks originating from inside her lizard brain. I felt like I was breathing heavy then too, even though I wasn't, lights of confusion and three simultaneously playing TV-screens' worth of signal sending my perception into a stuttering head-shake spiral. The world went dark.

Leaves *and* Circles

Green. The room was glowing softly with it from the handful of glowsticks positioned equidistantly and neatly around the floor, and I wished they were a different color just then, maybe a gentle orange or blue. Arm throbbing. If I weren't already lying down, I would have fallen over from the pain radiating out from the bite, which seemingly referred into some part of my back I couldn't quite define. I made a noise consisting of a staccato, high-pitched breath, air struggling to escape my throat, all I could manage. "Here," she said. She handed me a bunch of brown pills, probably Tylenol with codeine, and a Gatorade bottle. I drank deep, struggling not to cough. "Slow, slow. Easy," she cautioned, me obviously forgetting past admonitions. I was parched, but eased up on command, trying to make gulps into even streams. "At least we know they can be killed," she pointed out. That was true, but the comfort it offered was somewhere between chilly and frigid. It meant the two of us could probably survive fighting *one* if we threw everything we had at it. I nearly had my body crushed and my arm snapped in two, and it took Kat going into full-adrenaline-fueled killer mode to take just one down, the after effects of which made me do a one-cheek grimace sympathetically as I thought back to our first Covetous encounter at the hardware store. A last-ditch option, I supposed, but something. Better than them being invincible.

"What's the prognosis, Doctor?" I queried, weakly but playfully, trying to keep up the appearance of optimism in the face our deteriorating circumstances. Was Kat back? Murder-mode reconnected synapses of our other patient, the one with restricted affect, turning her back into the real Kat? If that was the case, I'd have been happy to prescribe a weekly dose of Covetous head-bashings for the rest of the month, were I the doctor.

She smiled and told me she'd cleaned, disinfected, and wrapped it with bandages and a small bottle of peroxide we always kept with us. The bone was OK, too, but I probably wouldn't be using the arm itself much for a few weeks, and the thought of doing so sent streams of pain out from it, possibly imagined. I grimaced again, abdominals tightening. We'd never needed to use any of our medical supplies until then, but I was glad we had them, and for her skills. I was even more glad to see a smile again, a real one, after everything that had happened and all her recent episodes. Maybe using her skills, her professional ones, had brought something back in her, causing my hopelessness to get dialed back a couple of notches, and momentarily taking the edge off the pain. I only half-smiled at the thought of that, not having enough energy for a full one yet, but I wanted to.

We were in the back of a moving truck, one of those boxy yellow trucks I'd guessed, or something that resembled one from the inside, anyway. Was the company that owned them even still in business before all this started? I didn't remember. The truck was empty, but oddly snug, or felt that way in light of recent events outside. We kept a lock with us at all times, and we used it to secure the door from the inside. Handy. I felt like I was starving, probably from the stress, so Kat laid us out some pretzels and beef jerky. I wished for that pizza square again, looking at the truck wall in the direction of L&B, still wistful. We had our picnic, the little fact that brains were probably splattered on the other side of the door behind us nowhere in my mind at that moment.

I didn't remember falling asleep. I slept past noon on the day after Kat's Covetous bashing, still weak from the blood loss and frazzled from the post-adrenaline rush, again. I barely moved. We listened for any activity outside, and it didn't take long to realize that yesterday's melee had attracted more of them. Sounds of scrabbling, grasping, picking. Trunks opening. Gibbering, as expected. It was hard to tell, but it sounded like at least five Covetous were out there based on discernible differences in pitch and babble-rhythm, all searching for their unknown prize, possibly searching for their compatriot. Probably not, though.

We sat there for the rest of the day, unmoving, almost rigid,

   Leaves *and* Circles

hearing them scrape the sides of the truck numerous times, and I thought one of them might have even tried the door. We didn't even dare to eat during that particular abeyance, instead spending our time just breathing slowly, evenly through our noses. I unwittingly bit half the skin on my bottom lip off and probably scraped a millimeter off the tops of my teeth from grinding them. I dozed off.

When I awoke next, Kat was finally asleep. Scrabbling continued, but less of it, and much of it more distant. Some had clearly already left. The street we were on, Shell Road, was only partially filled with vehicles, not bumper to bumper; it was never a particularly high traffic area, unless people were traveling for sun worship, so there wasn't as much for Covetous to search. Summer-only affair. That's where we were headed, too, the beach, so I was glad it was an off-season. I dozed off again.

Next time I woke up it was to the gentle shake of the truck, nearby car windows giving a tepid rattle in concert. Kat was up, eating canned tomatoes and peanuts, seeming lucid, giving me a reassuring half-smile and ignoring the mini-earthquake occurring. I ate, too, and started feeling like a living human again, sensation of hunger momentarily blocking out arm pain signals. The Covetous outside were gone, Kat was sure of it, having spent the morning listening intently for signs of them. It smelled awful in there, the scent of our own waste mixed with the blood and viscera just outside the truck making us both gag; I still wasn't in much condition to walk or do much of anything but sleep, but we needed a change of venue at the least. Kat decided that I should rest another day, my recovery barely having begun.

Unsteady on my feet, Kat gave me a shoulder and halfway dragged me to a red van just south of us, with one front tire completely deflated causing it to cant forward like a dog on bent paws. Not as good as the truck, but at least the back part of it didn't have any windows. We got in, locked it up, and balled ourselves up near the back doors, awkwardly, our bodies sloping along with the deflated tire. One more day, I hoped. Arm throbbed less, if only fractionally. We slept again, blissfully free of noticeable scents. The whole period in the truck seems to blink in and out in my memory, feeling fragmented, occurring in hazy flashes.

Morning, a low stone gray, slight tickling drizzle. Foggy, thickish, a sodden washcloth, hovering in front of us. We had to keep going, worried both about supplies and Wordless wandering back over to us, unprotected as we were in the vehicles. Kat walked, and I staggered, heading down Shell till we reached the housing developments near West Eighth, where one of them, I knew for a fact, was built by the senior Trump, rather than a junior. I chuckled to myself, thinking that new-world had let us dodge that bullet, at least. Most were twenty stories or more, mostly apartments, red and brown brick, soft, urban, American Brutalist. A one-story church of no particular style, doors flung wide open, half its roof caved in. What was left of a McDonald's, more like McBombsite. We stopped when we reached the train station, me needing to rest, still getting spells of dizziness, probably from blood loss. I felt better though, relatively speaking, and Kat was still smiling, endearingly crooked, briefly looking almost giddy. That was good at least.

There was a tremblor beneath us, weak, but unmistakable. Then another, then several more in quick succession. Barely enough to shake a coffee mug off the table, but enough to get us to stop, duck, and scan, though I knew what was actually coming next. When the shaking stopped, sounds of water rushed beneath us, coming from sewer grates and manhole covers on either side of the street. One long rush, a white-water rapid sound that tapered off, the taps slowly turned back to neutral. I rubbed my then well-grown face stubble and looked at Kat, hoping for some insight or a reaction, but her face told me that it didn't even register. I shrugged and we moved on, but the issue continued to nibble at the perimeter of my processing system, vacillating between background and foreground processing for a while. I still had no idea what it meant.

Streets seemed empty, but comforting again, waves of familiarity rising up pleasantly, smoke-like, starting at the abdomen, lightening my mood and pushing underground rumble and water-rush anxiety backward. It helped me focus on other than insistent arm-throb, too.

We arrived at Coney Island, the border of it really, and began to approach the boxy elevated train line crisscrossing from east to west over West Eighth Street, all faded turquoise and worn yellow. Hanging from the steel girders were more gibbets low enough to graze the top of our heads, swinging gently in the occasional breeze, soundless but no less unnerving.

I looked up at them, tensing my abdominals, halfway expecting the eyes to open to send their yellow warning-glow out, causing me to already imagine the taste of bile in the back of my throat. They didn't, though, and I gradually relaxed, stealing a look back at them several times as we walked until they faded out of sight, wondering what they really meant.

We arrived at the amusement park, just down the block from Nathan's, and I gazed up at the Cyclone, another quasi-kitsch monument to the glory of old-world, still majestic in its woody, old-timey kind of way. Can kitsch also be majestic? It seemed like it could at that moment; an exhibit in a city-scale museum of lost quirk and imaginary Kodachrome. I wanted crinkle-cut fries again, an almost automatic trigger on that stretch of road, the way one might crave cookies upon entering a bakery. I closed my eyes and tried to force myself back into dream-trance state, like the one back by the superhero statues, hoping to hear the sound of the coaster and the smell the scent of fries, but it didn't work. I looked south towards the beach, and could almost feel the sea-spray, though.

The sky was unexpectedly clear down there. It was mid-afternoon, still a couple more hours of daylight left, I'd guessed, though you can never tell with certainty in new-world. We needed a better look around, a lay of the land, so Kat unilaterally decided to climb up the tracks of the coaster, and I couldn't even begin to mount a protest, all energy diverted to keeping myself from falling over and yelping due to suddenly resurgent arm pain, maybe now due to worry instead of actual injury. I watched her slink past the yellow and blue sign with its ancient light bulbs, right up and over the gate, coming down softly on the rotted wood leading up to the coaster cars. I could hear her feet pittering on the damp wood, then fading.

A few minutes later, I saw the back of her red robe right at the curvy front peak, where another drop would start and your stomach would leave your body. I clutched my arm again, aching, bandage constricting just a hair too tight, my arm feeling like it decided that it was a good time to escape since I wasn't paying enough attention. Seconds later she was running down the tracks and skidding across the street like a cartoon character trying to prevent a cliff-edge calamity. "We've got to go. Now," she urged, grabbing my arm and yanking me to my feet, not waiting for any discussion.

I followed her, half-hop and half-hobble, and we automatically switched to our completely non-verbal system for communicating: where to step and how fast to go, with her eyes reading heightened caution.

Leaves *and* Circles

We traversed the main thoroughfare of Brighton Beach, which was strangely clean, as if somehow washed by the nearby waves. We skipped gathering supplies in our desire to get away from the beach, then made our way on to Coney Island Avenue. I doubted pierogies or poppy seed cake would be edible by then, anyway, though there were a couple of hardware stores we could have used. She looked back at me as I continued to lag, urging me to go faster with her eyes. I forced myself to try to go faster, grasping the arm and grimacing from pain radiating from it, feeling like it was being punched with each hobble-step I took, trying to heed her unspoken warning.

We reached Coney Island Avenue, and it looked more Mosul than Little Odessa, cars flipped over and turned at ugly angles, bullet-ridden and fire-scarred. An old bookstore, something Ukrainian by its Black Sea sign reference, was completely hollowed out, and the car service next to it looked like a Scud had hit it straight on. What exactly went so wrong there I can only guess at, though I wouldn't have been surprised if it was citizen vs. citizen. Not every calamity was caused directly by the Wordless while the events were first happening, but we couldn't stand around to figure it out; Kat's demeanor was still reading fiercely urgent since her survey of the sand, telling me that something was very wrong there.

We went off onto a major side street and found a pitstop candidate, a newer building that looked terribly out of place—all blue glass and steel, ten stories high, much higher than the surrounding structures, but cheaper, gaudier than what you'd get in Manhattan—that looked largely untouched. I think we really started to appreciate putting vertical distance between them, and us, so we were glad to see it. *"For rent"* it read on a green and white sign on the front, strangely only in English, likely having no retail tenants. Inside, it was unfinished; wiring hanging out from the ceiling and drywall everywhere we went, and it possessed a strangely non-building quality to it, like you were in some facsimile of a building instead of an actual one. We ascended to the second-to-top floor and found a solid patch to sleep on near the stairwell. Plastic sheets hung throughout, and cans of white paint still sat on paint-smattered floors, waiting forever to finish their work.

Another meal of nuts, honey roasted and delicious, and canned tomatoes, tasting slightly tinny. Then she started explaining what she saw.

The beach-top was swarming with them, *hundreds, maybe thousands* by her count, little cowl-clad bipedal ants on another silent work site run by invisible masters, but far larger, stretching down the beach in either direction as far she was able to see. Digging, pushing wheelbarrows, planting, cultivating a layer of beachgrass all around them, using lifeguard chairs repurposed to hold plastic shopping bags. *The earth belongs to us, the workers.* A sand-covered nursery with yet another unknown purpose. First the golf course, with however many hundreds were there, and now this. Were other parks starting to see these numbers? Why were they spreading out now? How many of them were there? We abandoned Prospect Park due to their increasing activity there, only to find them seemingly more active here. Or maybe they were even more active back there now, too. Disconcerting. I worried that they'd continue to spread, metastasizing onto every stitch of urban parkland that New York had to offer, and I wondered if anywhere would be safe from them. What was it that made them choose these places, but stay clear of so many others? Did they ever coordinate in their work, to make decisions about necessary resources or labor, or did their programming just choose for them? How many were back at Prospect Park now? Did we really make the right decision in leaving? Just more questions, as always. We'd need a new plan. Again.

We slept on it, exhaustion overtaking arm-throb as my most pressing issue for the moment. I woke, head with a suggestion of lightheadedness, disoriented, stomach growling with discontent, but feeling like I'd slept a good amount. It was still pitch dark. Temporary windows, all apparently undamaged, were installed in the building, so at least we weren't exposed to the elements. Small mercies. There was no suggestion of sunlight then, weak as it tended to be, and I was worried, thinking back to the extended day-night in the clubhouse, wondering if this time would be any different. Everything felt so distant at that moment, like I went to sleep on earth and woke up on a darkened alien planet. I stared into the night, daylight so far away.

"It's eleven," she offered with a tinge of concern. Indeed it was. Eleven in the morning and no hint of gray, no sullen clouds, no anything. The building didn't have a useful thing in it, either, unless we wanted to practice our scumbling with wide wall brushes, so it wasn't the best place to get stranded if it came to that. The thought of going outside in the pitch darkness with our flashlights switched on was not a comforting one.

We only had food on hand to last another couple of days; we certainly weren't planning on being stuck in the dark in an empty, half-built building with no usable supplies for any length of time when we stopped there. We decided to give it one day, hoping that maybe it was a just a fluke, some kind of freak new-world eclipse on steroids or previously-unseen side effect of the filter passing over. We sat in the flashlight-lit pitch, going over the things we'd seen recently, checking the wound, rechecking our dwindling supplies, me trying to dream up some sort of silver lining to the situation. A chance to rest and regroup. Weak, but I had nothing else. My arm was pulsating, so I popped more brown Tylenol, codeine doing its thing, dialing down the edge and helping me focus on doing exactly nothing about the predicament. In spite of all the new awful, I felt like it could have been worse. Kat was talking again, present; I didn't feel alone, at least.

We gave up for the day, knowing nothing would come of it, so we went to activity defaults: sleep. When we woke again, we were still encased in ink. Eyes closed, blackness. Eyes open, blackness. Something told me then that we were hoping for too much, thinking it would go away after a single day. In spite of all we'd seen, put up with, been through, I don't think we were quite ready for *that*. Not complete darkness twenty four seven; if Scandinavians couldn't come to grips with that having lived with it their whole lives, I doubted we could, and at least they would have had electricity. We expected the power would go eventually, sure, and we did have sources of illumination, but it was still too much, just too much. I sighed hard, grumbly sounding, not even trying to mask it. I took a hard swig of water from a plastic bottle, and I didn't even bother to put a light on to find it; it just seemed so futile. Didn't we have enough stacked against us already? Frustration was returning, and I made sure to hold on to it to avoid letting despondency take its place.

I stared out into the black again, trying to make out anything, squinting hard, willing my eyes to adjust, hoping for a glimmer or a bit of movement, anything, but it was impenetrable.

We really needed to go.

Leaves *and* Circles

CH29
WELL, AS LONG AS YOU'RE HAPPY

Food had become the immediate priority again, as it always did, with us having eaten through the canned tomatoes, nuts, dried fruit, and Kind bars. The water situation wasn't great either, but rain was common enough that we didn't worry about it too much. We had to chance going back outside to try to replenish our stores if we were going to be stuck in the dark for a while.

We crept downstairs with flashlights switched on under the outer layers of our jackets to attenuate the light, our footsteps patting on the hard, dust-covered floors, reverberating gently off the naked steel columns. It was stagnant out, an inert kind of windless dark. My watch, which thankfully possesses a backlight and not just a twisty rubber band, claimed that it was just after ten in the morning, but there was still no sign of slate-masked sun anywhere, a state starting to shift from oppressive to almost welcoming in my memory.

Being the only things with illumination, we became much easier targets. I thought about the fire pits from when we'd infiltrated the park, thankfully boneless, or so it seemed, with ash and charred pieces of wood, but they'd looked dormant for some time. I wondered if they even had any use for them anymore.

I never believed that they could see in the dark or that they had some kind of thermographic or infrared vision, but something does seem to allow them to perform their delegated tasks without any visible light. If they do have optical enhancements—some kind of

Predator-mode—then it would have been impossible to hide from them, particularly the Covetous, using just old cars and dumpsters as we did. My guess: their programming somehow facilitates their work, imbuing them with senses or guidance specially designed to allow them to perform specific, predetermined tasks even in the most adverse conditions. Maybe it's insectoid, with them following chemical trails to guide them in specific patterns, or maybe there are some non-obvious visual cues involved. None of that, though, seemed to apply to tasks like "hunting" (us), which would require at least some basic reasoning, as the Covetous display. Whatever programming they have, it's seems extremely rudimentary. Once they switch to "reasoning" mode, they're forced to use their senses again, which don't appear to give them any particular advantages. So no night vision. None of that helped us at that moment, though.

We slinked down the sidewalk, crouching low and breathing in shallow, measured breaths, careful to watch our step. We found an unlocked mini-market just down the street, a rundown place creatively named *"Food Mart"* on a weather-beaten sign in English, Russian, and Arabic, welcoming us in. Inside, there were plastic bottles of flat soda and oversugared iced teas sitting in long-dead branded commercial refrigerators; pork rinds; beef jerky, extra spicy; and more putrid candy than we'd know what to do with. We sat up against the flaking, off-white plaster wall, flashlights switched off, munching meat sticks and soaking in the blackness. She suggested staying for a while since there was food, which was our main concern, and considering the state of things, it seemed about as safe as anything else for the moment. No use going back outside and risking attracting attention. There was a small storeroom in back, messy but mostly intact, that we could camp out in, and the food could probably have lasted several days, allowing us to ease up a bit, despite the impenetrable dark. Food and staying out of sight trumped vertical separation and a good vantage point for now.

I sat in the ruined front area up against a wall by the counter, cradling my arm and wishing for a chopper rescue while Kat reorganized her bag next to me. It wasn't a tree-heavy area, but I was able to discern the sound of a breeze through leaves down the street. I tilted my head back, expecting the whispers and guttering again, and it came, not surprising me at all this time, practically causing me to scoff. It continued for much longer than in the past, defeating my efforts to ignore it. I kept trying to push it out of my mind, to refuse to care about it, but then there was something else: light.

Electric. Green. Light.

The wooden circles had become a default feature up until then, unbloomed flowers, blending more or less seamlessly into the hybrid fabric of the new arbo-urban landscape. Doors, lamp posts, fences, sometimes just lying on the street; we didn't notice them much anymore unless we were tripping over one.

We crawled from the wall over to the grime-caked window, and I rubbed a hole out with my balled fist, creating a messy coffee stain on my hand, and we peered out.

Directly across the street from us was a circle, bobbing slowly above the ground as if floating in liquid around ten feet off the ground, beaming an electric green cone of light onto the area just below it like some otherworldly spotlight. That same color, that same feeling, drawing us; subtle, calming, relentless. We went outside, working our way towards it, eyes and heads averted hard sideways, trying to avoid its powerful pull. Even without looking directly at it, I could see the cold dancefloor glow hinting at the edge of my peripheral. Then it was too bright, illuminating half the block, blanketing everything around us with its icy neon cast. I was worried that Kat would be staring at it, unable to resist, going full hypno-bridge mode and walking into it, leading to who knows what, but she wasn't. She was looking east. More lights. Down that way, it was pure white, a light coming from a floating circle in an identical beam shape.

Further along, white again. Then purple. Another white. An occasional green. The odd purple again. Every direction, white, white, white, green, green, purple. Mostly white, but in no particular pattern. They were everywhere within view, and I immediately assumed that it'd be everywhere else, too, since there was essentially nowhere in the borough without an adornment of circles. We rushed to the top floor of the building, clanging loudly on the unfinished metal steps, something reverberant, practically tripping over ourselves and careering backwards down the steps multiple times. We ran past some columns, skidding on the hard floor up to a clean window, and we had a clear view over the low structures in the area. The lightshow was starting around up us like a street-level *Luxor* on overdrive. One after another, then in fives, thirteens. Then it was everywhere, just about as far as I could see. Streetlights of a sort, on again, city light replaced by no light replaced by hybrid-city light, *"urban," "local,"* and *"organic"* now taking on very different connotations than the ones from their previous repurposings. Then, noise. A rising cacophony, the roar of a sports stadium growing in excitement, started surrounding us, enveloping us from every possible direction. Deafening. I started breathing fast, hard breaths, blood pounding in my ears, heart racing, emotional state going from moderate worry to full-blown panic. It grew louder, drowning out even the suggestion of other sounds, culminating in an almost singular sound, overtaking absolutely everything around us.

They were cheering.

CH30
THIS ISN'T VEGAS

We mashed our hands onto our ears, heads down, vainly trying to block out the white noise of the death-cult celebration. I never thought to look for earplugs in new-world before, as there was little need, it being car-less, animal-less, bird-less, and various other -lesses, leaving it rather subdued so long as you weren't being chased by a Covetous or yourself smashing plate glass. I couldn't have thought of another item I wanted more just then, other than a helicopter and the ability to pilot it. One solid sound of white noise, continuing, reverberating through the streets, seemingly shaking the fabric of the city, drowning out my ability to think.

A good five minutes passed before it finally stopped with a decrescendo, weirdly sudden and synchronized. I stood up and looked out onto the newly illuminated streetscapes, placing my hands on either sides of the top of my head. I felt woozy. Eyes unfocused. The room listed, and me along with it. Kat was in the corner, arms around her knees, trying to disappear her face, and I imagined, herself, into them. We both knew that we were entering a completely new phase, one representing a major shift; an escalation of some kind. Definitely not on the good side of the ledger, I thought. Our dreams of safety and solace melting under the cold glow spilling from the death-cult *Better Homes and Gardens* display now dotting the whole of New Brooklyn.

I forced myself to look out again and behold their nebula of light. From nearby wide beams to faint dots in the distance, I gazed upon them, trying to force my mind, wracking it, to understanding their significance. Light-circles weren't spaced evenly or in any reasonably discernible pattern, and nothing visible to the naked eye appeared to be holding them up or powering them. They simply floated, a gentle liquid bob, mute, and almost soothing. I spent some time staring, my body quivering, eyes taking in a sweep of our new city, and willing my mind to adjust, but it wasn't anywhere near accepting.

To learn more about what it all meant, we'd need to run experiments, but we were in the completely wrong headspace to even attempt it right then; I was still shaking, Kat was huddled, immobile. Still, the wheels were already turning for me, curiosity battling with fear. Maybe they were just decorative, the new-world death-cult version of home improvement or street beautification, I joked to myself. It all but confirmed that they really didn't have built-in night-vision goggles for non-programmed tasks, and it potentially solved the night stealth issue, which ticked up the encouragement meter back up a hair, I supposed, while simultaneously creating new worries about a myriad of other potential problems. Night trips now seemed both potentially more and less risky, presenting a new set of tradeoffs to think about, and I wasn't sure what to do with that yet. It didn't matter that day, though; our nerves were utterly shot, cortisol having dragged our systems into a dark alley for an extended beatdown. We crawled back into our sleep cubby on the lower level, curling up in the bag, and fainted asleep for a long while, this time pure exhaustion acting as a sedative.

We woke up around three AM, nerve-frazzle dialed back thanks to our extended nap session. We felt well enough to start testing, physically, though I shouldn't understate our hesitation or misgivings about doing so. The lights were a drastic change, much larger than any we'd seen in new-world so far, and we were worried. Extremely worried. Still, we needed to get at least try to get a handle on it.

    Leaves *and* Circles

We tiptoed downstairs and back towards glow world, sky no less black, utterly devoid of any hint of moon. The white ones, whose color reminded me of white LEDs, were the first ones we tested. We grabbed a piece of rebar and some paintbrushes and cautiously went outside, scanning both ways, up, down, everywhere to make sure it was safe to continue. No Wordless in sight, and no sounds. With the lights on as they were, mute and cold, the silence felt even more eerie than before. The world felt like it had died, then come back to life as something else, some kind of alien crypt. Kat underhanded a paintbrush into one light cone, skidding as it went, bullseyeing in the middle. We stood staring for a few minutes, staring at it intently, crouching on one knee, tensed up and ready to run, heads leaning left and right trying to pick up any signs of a reaction. No change.

Next was a purple. I started by tossing the rebar, overshooting a couple times, then got it halfway in, the metal clanking uncomfortably as it bounced along the moist asphalt. We avoided getting too close to them for the moment, worried that they could be hot, or radioactive, though our distance from them might not protect us from that, I'd guessed. We couldn't feel anything emanating from where we were, roughly six feet away from them. We made more attempts with other objects: a plastic milk carton, some pennies from the bodega register, packs of useless candy. Still nothing. Kat tossed a pack of cigarettes, this time into a green one. We looked at each other.

Everywhere, all at once, came a sound like hitting every key on a synthesizer keyboard at the same time funneled through the blast wave of a bomb. We about-faced and bolted directly up the stairs right to the roof. I slammed the roof door shut and started looking for anything to block it up, but we were stopped cold. A new sound replaced the old, a sound like a corroded steel beam fitfully scraped over soaking wet asphalt and sewer grates. We held our breaths and peered over the lip of the roof, necks oblique, trying to look with just one eye, us barely having recovered from the impact of the previous din. At first we could only see part of something, something not yet having a definite shape, passing as it was just on the outer edge of a green light cone some ways down the block to the east. Then it walked right into a white one, obscuring most of the beam with its heft, studying its surroundings, ambient light from nearby cones illuminating it in eerie tri-color.

It stood at least nine feet high, human arms and legs elongated down to the ground, awkward and gangly. It walked on its feet and palms of its hands, scuttling forward like a runner starting a foot race. Its face was clearly human, but not quite. Its teeth had been replaced by solid ridges of marigold, resembling flat bullets inside an unclosed maw. It was completely bald, pupils covering nearly the whole of its eyes, except for the barest hint of white around the edges, giving it a look of black olives in milk. A shiny-headed human filtered through a giant ground sloth. Its torso was human, too, but stretched beyond belief, with a flat abdomen, rippled with muscle. Its breathing resembled air being pumped out of a compressor at regular intervals, thin, measured, cold.

Its head moved back and forth, eyes darting, or as much as you can have eyes dart with pupils that large. The feet had some cloth over them, which seemed quite out of place. We'd only seen a few of the Wordless without their robes on, so we honestly had no idea what, if anything, most of them had on underneath. We just assumed they'd all be nude, but clearly some had retained vestiges of their pre-robe outfits. This one was still wearing its socks, filthy, stretched, and ripped, but still hanging there. We sat staring, shocked, dumbfounded, motionless.

It spent nearly an hour searching for us, peering through the windows of cars and looking in doorways, behind trees and right on the street, patiently and methodically, if not particularly thoroughly. Like its brethren, it never made an attempt to go inside any buildings or vehicles, not that it could fit through any of those doorways, anyway. We observed it intently, trying to learn its patterns, tense though we were. Eventually, shock gave way to boredom as we watched it execute its repetitive program. When it seemed satisfied or its search timeout finally expired, it hopped off, metal scraping on wet stone sounds following unsettlingly in its wake.

CH31
A SWIFTLY SHIFTING PLANET

The bridges began to make sense to me, the color of the lights finally neatly fitting together one long-dormant puzzle piece with another. The green light must serve as a kind of alarm system, their version of a tripwire. Better, though, because it tags you, making you *want* to approach it, *want* to be detected. As you stare it gets more alluring, more enthralling, eventually overriding in you your interest in your surroundings, forcing you into the light to reveal yourself to them. An alarm system that burglars want to trip.

I felt relief that we never seriously tried to cross the bridges, a previously undetected chest-weight shaving off a few pounds. Based on this new deduction, it made sense that human-sloth-hybrid would show up when a green beam was disturbed in order to presumably collect—or dispatch—the source of said disturbance. I wondered what would have happened if we'd actually stepped onto one of the bridges; we could have been caught out with nowhere to go but over the side. Unsettling.

I was initially lost at what to name them, these gangly, twisted taffy-creatures, Kat uninterested for the moment in playing researcher. Leggers? Too comedic. Guards? Boring. The little things, like good names, still mattered, serving as a tether to sanity, which meant that one was out. I pondered it briefly, opting to stay simple and to the point: *Hunters*. I hoped that this would be the last member added to the Wordless taxonomy, a growing unease at the increasing dangerousness associated with each entry.

I went back to thinking about the green lights, their nature and design: were they actually meant for *us?* That seemed oddly geocentric, like we'd be promoting ourselves to pre-Galilean earth-status. It reminded me about the story of a woman I'd read about, some kind of cool-hunter who could recognize patterns in things others couldn't, and whose father was involved with security; the father said that paranoia was fundamentally *egocentric*, and I think he was right, with both ideas essentially saying the same thing about mistakenly putting yourself at the center of something that you shouldn't. These lights, whatever their nature, were likely not designed or evolved specifically to deal with us. If that *were* the case, then who, or what, were they for? Were the Wordless expecting something else to become a threat to them? I began to consider the possibility that we were going to see even more new denizens on the streets of this New Brooklyn, maybe something that *wasn't* a Wordless, but something only they or their unseen masters were privy to—and potentially feared. Things were getting harder to plan for.

The Hunter was gone now, and we didn't see any others. The streets felt abandoned amongst the terrestrial light nebula under the flat black sky. Before the light-cones appeared, we had most of the city to ourselves (as long as we avoided parkland): our own mist-shrouded, soppy, but quasi-familiar playground where we could scavenge for supplies and find pleasure in little in things. Discoveries; bits of knowledge; new food stores; books; architecture we didn't have enough time to enjoy before; those intermittent feelings of comfort and serenity associated with returning to an old neighborhood, even if it was changed. Now I worried that this place would be changing even further, and I wasn't sure how we were going to fit in with the new order.

May, year two

We were more cautious in the weeks after the light-cone and Hunter incidents, keeping our pace slow, crouching low to the ground, darting from dumpster to vehicle to trash can, constantly scanning for possible threats, with my arm-throb serving as a reminder slash commitment signal for attentiveness. I almost appreciated it considering all the new dangers popping up around us with seemingly each passing day. I briefly looked down at the bandage as if to acknowledge that fact, nodding at it slightly. We avoided the lights, treating them as pits or those red laser beams you'd see in action movie break-in scenes, and ducked into buildings to get our bearings, peering outside through a window or a well-placed crack in a wall before venturing back out after deeming it safe. We slept on high floors away from windows, preferably inside closets or small rooms, and made sure to block and lock any place we called home for a night. I didn't feel confident that Hunters wouldn't eventually figure out a way to get inside, perhaps by scaling a wall up to a window, despite their size; there were several times we were able to hear their telltale scrape, putting me on edge, causing my far-too-familiar teeth-grit and abdominal squeeze. The thought of one of those ashen faces with their bullet-maws finding us while we slept froze every vein and capillary in my body.

It took about a week after the appearance of the light-cones for the sun to finally return in any fashion; during the days leading up to

their appearance, sleep and wakefulness blinked in and out, a rolling blackout of consciousness and unconsciousness, leaving me feeling perpetually disoriented. Three-quarters past ten rolled around one day, and we had a dull cement sky once again, an actual comfort, the scaling back of expectations making me snort to myself. The light-cones stayed on even in the daylight, and I wasn't really surprised.

After heading back out into New Brooklyn's silent, arbo-urban disco, we avoided parks, beaches, or anywhere else we thought were especially likely to have Wordless. We would see them even in small, proper parks, not just the larger ones, and in Greenstreets mini-parks, those semi-random bits of old-world hybrid-city with a single tree and a bench off to the side, surrounded by low, black iron fences, giving you a bite-sized nugget of naturalism wherever you were, little islands of life in seas of concrete and steel.

Without fail, each park or park-like space had at least a single Watcher on patrol, steely gazes probing the area out in front of them. The Forlorn continued their autonomous program of circumnavigation, and Diggers continued to dig and plant, ploddingly, still with bare hands and no hint of exertion. We hadn't seen a Carver since the lights went on; perhaps they got reassigned, I mused. We also came across the occasional Covetous rifling and complaining in gutter-speak, and we were careful to avoid them as usual.

Mid-May, year two

Something unexpected. Filthy, black-robed Wordless standing in circles of three around trees in a small park off a three-way street in Gravesend. *Weepers again.* Something had finally pulled them out of their misery, and they stood silently, mostly still, hands joined. Their faces were no longer filled with despair, instead replaced with something else, it seemed to me: expectancy. Tears streamed down their faces, endlessly as before, falling into the soil and flora below them, perhaps nourishing the short green grasses and sycamores and firs around them. Tears of *hope*. I don't think they ever saw us, but then, they never appeared to look away from tree they were "caring" for. I struggled to guess the meaning of this new development, but it felt ominous. What was this all adding up to?

Home search continued. We were heading west, then north again, this time to Red Hook. There were actually multiple reasons for this choice, which I detailed at the beginning of this work. Fewer parks and distance from Prospect Park were two of the main ones, as a reminder. In retrospect, we probably should have gone east into Queens, maybe South Ozone Park. Despite its name, it was mostly one and two family housing, without much in the way of dedicated green space. It was leafy, sure, but nothing that really qualified as a park *qua* park, which might have been safer for us. Maybe a place like that, away from green spaces, could have survivors. I wanted to think that, anyway.

Not going there when we had the chance was probably a major mistake.

It took nearly a week to safely reach our new neighborhood due to our go-slow approach and our need to avoid the lone Hunter we encountered during the trip. As long as we didn't touch the green beams, we weren't likely to see them, I believed. At one point after espying that one, I was sure it was going to spot Kat since it had stopped short and looked in her direction, scanning left and right and sniffing the air with its slightly over-wide nostrils. Kat was frozen in place, staring directly at it, or maybe staring in the direction of the bridge, its soundless siren calling her again in her memory. I yanked her by the arm, pulling her into an alley behind a chain link fence, ducking down behind some crates filled with fruit, putrid in a quite unfamiliar way, trying hard not to gag. She wasn't gagging, though; she was still dazed, staring straight

        Leaves *and* Circles

ahead, the scent having no effect on her. I held on to her for a while, held her down in case she started going on bridge-call autopilot. I waited for the Hunter to leave, listening for its tell-tale scrape, wait for it to grow distant, then scuttled on, two beetles weaving through the dung instead of rolling it. I led her by the arm until she came back to me, with her having no memory of her staring episode, as usual. I shook my head, again unsure of what to do.

The weather was getting warmer in mid-May, up around sixty, and it seemed more humid than ever, which felt psychologically like it was making us go slower. I noticed a few new things during the trip to Red Hook. One, leaves on the streets were finally disappearing. I'm convinced now that they were being picked up by the Wordless, their disappearance too sudden and complete, with no traces of broken ones or bits of stem, for them to have disintegrated. Two, the colors on the circles didn't always seem to correspond to the colors of the lights shining out of them, which I honestly found surprising, since the connection seemed so fitting. Obviously, the white ones never would never match up, but the greens and purples were frequently mixed up as well. My thinking now is that the colors never mattered at all. My theory: they'd somehow become convinced of the importance of the colors for completely spurious reasons. Perhaps it was a mistranslation or a confusion of cause and effect in some distant past when other groups had experimented with bringing about new-world and were documenting it. (I'm also speculating that someone was kind enough to document the apocalypse initiation process. *The Eco-Death-Cultist's Handbook.*)

This made me wonder about some other things, namely: how many times whatever process caused this was (vainly) attempted in the past; whether there was anything written down about it anywhere; who might have known about all of this; and who communicated it to the people who would become the Wordless. Surely these people didn't spring fully formed as would-be robe-children, just biding their time to turn the world into a forest-green murder-hole.

There had to be more information out there somewhere, but that all seemed so very far away.

We took the longest way we could to get to Red Hook, wending our way through a sliver of Carroll Gardens and her stately brownstones. The dissonance was eerie, and even a bit amusing. Thick, attractive structures, always so powerful looking and faintly regal in their own non-monarchial American way, now in the middle of an otherworldly movie premiere, blissfully unaware of the set they were the backdrop of. There was just something about the neutrality of objects, their ability to witness, which fascinated me.

We made our way across the northernmost streets of Red Hook, my tension decreasing with each step into the neighborhood and away from the big park and the beach, down to the hulking, almost prison-industrial ambience of Inlay Street, with its stacked containers, boxes of building materials, and an unadorned but heavily balconied building of monochrome tan. We passed some dilapidated, half-repaired sites of former warehouses, which looked more like half-built jails, abutted by decaying, wooden, blue tarp-covered scaffolding erected along the sidewalks. More ghostly cones of light helping to guide us, mute will-o-wisps just hovering in place, occasionally unnerving me.

Signs of decay on things that were previously in a state of suspended-decay-animation started to appear again, I noticed, the growing calm induced by our arrival in Red Hook serving to remove clouds from perception. Certain kinds of organic matter like wood, tree leaves, and other items of a green nature that weren't generally considered human-edible (unless you were a budding urban foraging-revivalist) seemed to previously have a kind of immunity to the passage of time, but that had apparently come to an end. I took that as evidence that some kind of new cycle was beginning, and that this might mean that even more radical changes were ahead. I rolled around the possibility that the fundamental laws—the biology, the chemistry, the physics—of new-world might

      Leaves *and* Circles

differ from our own in more ways than we believed, requiring us to rethink even more of our assumptions. Or perhaps it was all transitional, I thought, some sort of special rules of interregnum, part of some kind of bootstrapping protocol, before reverting to the rules of old-world.

CH32
AS FAR SOUTHISH AS SOUTH GOES

Summer, year two

The distant echo of arm-throb resurfaces in other body parts sometimes, but I feel that it must be psychological. Not that it helps. Maybe it's the recency. Everything has been feeling raw lately, alternately real and surreal. We never know anymore which series of actions, no matter how insignificant they may seem, could lead to disaster. Formerly simple, everyday things take on a new significance, magnifying in import, especially in memory.

We found this building, the one I write this work from here on Van Brunt, with little fanfare. We walked right in right past the Shop of Unremarkable Trinkets (actually named *Bacchus Collectibles*), closed the gates behind us, then blocked up the doors and placed some dismantled furniture by a few of the windows, which I'm not sure actually helps in a practical sense, but it does make me feel better. Doubly so when I can hear the rusty, wet scraping of the Hunters outside. A thin security blanket made of old wood that used to be chairs and table legs.

We settled in on the level-spanning apartment on the second floor, even more wary of ground level anything, especially since Hunters started appearing. Woody, quaint, sparsely furnished. A few unremarkable mahogany dressers, a plain bed, and an oaken *Ikea* bookcase, possessing a shine from its lacquered finish. An empty kitchen, untiled, with amorphously tannish-white wood slats on the walls. Unfinished wooden floorboards spackled with white made to resemble paint splatters. No pictures on the walls, barely any clothing in the dressers. Whoever lived here likely didn't spend much time, or grabbed everything and left during the events. Sturdy door, almost medievally thick, wood with solid metal trimming and a small round peephole, somewhat scratched up. Two standard windows on the east and north sides, openable from top and bottom. A barely detectable hint of mustiness, nothing terribly offensive, like a well-maintained attic. Clean blankets and sheets, plain white everything. Some books on art, mostly pictures. A few sweaters, wool, two-tone checkerboard patterned, and pairs of blue jeans that didn't fit either of us, but would do fine as rags. It felt purposely unremarkable, like whoever lived here just liked being surrounded by *tabula rasa* so as to not mess with the frequency of their thought waves or creative flow. This was home now.

We needed to replenish supplies again with our food stores running critically low. Red Hook never had much in the way of shopping or food establishments, but large public housing developments not far away seemed to hold some promise, and the area seemed almost untouched by fires or looting. A small comfort, I thought with a touch of frostiness, feeling almost sarcastic towards myself.

We spent most of the summer, full of unremarkable gray and white days, mostly windless and under *fibratus* clouds, with a weak sun struggling to illuminate the cobblestone streets, breaking into and gathering supplies from adjacent buildings. A familiar ritual by then, all our procedures honed and needing little active communication. We encountered no resistance, the Wordless presence being essentially nil here at the time, so we were able to restock easily. This was just as well, considering Kat's increasing taciturnity, causing my insides to see-saw from the serenity of familiar, repeated activity to vague dread and back again.

We found a decent amount of food: hard, round pretzels; bags of jasmine rice and soba noodles that still looked decent; questionable looking cans of yellow corn and green peas; a box of off-brand energy bars, stale, but edible, and a whole box of tiny batteries, with no signs of damage, for the watch. Batteries for flashlights were less needed because of the new lighting situation, which was just as well because we were only finding terribly corroded ones for them lately, unlike the watch. It was almost like time and nature were catching up, all the previously slow decay snapping into place like a rubber band after a long pull, bringing with it shades of brown and red and splattering them on things, in the form of corroded steel I-beams and rusty sewer grates. What objects were previously on the delayed schedule seemed nearly random, with things like batteries or rebar on a normal schedule and manhole covers on slow-burn. Or maybe it was purely compositional; my memory, combined with some warping effects of new-world perception were experiencing a kind of decay patternism, seeing patterns of decay and non-decay that weren't there. Now I wasn't sure, but the feeling that I was right about it nagged on.

The summer brought with it the scent of mold, back in the air some days after its long absence, competing with the heretofore more prevalent wet leaves and cement scent, forcing me to occasionally stifle a gag and giving me the urge to zig-zag through streets away from it. Kat seemed unaffected, just like with the rotting fruit, passing in and out of seeming presence, but never missing a step, never coming close to tripping on the damp stones underfoot.

Things were living—and dying—again, it seemed, and not just the things that Kat bore down upon in berserker-rage. I came back to the idea that it might all be part of the new cycle, and wondered what else might come with it. It might mean that we could grow some of our own produce, assuming we could find seeds, equipment, and books on it; I started to regret printing out more web pages on identifying plant species than actual gardening instructions. Maybe the waterfront Ikea could provide.

We got our first clear look at the cranes rising by the water's edge one day that August during a canvass of the area, mists having abated temporarily. As soon as I spotted them, rising in corroded splendor, *I was hit with the feelings of a time and things I'd never even experienced, a kind of temporal* Fernweh: the ringing of work bells, the sedate clanging of buoys; crates being hoisted up and down from ship to dock, colorful steel cans strangely replaced by wooden ones; stale coffee and the choke of cigarettes; rough shouts and grunts, indistinct and devoid of treble, from grizzled men with calloused palms. I stood on the edge of the water, head swaying by micro-increments, filtering the present through imagined visions of the past, entranced and remote, gentle laps of the river below eroding the stone edge by imperceptible degrees as it had countless times in the past, almost synchronously, in both the envisioned past and the unreal-real of the present, both overlapping and undulating past each other in my perception. Kat confirmed the area was clear with a word, breaking me out of past-present filter trance. I looked back up at a crane, trying to will myself back for a moment, though I knew it was hopeless after my other attempts, and then turned to go back home.

Late summer, year two

That was an industrious, but calm, period for us. We rebuilt our supplies and dove into books we found in nearby houses (the aforementioned art books, mostly modern stuff, unexpectedly compelling), along with Atwood, Dr. Seuss, some drug-store book aisle thrillers, and a fascinating history of doors in NYC. We counted the bricks on the buildings across the way: rose, chocolate, pink, burgundy, and the occasional white or black, writing our counts down on a yellow legal pad along with a concocted descriptions of the building's history and former inhabitants. This activity kept Kat present and engaged, a strange remedy, more so than others where she seemed more docile and distracted, frequently staring out into nothing even though she showed no loss of physical coordination. Or maybe she was back at the dock or in L&B, where I wanted to be. No, that wasn't true. Most likely she was back at the bridge yet again, its icy glow never seeming to loosen its grip on her. I felt at a loss as to what to do about her condition, and she only stared at me vacantly when I'd attempt to discuss it, causing me to sigh with discouragement, which elicited no reaction from her. Not like her at all. My sense that she was slipping back—or being pulled back—began to grow, with me feeling a growing sense of helplessness.

September, year two

Temperatures started dropping. Dampness notched up again, too, causing the smell of wet stone—which I much preferred—to strengthen, fighting back against the stench of mold. Drizzles, frequent, light fog perpetually tracking across cracking stones. Looking down at the streets, it was easy to forget how much work had gone into the accouterments of a city, things that seemed somehow to automatically care for themselves, some sort of self-trimming urban hedges, before it all began. Now the stones' neglect had become obvious. Pock-marked, cracked, chipped, and unloved. Street-sweeper truck whoosh was stark, vivid by its absence now.

It was this time that we first had the first visitor to our sleepy coastal nook. It was a Covetous, clearly visible from our window even from a distance of some blocks, springing awkwardly, reminding me again of a poorly coordinated dog, but in a robe the color of dirty lakewater. There wasn't much on the streets here to look through, maybe half a dozen vehicles on the whole of Van Brunt, and nothing but dark yellow confetti leaves blown in from adjacent blocks, as we'd cleared the street itself of non-vehicular obstructions. It pried open a few car trunks and scrambled away quickly, not even finding much to toss aside, as we ourselves had picked through them all by the time it arrived, leaving things we couldn't find a use for: heavy

      Leaves *and* Circles

spare tires, an old DVD player with a cracked window, and some cheap, flimsy, green-corded holiday lights. There was one exception to the useless item finds, though it wasn't from a car: a pair of binoculars we could use, picked up from a water-damaged house near the bay in the south part of the neighborhood. Probably our best find since we started.

There was something different about that Covetous, I noticed after observing him for several minutes from up here. He (and he was clearly a "he" based on the clues visible through the rents) still wore a long robe, slightly faded and mostly in tatters, noticeably worn on the bottoms due to dragging; he was still doglike, running on all fours, as I'd mentioned; he retained a dissatisfied demeanor, seeming unable to locate whatever mysterious object Covetous perpetually seek (their search system clearly still needed a lot of work.) All the things we'd expect to see. His back, though, had started to curve, like a person with a lifelong hunch, though he couldn't have been older than thirty. He was hairless, skin developing a dark greenish-yellow, vaguely Dijon mustard hue with hints of liver-spot mottling starting to show. Emerald-green irises covered his entire eye, visible clearly near the white-light cones, with no sclera visible at all now. He was gaunt, sinewy, fingers and toes elongated, and nails longer, slightly curved and coming to a fine point and acquiring a faint chestnut hue, almost avian.

Then we saw something even more unexpected. He stood up straight and curled his mouth upwards, revealing yellowed human teeth, a bit too long for his mouth now, but perfectly straight and just barely fitting; the Cheshire cat badly in need of a dentist. He was smiling, broadly, madly, and was clearly staring at the lone purple cone of light at the end of our street out front. Forgetting the useless trinkets around him he'd been rifling through, he ran straight towards it, arms high in the air, eyes widened and brow furrowing up, a look of what appeared to me was *unmitigated joy.*

In a moment, he was under the floating circle, inside the cold, purple disco beam. He immediately started changing, growing, shifting, body appearing to stretch and convulse in every direction. Muscles grew, then shrank, then grew again, body parts elongated and thinning. The beam disappeared seconds later, its wooden circle lamp clipped from its invisible string, clattering across the cobblestones below, unnoticed by the Covetous. He was taller, lankier, a bit more sinewy now; he also appeared dejected, the look of a child whose promised toy turned out to be pale imitation of what existed in the imagination. He went back to all fours, now completely naked, and strode off the way he'd come.

We both pushed back against the wooden wall and slid down, heads knocking back against the hard, cherry bricks with a thud. "Really glad we never touched one of those," she cheered, weakly, but reassuringly present. I smiled at her broadly, effusive, glad to see her back, but with thoughts immediately returning to the changed Covetous, trying to connect what we'd just seen to previous events.

We finally had a partial answer on the lights and their uses. Whites appear to do nothing but illuminate, having no other visible purpose; greens serve as tripwires, alerting them to the presence of non-Wordless; and purples transform what steps into them into something... different. To what end, I wasn't sure, but I knew there was no possible way it could be good for us, not after what we'd just witnessed. Maybe it gave them abilities they themselves weren't able to perceive yet, or maybe the abilities were simply delayed, on some kind of timer or development schedule. Maybe it was just another broken vow or misunderstanding of purpose, the promise of salvation or power ripped away just when they'd thought they'd finally obtained it. Or maybe there was another purpose, one that we had no current ability to perceive. By the look on his face, the beam did not have the desired effect, or maybe they were just programmed to look that way, face reverting to a default expression. I didn't believe that, though; there are times you can see flashes in their countenance, in their eyes, that give away a hint of humanity

          Leaves *and* Circles

buried underneath the layers of death-cult-code abstraction, indicating a n all-too-recognizable human emotion. To me, that's what it read: disappointment.

We sat in an empty silence for the remainder of the day, Kat's cognizance receding, eyes looking glazed and heavy. I probably should have learned to expect that, but my brain refused, only willing to accept that she was old-world Kat experiencing some temporary issues. She was probably tired, anyway. I sat there for a while, thinking about the Covetous, trying to force my brain to make some sort of connection, wishing I had my Observer team again to help me gather data, send it through the network, and process it, so that we could understand everything. That was all so far away. Kat fell asleep, and I followed, slumping against the wall, still fully dressed.

CH33
YOU SHOULD BE MORE CAREFUL

I woke up with side of my face on the floor, drool pooling up, uncomfortably cold, stretching into wet, gossamer bands as I raised my head up. Bleary-eyed and parched, I staggered to my feet. It was dark. I called to Kat in a loud whisper, throat scratchy. Nothing. Again, this time in a normal voice. No reply. I looked around the place quickly using a keychain flashlight, one room to the next, then again, double-checking, still calling her name. No sign of her, and still no reply. Then I noticed it: the door to the apartment was wide open. Maybe she heard something and didn't want to wake me up, but that wasn't like her at all, but then a lot of things weren't like her lately.

I went to the south-front window, pushing aside the thick curtain, blood turning instantly into solid ice. She was walking slowly down the block south, head tilted slightly to one side, heading toward the light-cones situated there. We slept with the curtains drawn, always, and we had a good pair of blackouts besides. How did she even see the lights? Then I turned to look at the front windows and saw it: we fell asleep with the one nearest her, that north one, still halfway open, curtain and window alike, incredibly careless. Stupid, *stupid*. I yelled for her through the window, parched throat making it come out like a short croak. Again, again. No reply. I started running down the stairs, swallowing profusely, too scattered to find a water bottle, half staggering, nearly tumbling down the whole set, careering from wall to wall.

The front gates were wide open, so I crashed at the bottom after jumping the last half-dozen steps, rolling down face-forward onto my palms, scraping against a scraggly concrete sidewalk tile. Stunned, I watched her walk forward, forward, slowly, *straight into the light*: the beckoning, cold, electric green. Before I could even get up again, the now familiar ear-shattering synth-sound rolled over me, making my body feel like a mini-earthquake was originating from within, sending undulating waves through me and forcing me to bounce up and down on the concrete, some kind of comic-horror breakdance move. It was a Hunter, obviously close by, and then it was *there*, passing just feet in front of me. My head was only able to make out the bottom half of its overlong calves, pale green-white, sinewy and still with a piece of blue cloth fluttering off like a denim flag from around its ankle. By the time I was up on a knee, head still reeling, he was already well past me.

Kat was standing in the light, motionless, head still tilted, her body listing to one side. I started scrabbling up, trying to will my equilibrium back into its proper place and failing miserably, mind and will overpowering by body.

The Hunter was on her, and my endolymph was refusing to cooperate. I was on two feet, extremely wobbly, veering from side to side but still attempting to run towards it, fists clenched, screaming. Before I could even reach the cone, it was already most of the way up the block, headed north, and Kat nowhere in sight, not near him, not on him, just nowhere. I was still trying to run, tripping on every broken stone and crevice beneath me, unbalanced and staggery, my palms bloody, hoarse from screaming, blood pounding in my ears. It was out of view in less than minute, its body bouncing away with its race-start spring much faster than you'd expect based on its size and awkward configuration, me lagging far behind.

I half-ran, half-crawled until my legs gave out, my brain demanding that they comply. Breathing heavily, chest on fire, bawling hoarsely and loud.

One mistake. That's all we probably get now. One. The line between success and failure, sometimes life and death, was narrow in old-world. Here, the delineation may well as not exist at all. We're no longer at the top of the food chain, just weak little creatures trying to eke out the barest resemblance of an existence off the scraps of a ruined world. We're insignificant here. *We're nothing.*

I slumped down, face flushed from crying into my soaked hands, blood leaking out from speckled, cement-top-shaped holes in my palms. I glared right at the green light cone. Hard. Blinking rapidly. I considered it. Maybe it would come back with her. Maybe I could follow it. Maybe I could fight it. I kept staring, almost wishing to antagonize the light, trying to mentally goad it, telling it to try what it just did now that I was ready. Fury squeezing out reason from my frontal lobe. Teeth scraping back and forth, gritted. Abdominal muscles tight. Stomach swirling. Every muscle beginning to go rigid, neck and head quivering from anger.

I bowed my head, looking down at the blood slowly pooling on the cobblestone, leaking into a shallow, diagonal crack, filling it, irrigating a river of blood made for dolls. There was no way to know I'd get the same one, them having locations all over the borough, and little chance that he'd just bring Kat back with him. They could come back with more next time, and I'd be completely outnumbered. A thousand things could go wrong, and I'd probably get taken too, or I'd die, and then there would be no chance at all of finding Kat. I breathed out and sat cross-legged, head alternating, fascinated, from side to side, watching the bloody doll river flow sluggishly, pooling up in an oval depression in some light gray stone, becoming a lake, trying to keep reason and sanity intact to prevent the overriding of self-preservation.

It was silent again, even tranquil, post-storm-like. I sat there, watching my doll river, trying to force my legs to move, but they didn't, instead just pulsing, almost soothingly, like some high-end massage bed for legs trying to force me to stay still. Maybe some sort of lizard-brain reaction to extreme trauma trying to keep me from doing anything self-destructive, a pacification device for elk considering jumping into the open mouth of a lion, because hey, the savannah can be tough sometimes, so might as well just get it over with. When I finally was able to move again, time had a feeling like it had paused then unpaused. I inched back to the apartment, barely able to hold myself up, head slung low, dragging myself up the steps, leaving hand-shaped prints in drippy red along the walls. Knees, too, were bruised, scraped, bloody, and I hadn't even noticed till then. I closed the door behind me, collapsing onto the floor. I don't even remember falling asleep; it was more like the awake was suddenly sucked out of me, some sort of somnolence vacuum.

I woke with a start. My eyes flicked open and I sat straight up, sliding across the wood floor to the wall, the same one we'd fallen asleep on so carelessly, flattening my back up against it, then looking left at the spot Kat was the previous day, somber. Post-nightmare anxiety kept me rattled, unwilling to get up for the better part of an hour, though I couldn't remember any part of it. A mouth-shaped pain pattern returned to my arm, throbbing in time with my pulse, causing me to grimace and wince. I removed the bandage Kat had set up, yelping, feeling like it did just days after the bite, and saw that it had reopened on me. I sighed, filled with frustration and discouragement. I spent some time re-cleaning it with peroxide just in case, then bandaging it clumsily, unused to having to do so, especially with my offhand. And without Kat.

The inner part of my bottom eyelids felt like I'd been rubbing sand on them for days, tear ducts feeling drained of all liquid. My body ached from dry heaving and falling down the stairs; hands were raw, speckled with lacerations and scrapes; legs were covered in bruises, appearing more black, yellow, and blue than any other colors; throat had that gargled-glass feeling from screaming. There was essentially no part of me that wasn't in some way damaged.

Arm throbbed again, seeming angry at not being the sole injury any more.

Kat and I had been together this entire time, two people keeping each other alive, keeping each other safe, keeping each other sane, and now she wasn't here. She'd saved my life twice, first through her initial planning when I was busy info-bingeing, and then later from the Covetous when she went fully bloodlusted Viking back near Coney Island. She took the first scouting run, a very risky move, learning important things about the Wordless for us. She was the one with medical training, and the only one of us that knew how to drive. She was the anchor of the team, my constant companion, my only friend, and possibly the only other real human alive on this perilous stretch of rock. To say that I was devastated would be the understatement of this one-and-a-half-year ordeal. Was? Is? I shouldn't be talking about her in past tense. No.

She was out there, alone, but alive. I had to believe that. What exactly would they, or could they, do with her, based on my knowledge of their interactions with us? Who knows what their protocols specify for "recently captured biped that triggered alarm system." I tried to imagine best-case scenarios, but they weren't particularly reassuring. *"Make her join by reprogramming her mind"* was the most optimistic I could come up with. *I needed to find her.*

I was determined to start the very next day, body-wide pain and injury be damned. When I awoke, I felt like I'd been imbued with a new sense of resolve after removing nearly all water and salt left in my body through my tear ducts, then replenishing it from our water reserve, drinking probably two bottles solid. I had a pleasantly empty feeling, despite all my other problems.

Where to start? Parks, obviously. The beach. Greenstreets. One of countless numinous, urban naturalist spaces, now repurposed and used against us, mosques converted to churches or churches to mosques in an occupied land.

All the places we so carefully, studiously avoided. Those were the places I needed to be now. They all needed to be checked.

My first stop was going to be the tallish public housing developments just northeast of the apartment overlooking Coffey Park. At least fifteen stories high, dull, brownish brick with classic *NYCHA* minimalism, but not at all high enough to be really vertiginous until you reached the top, not like what I imagined taking the stairs up in a Manhattan megatower would be like (and some buildings didn't have windows in the stairwells, which gave them a subterranean feel even though you were moving in the vertical), it would hopefully provide me with good views of the area. As I approached some trees on the sidewalk next to the building, a whisper-gutter breeze started pushing through the branches hanging overhead, making me wary, causing me to look back and forth, somehow expecting something else to follow.

I'd have a good view of the whole ambit of Coffey Park on the roof, or so I hoped, but before I went up there, I wound up taking a slight detour first. It was a rare moment of opportunity: the park appeared empty from street-level, currently devoid of any Wordless, giving me an opening to explore more closely without risking a reaction. I stepped past stubby black traffic poles lining the park entrance onto the damp gray honeycombs of stone, and headed over to a patch of grass hosting a couple of fir trees. Inside the park, I noticed a faint smell, the one from Prospect Park, the one I couldn't place, and got that same queasy feeling. Wrongness. Something about the way the soil and grass sat, textured unevenly, like something was buried underneath. I flipped my bat around and jutted the hilt into the ground, hitting something solid, possibly rock. I scraped around, moving dirt to and fro, trying to get at the source of the unevenness. I reached down into a section of soil I'd excavated and pulled, but it barely budged. Dusting another layer of soil off, it started becoming clearer, whatever it was. That's when I decided to wipe the solid parts down with water and some stray leaves.

I wanted to feel surprised, but I didn't. Underneath the ground in a circle roughly ten feet in diameter were bones, dirt-stained white. They were connected together by their epiphysis', using carved depressions, into the next bone in the chain, and wrapped around at six-inch intervals with what appeared to be tree bark, three layers deep. *Humerus, Radius, Femur, Tibia.*

It was obvious what had happened in retrospect, and it was clear that I knew the truth, that truth at least, already. I knew I must have known the entire time, but I wouldn't let myself think it until that moment, mind-circuits of denial refusing to let my conscious even countenance the likely reality.

I sat next to the bone pile, thinking about the former owners, trying to imagine their existences, trying to imagine if they could have envisioned ending up as post-apocalyptic death-cult garden decor. Wondering about their jobs, about their desires, about their Internet habits. Had I looked at one of their posts on Twitter? Viewed an image remix on Reddit or imgur? It's strange to connect times and events like that, the then and now, a before existence of everyday actions and pleasures; there was a grisly delta between that world and the one we found ourselves in now, me and those bones.

An expanding bellows of somber expanded through me then, with me not even dwelling on the possible purpose of the bones, instead thinking about where the rest of their owners might have ended up. I decided that they were probably in the middle of the bone-circle itself, probably buried as shallow as the bones themselves due to the way the ground extruded unevenly. That solved at least one mystery, though I wasn't even trying, too distant and myself *forlorn* to care. Those bone-circles were probably everywhere, in every park, in every patch of grass that surrounded a tree.

There was nothing I could do for them, and nothing they could tell me about their killers as I sat there in my silent vigil. *So many corpses roll away unrevenged,* a famous detective in a moderately less rain-sodden city once said, and here they were.

I looked up, and was forced instantly into flight mode, heart thumping, but with focus rather than alarm. Dozens of Wordless were heading towards the park slash newly-discovered ground-level ossuary from the north. I needed to get out of there quickly, the first of the hoods starting to pass the treeline at the far end of the park. I jumped to my feet and dashed south towards the public housing development, working purely on instinct, grimly focused, far from panic-mode for once.

I made my way through graffiti-covered glass doors, more cheap bubble-letter and plain line stuff, then up rough cement stairways, cracked and rutted from constant use, with metal railings covered in tag names done in scratches, and dried gum turned gray and black. Westerly Brooklyn could have really used some Ficalora curation, I thought, but a bit late for that now. I was huffing by the time I'd reached the top, stepping through the scuffed silver door, already open, onto the roof, which itself was covered in crunchy pebble carpet speckled salt-and-pepper. No wind that day, thankfully, so no chance that a sudden downdraft would suck me down onto the parking lot below, ending my scouting mission in a grave of aluminum and rubber. There was no haze to obstruct my views that day, either, with the air feeling somewhat less weighty, more breathable, almost buoying compared to typical days.

I surveyed the park, fully populated by the time I'd reached the top, and saw all the usual things I'd now come to expect: Forlorn processions in endless circles around the edges, moving still to their own transparent frequency, in and out; Diggers pulling up dirt in small mounds, then moving the contents of those small mounds to larger ones out in the middle of the street nearby; Watchers making their rounds, looking for deviants or interlopers, though I was sure they wouldn't be seeing any of those; gibbets with their robed, human-shaped contents, being hung from tree branches.

Something new, too: Covetous, going in and out of the park with bags, obviously filled with something, in their hands, finally doing something other than fruitlessly searching every container in sight. Diggers would open the bags, and then pour their indiscernible contents into small holes in the grass. The Covetous appeared to me almost pleased for a brief moment (though the distance was too great to tell for sure), before their faces reverted to their usual morose visages. Then they'd scuttle back out of the park. If the parks weren't perpetually full of Wordless, I might have been able to dig up a hole and see what it was they were burying, revealing the answer to the long-standing mystery. Weepers, too, still looking hopeful, stood around trees while their tears flowed freely into the ground below, seemingly never running out of liquid. Could they have been taking breaks when I wasn't watching? If I had batteries to spare, I could have set up cameras to watch them. Should have thought of that earlier. This was the first time I'd been able to observe the Wordless so close up since light night, and everything they did now seemed simultaneously engrossing and repulsive, as opposed to just robotic and cryptic as they did before. They had a startup script of a kind, that was clear, one that ran all the initialization routines associated with taking over a new place of urban-arboreal space, and I was watching it run up close.

I spent weeks like that, gazing from the tops of the tallest buildings I could find. When I was on the street, it felt to me at times like I was meeting no resistance anymore, the Wordless seeming busier than ever with their mysterious new project. I passed through broken street after broken street without issue, not seeing a single Hunter on any of my trips, though I did make sure to continue to steer clear of any of the green light-cones, knowing how quickly they could change things for me. I did come across some Covetous while out doing observations, keeping my distance as always, but I noticed something different in their actions and demeanor. They seemed preoccupied by what I assumed—correctly, it turns out— was their long-stymied search finally bearing some fruit. Maybe I should have renamed them.

October, year two

A year had passed, I noted with a hint of glumness, since things really started to go downhill. It was growing cooler in that subtle way that autumn tends to do, distracting you with changing leaves and falling nature-detritus, damper, and with a petrichor scent growing stronger again. The white mists, wispy and frail, began returning to accompany the wreckage in the streets.

I was frustrated, hints of despondency creeping in through unguarded breaches of my psyche, but I tried hard to push those feelings back down in the hole, away from the surface where they could impede my mission: finding Kat. Even though I'd learned the new set of behavioral patterns the Wordless were displaying, I had no illusions about their patterns remaining dependable anymore, not with all the changes over the past year, and I felt like what I did know wasn't really helping me all that much, anyway. It was so much easier at the beginning.

So what did I learn during that period, that second autumn? I learned where they had their largest groups. I learned how they react to me, or don't. I learned how to avoid their alarm system. I learned the routes that had the fewest of them so I could move unmolested. I now knew them as well as one can know things one can only study from a distance, and can't communicate with. I badly needed some new data, something that might actually get me somewhere useful. Something that would lead me to Kat. I needed a breakthrough, next-level knowledge, a multiplier. The limitations of remote monitoring were starting to wear my patience threadbare. Nothing seemed forthcoming.

It was a strange time, that October of year two, with me not knowing exactly how to feel when I wasn't brooding over Kat's disappearance and silently cursing the Wordless. The leaves, formerly fused to trees, seemingly not even separate objects before, started falling out again, with no hint that they'd just recently been part of some temporary ecosystem that suspended them in a perpetual autumn twilight. The streets were again choked with them in every hue of deep brown and dull gold, rusty crimson and rich chestnut. Life had returned, decay had returned, and now, apparently, cycles of life, death, and possibly rebirth had returned. The black asphalt, with its faded yellow lines, was lined and caked with mats and carpets of litterfall, squishing and crunching underfoot, again quite pleasantly. For the first time since early on in the events, I spotted what I could have sworn was a squirrel. It was just a moment; a rustle, a quick scurry, but it was there. I stopped and stared at the spot, contemplating, trying to connect it to everything else I'd seen. Everything pointed to some ecological unpause button being depressed, causing life to start trickling back one leaf-drop and possibly invisible maybe-squirrel at a time.

I also felt that my presence was, for the moment, seemingly less important to them than it had ever been, being downgraded from vague nuisance to utterly irrelevant; I might have felt insulted if I hadn't wanted to torch them all in their robes in their commandeered forests with such vehemence, right down to a one, and watch them writhe in agony as their becowled bodies roasted alive, preferably opting to scream rather than remain silent for the duration. They'd taken the world, they'd taken history, and now they'd taken Kat.

Park after park searched, plaza after plaza scouted. I rechecked the beach, hoisting myself up by the red-and-yellow plastic sign to get a good view from the top of Nathan's, and surveyed the sand. The beach was thick with giant, scraggly, yellow-green piles of beachgrass, their gardening efforts evidently having paid off. Did it always grow so quickly? I don't think I ever even thought to consider things like that before. How quickly did grass grow in general? I felt like I should have known that stuff by then. I had new things to think about since *suspension season* ended. "*Get more botany books*" went into the seemingly endless mental note list. I spent the

     Leaves *and* Circles

remainder of the month cataloging more locations, more numbers, more rituals, looking for some evidence of Kat, but I still didn't feel any closer to finding her than when I started. Their operations were unceasing as always, day and night, and the pulse of their activity seemed to be quickening, I felt certain of that. I continued my habit of sleeping on top floors of tall buildings so I could scamper up and get views right after waking, perversely thankful for their borough-wide light installation.

Then it was dawn, the air strangely crisp and refreshing, the light breeze possessing just a bit of bite, reminiscent of certain past autumn mornings when the leaves were in that stage where they appeared in perfectly polychromatic hues, *reminding me of what it was like to imagine a beautifully spectral, haunted world rather than live in one.* It was the last day of October.

CH34
THAT MUIR MOMENT

There are moments in life that you're wholly unprepared for. Things that your imagination, your experiences, your most vivid dreams cannot hope to help you come to grips with; they simply have to be experienced for themselves.

It was much brighter that morning, patches of gentle blue and actual sunlight, making visibility near-crystalline. *Komorebi* through the leaves of trees, feeling strangely anomalous, peeking through for the first time since I could remember, a long distant, half-remembered dream smoothly dissolving, then reforming into extant reality. After coming back from the memory of old autumns, those haunted ones, it started to feel unexpectedly profound. That same sun, the one that humanity had been waking up to for millennia, now shining down directly on New Brooklyn for the first time.

During that October I'd been staying in a different building almost every night, not wanting to trek back to the Red Hook house just to sleep, ignoring that nagging need for familiarity. I decided to hew to my new routine, to focus, to push the feeling out. I'd been methodically making my way northeast, looking for ever taller buildings to get better views from, to maybe catch a glimpse of something I'd so far missed, some clue to Kat's whereabouts. Skipping Gowanus, with its low-slung shab-realness altogether, I made my way to the area around Barclay's Center, that vague nexus-hood made up of Boerum Hill, Prospect Heights, Park

Slope, and Fort Greene while simultaneously not feeling like any of them, a quasi-autonomous zone. It felt like a DMZ, full of the polished, flagship versions of everyday brand chain stores and dark-Jetsons-reboot subway entrances, with a spaceship covered in steel latticework painted to evoke a brownstone at its heart.

I thought about how long it'd been since I'd ridden in anything mechanical, be it a subway train or a bus or car, and how odd that seemed. After riding the subways by myself since I was twelve, not having done so in over a year felt somehow foreign and hollow, reminding me again of just how much the world had stopped. Humanity walked around on foot, then horseback, carriage, steam train, then motor vehicle. Now we were back where we started. I thought about people picking up the pieces of their bombed-out cities after a blitz, staring mournfully at their rended infrastructure that'd probably worked only days prior.

I started to walk right by the Center, which was in surprisingly good shape, with even its front Starbucks windows fully intact and looking almost new, just closed for the day, evincing a brief blip of desire for coffee, even terribly burnt as long as it had milk in it. Across from the Center, though, it looked like a bomb site, a mini-Dresden out of what used to be a sparkling new subway entrance from the seventies-imagined version of the future; it was a pile of rubble, shelter-top bent and partly melted from what clearly seemed to be some sort of violent explosion. I wondered if other subway entrances looked the same, and realized that Kat and I hadn't paid attention to them at all, having discounted using them early due to the risk of getting trapped down there with few degrees of motion. Maybe we should have investigated them.

I found a suitably high building to use as a vantage point, and I started to approach its spider-webbed glass doors, next to which was a black wooden stool, looking lonely, where a door-person would have once sat. I tried to picture one sitting there, but came up empty. I felt a deep rumble from below, powerful this time, causing the stool to double over and me right with it, grabbing, just barely, a cement post to keep myself upright. Steel beams from inside buildings groaned, and the structures themselves swayed, unbroken glass windows rattling disconcertingly, causing my panic to ramp up in jagged steps. Then it stopped, and I could hear the sound of metallic rapids pushing through huge underground pipes once more, which I now felt sure were actually the subway tunnels themselves. Metal garbage cans rolled up and down the street, unsure of which direction they should be going, clanking against *"No Parking"* sign poles and thumping car bumpers.

Then it finally stopped, and I was able to pull myself up, pushing through the glass doors and up the monotonous series of emergency steps.

Up on the top floor of the building, one of those mixed green-glass and plain pale-brick hybrids that took the worst features of both old and new styles, combining them into one sickeningly chimeric whole, I gazed out of the windows towards the south. I smashed the windows out with a metallic bit of pipe I'd found, as they were of the non-opening variety. I surveyed west to east, then toward where I imagined Prospect Park would be, though I was too far away to see much of it from there, even with binoculars. It turned out not to matter, though.

It started right then. First, a rumbling, like a scarcely-detectable, far away earthquake which gradually crept closer, causing the windows to rattle, and forcing me to hold on to the apartment's sole piece of furniture: a flimsy, white trellis table, strangely out of place in the luxury environs, which barely helped me stay upright. Struggling to maintain balance, and staggering to my feet with the building still trembling violently—but seemingly holding up—I scrambled up the last flight of gray stone steps to the building's top. I ran across the coral-like cement of the roof, stopping a few feet from the edge, holding on to the beveled lip to prevent myself from pitching over, though I wondered if I wouldn't have been safer lower down.

Then it happened. At that moment, rising up from the south was a thing of such size, such enormity, that distance sank away into irrelevance. Higher and higher it rose, leaving me slack-jawed, sucking seemingly every molecule of air out of my lungs and causing my head to pirouette in place, the frame of my vision itself seeming to capsize in the violently churning sea of perception. A redwood tree, perfectly sienna and unimaginably wide, rose to what looked to me to be the clouds, practically touching the blue rents now torn in the floating *spissatus*. It was split in two at the bottom into thinner trunks, a wooden titan with its legs spread wide, and two gargantuan branches resembling ricket-ridden arms, bending slightly in the middle before coming back up again, and gaggles of much smaller branches covered in enormous chlorophyllic leaf buds, looking like oversized pupae emerging smoothly from their chrysalises.

I don't think I took a breath for several minutes. Time dilated, swayed. My head swam at the immensity of it. I'd never been to the Grand Canyon, but I imagined that the first of those to see it, long before photographs, must have felt how I did. In a way I could never have previously understood, Muir and his awe at the Range of Light now made perfect sense to me. The vastness, the majesty, the *awesomeness*, in the older sense of the word. I felt that time had collapsed, folding over itself, me in his time and him in mine.

More colossal flora sprouted up from every park in the borough. South. East. North. Everywhere I looked, there were more, sprouting, growing. For the first time in ages, Manhattan was perfectly visible, mists having cleared, with barely an inch of that borough seemingly uncovered by plant life. Nestled among the skyscrapers—the Empire State, the Freedom Tower, the Chrysler, and all the rest—were more massive woods of sycamore, oak, fir, pine, chestnut, and redwood, most having nothing adorning them but enormous leaf buds yet, their nascent state doing nothing to detract from their magnificence. A new nature in all its glory, bursting forth from the soil, the concrete, the steel, and the hard black asphalt. I don't know how much time passed, but when the rumbling finally stopped and my vision and consciousness synched back up with the present, and my stretched out perception returned to its original shape, I stood among, within, but nowhere near the top of, a city-forest sized for titans.

I went down to a knee, all bruises and arm-throb temporarily consigned to limbo due to immensity drown-out. I breathed deep, crisp breaths of autumnal perfection, holding them there, trying to regain composure and restore my own perceptual core. I looked down at the coral floor of the rooftop, then back up towards that first redwood that had risen, thinking laterally that I should still be bewildered, but I was instead entering post-awe disbelief, still trying to process the size and scope of it all.

When my mind and body were willing to cooperate again, I sprinted down every flight of the stone steps, probably thirty floors, on what felt like a single breath, lungs still full of crisp, invigorating autumn.

I meandered dazedly through the mega-forest that was New Brooklyn. Staring upwards, mouth still agape, I took in the sheer enormity of it, gaze surveying upwards along brown bark columns whose tops were invisible to me from street level. Trunks extruded through patches of grass and pavement alike, sending broken blacktop stone and deep ravines through shattered streets.

I walked southwards, slowly, deliberately, touching the bark of each tree I passed, trying to accept the reality of the thing. Leaf buds the size of fists hung above me in their muted pistachio and forest greens and deep crimsons and oranges, just waiting to sprout their oversized output.

Branches, budded or bare, hung over short and tall structures alike, practically mocking them, giants hovering over small children with arms outstretched. The bases of some trees were split in two as

  Leaves *and* Circles

I'd seen before, having an almost bipedal look, gnarled gargantuan archways somehow looking both ancient and completely new.

Shaggy lime-green shrubs and bushes the size of elephants, minuscule compared to their titanic brethren, adorned the sidewalks along Flatbush Avenue, some tall enough to completely obscure the bodegas and bakeries and hardware stores still offering free popcorn behind them, giving the world a neo-imagined Aztec look with a Brooklynian cast.

This was now a kind of lost world, filled with the ghosts of baristas and stockbrokers, and probably grown from their bones and flesh. My mind reeled, causing me to list again, skies circling vertiginously. I stopped to hold on to a walnut tree, an old-world one, now looking dwarfish, almost sympathetically short now.

I'm not quite sure how long I wandered for, or even which direction I was going initially, but somehow I found myself in Gowanus, some ragged stretch of street hosting a grungy auto body shop and not much else. I went into a building, though I'm unable to remember enough about it to describe it now, the hugeness of everything pushing out parts of memory just then, and headed to the roof. I wanted to take it in once more; to make sure it was all real, this even newer new-world. I gazed south, my directional sense momentarily returning due to the visibility of obvious landmarks, and slowly swept my head left and right, just like I did that first night looking over the variegated bands of color spread over Prospect Park. Was there any way I could have imagined at that moment under the cobalt sky that things would come to this?

I wandered out of the building, dazed again, walking in a direction that didn't register consciously. At some point later I found my bearings, my internal navigation system finally deciding to cooperate as confusion and head-swim begun to taper off. My chest was still burning slightly, but I started to run south down Flatbush Avenue anyway, picking up my pace through streets and streets of wreckage and trash, trying to get closer to where we started. I arrived at the old apartment building, snapping a quick gaze at the entrance, half-expecting Kat or a Watcher to be there, then ran upstairs, right to our old front window.

Wooden circles, formerly floating, now adorned the ground, lights all extinguished.

The processions had stopped, the Weepers were gone. No more digging, no more carving. No Watchers in sight, not a single patrol. They were all gone, it seemed, swallowed by the New Brooklyn.

I ran back down and walked straight into the park from the north entrance, stepping through the Soldiers' and Sailors' Arch, almost expecting the fountain to come to life to feed the colossal, open-air greenhouse.

To call the feeling I had *strange* would be a terrible understatement. The buildings that I knew so well were still all around me; the streets were there, if broken in places by new growth; the arches, too; the lamps, the cars, the trash, and the fences were still where they were, for the most part; and so was the fountain. All the old pieces remained in one form or another. But there was all this now, a massive arboreal-urban improvement project, the product of a paintbrush that used flora as paint or a city-building simulation game gone haywire, I wasn't sure which fit best. It was familiar and unfamiliar, but pushed to extremes at either end, stretching, thinning the gray middle zone that centered the place. It was an aberrant feeling, to have both things in you, on you, all at once. It felt like the same place, but also didn't. It had all the old memories, but half-faded and partially grown over, warped in some places and untouched in others, recolored or simply rearranged in multiple contexts. Dissonance. I felt nauseated. The world stopped making sense, everything that formerly existed in two places, both physically and in mind-space now occupied both simultaneously. *That liminal nether time that lead up to this moment now felt more like old-world than this ever could.*

I reached an opening, a wider part of the park splitting out

 Leaves *and* Circles

into multiple roads leading to different sub-areas. *Then, a noise. A great chirping sound.* A massive cello getting its strings plucked with bare fingers. Up ahead, I saw them. Wordless. Not marching, not carving, not digging. Instead they sat, walked slowly, alone or groups, in epicycles to that invisible frequency, or laid down spread-eagle in the grasses, hoods rolled back, splaying messily on the green. Filthy, mute, unblinking. Some faced me, looking puzzlingly docile, heavily lidded, almost dazed, with others looking away in various directions. Some appeared to be eating fresh grass, bits of brown bark, green and yellow leaves, and other unidentifiable bits of plant life. Others just lolled in the newfound sunlight. Their ant-like organization and their monotonous, repetitive tasks and behaviors that dominated everything—new-world, our notes, our observations, our ability to *live*—for the past year and a half were gone. Then, chirping and twanging sounds past a group of Wordless ahead of me, towards the south. Loud, but not overpowering, semi-familiar, but still difficult to place.

Then screaming.

It must have been fifteen feet across. Shiny lime green with an oblong orange underbelly segmented by circumferential spiracles; enormous eyes, compound deep brown with dull red ommatidia, bulbous; antennae, a rough gray, pointed down in an arc towards the ground; wingless, but looking strangely armored, almost plate-like. In a second, *the Wordless were screaming,* scattering in all directions, most disappearing deeper into the woods.

One tripped on his tan cloak, strangely clean looking, and struggled to untangle himself from it, the bottom half wrapping around his calves.

He was split cleanly in half, blood pouring, slimy internals sliding out of his abdomen, slapping the grassy ground around him. The grasshopper-thing pounced on top of him, swordlike jaws of the same color stabbing straight down through the Wordless, burying its maw inside of him, slurping noisily, like someone eating soup and snapping the ill-placed bones between their teeth. The Wordless gurgled out a scream, causing me to wince. He began writhing, insides swinging back and forth, limply and messily around his destroyed form as the thing gorged itself, rib-bones jutting out in a jagged mess, his body shuddering, then quivering, then silent, with his eye-spanning blue-irises looking empty as the sky. The grasses and tiny yellow confetti leaves around him were repainted a deep reddish orange, at which I stared for a moment, fascinated, thinking back to my sewer-void leaf, mind unconsciously attempting to erect a domino-filled tunnel of causation from that moment to this one. I shook my head and started backing straight up on the tips of my toes, deliberately, one step at a time, still staring right at the size-magnified predator-prey scene unfolding in front of me, then turned around and sped as fast as I could, pushing my body to its absolute limit. I felt a brief flash of connection to something else, but not the falling leaf this time, mind traveling through a vibrating string of experiences, swirling with color: my first time witnessing them that day with the dog, then running away, just as I did now. *History doesn't repeat itself, it rhymes.*

Unfortunately for me, turning was a mistake. The world pinwheeled; I went from my familiar park to a seemingly infinite sameness of trees around me, circling in my perception, turning from well-trod thicket to outlandish chaparral, a place I couldn't recognize nor properly reason about. I staggered, one hand falling behind me to keep myself from doubling over, trying to right myself, trying to remember that I was still in the middle of Brooklyn, but it didn't matter; dumbfounded terror was in control of navigation. I ran forward, no longer able to convince my body to worry about direction, lizard-brain reaction screaming to get as far away as possible, as fast as possible. I came to another boscage, tall, filled with old-world oaks and some smaller greenery, with no idea where

I was in relation to the park's boundaries. I maneuvered through low bushes and scrub, still trying to push more distance between myself and grasshopper-thing and whatever else might be back there, breath ragged and temples pounding with each heartbeat. I stopped again, woozy, swaying forward and back, then stiffening, vision still pinwheeling but at half-speed now, feeling the sensation of being on a Rotor ride in slow motion, centrifugal force keeping me upright.

Arrayed out in front of me was a scene that, if not for the previous horrorshow, might have sent me into a one-eighty again, screaming. At that moment, though, the fear-needle was already pinned hard right, so I didn't have anything left but lateral terror-reactions. I looked over a vale, light yellow-green grasses on a large expanse of land, occasional hillock giving the landscape some kind of lumpy green pudding texture. Mostly, green, that is. Roughly thirty feet in front of me was painted vermillion, alternately viscous and runny, littered with unrecognizable chunks of flesh and bone, and perfectly recognizable chunks of body: legs, with large pieces torn off; naked feet, well-chewed; arms, hands, and partially caved-in skulls, most already missing their flesh; and torn and shredded cloaks of every familiar autumn color, stained with blood. There were also torsos in various states of being devoured, piled haphazardly in the center of the vale, serving as an entree for the creatures feasting on them.

At least twelve feet from nose to hinds, with the tails adding another two, having amber canine eyes, with bristly coats running from mottled gray to snowy white to a rich, rust-brown. Wolves, unmistakably, but at least twice the size of their old-world cousins, slavering human liquids from their enormous jaws. Front halves were covered in viscera and blood, bisecting the creatures into red and non-red halves. Some were already sated, clearly, rolling around in the grass-shambles or playfully tugging a leg bone between iron-grip jaws. Some howled, longer and deeper than old-worlds, but unmistakably wolfen.

Centrifugal force-feeling started spiraling out of me, in reverse somehow, and I staggered back, mouth halfway open, eyes narrowed slightly, body seeming to communicate that it had begun its quitting protocol. I kept stepping backwards, then felt the sensation of falling. Everything went dark.

I woke up to a pulverant substance sticking to all exposed flesh, instinctively making me start brushing off my face. It was ash by the taste, clearly, though I couldn't see anything since I'd apparently dropped my supply bag sometime between fleeing in terror from grasshopper-thing and tumbling backwards from stupefaction after witnessing wolf-feast. I was parched, ravenously hungry, and nauseated after remembering the wolfpack and their banquet. I retched, only bile coming up with no food in my system, stinging the back of my throat and forcing me to spit into the invisible ash. I righted myself, pushing my back up against an unseen dirt wall, which curved around in a circle. I felt the area around me, guessing it to be roughly six feet in diameter. Feeling through the ash, looking for some clue as to what I'd managed to get myself into, I came across what I guessed was bones. Too small to be human, probably squirrel or pigeon, long denuded of any flesh. I sat there for roughly an hour, streams of daybreak the color of fire starting to spill in, giving me some ability to see.

None of *my* bones seemed to be broken, and I didn't even feel bruised, probably having had a perfect fall into the soft pile of ash that was likely several feet thick (which I determined by plunging my arm in and feeling around for the bottom.) The walls were hard soil, a rich muddy brown with small rocks scattered throughout, smooth, making me think it was hand-dug and hand-manicured. It was probably one of the fire pits Kat had seen but I hadn't, and its bone-contents partially answered at least one question: the one about the disappearances of some of the first animals. It was too wide for me to chimney up, and too smooth for a straight-up climb, so I spent some time rifling through the ash, trying to locate

   Leaves *and* Circles

larger bones I could use as spikes, like a dog bone. After twenty or so minutes of digging, trying to focus on the strangely gratifying feeling of the ash on my palms rather than the possible contents of the pit, I found a few bones that could work. After some laborious effort—especially grueling in my post-awe, post-trauma, near-starving state—I was able to break the bones in two. I was trying to get an even split and a sharp edge, both requiring considerable filing from a makeshift whetstone of unspecified slate-gray rock. It was almost twilight by the time I had something workable.

I took my improvised climbing spikes and set about hoisting myself up, reassuring myself that it was only about fifteen feet up, and that a fall back down would probably be painless due to the softness of the ash. I worked them into the walls, my bone-spikes, pulling myself up with minimal strain, the ascent being considerably easier than I'd expected given both my hunger and the circumstances. It made me think I'd entered some kind of warped, affected monk-mode, but instead of extreme discipline giving me control of my body temperature, I had some kind of increased strength and self-command that was at odds with my perception of my own capabilities, and fueled by vague terror rather than inner peace. I got my arms over the edge and started to pull myself over, but instinctively let go as soon as I was able to see what was out there. Amber yellow eyes gleamed under the unobstructed bone moon and gaseous blue-twinkle of stars, crystal clear in the startlingly unclouded sky above, which I had a perfect view of flat on my back in the pillowy, gray-white ash pile. Howling and scampering sounds above, followed by the growing din of oversized insect life. A cello sound again, too, but more high-pitched, ending in a short trill with half-step note alternation. Mutant ninja grasshopper sounds, probably deafening up top, but weirdly soothing down there in the soft bone powder, as long as I didn't think about the size or nature of the things making them.

I sat there, eyes open, enjoying the expanse of stars, something virtually impossible in old-world, trying to remain neutral towards the reality of my predicament. I tried to focus on the pleasure of natural experience, its unique magic, its universality across time and culture. The air was gentle and crisp with a hint of chill, but still comfortable, blowing soft breezes through the oaks above. I stared up there for hours, body eventually ignoring my stomach's mad demands for food, an impossibility unless I was willing to eat ash or bone. I tried and failed at sucking out the marrow.

I awoke to a soft cerulean sky smattered with fibrous *cirrus* clouds, and the air felt dewier, but not unpleasantly so. It was cool, that early morning coolness that feels like it's holding back warmth rather than having its own frosty core. It was mostly quiet, too, the only sounds being the continued gentle sway of oak branches and leaves topside, making me close my eyes, placing me back on a lawn on Staten Island, aged six, facing a freshly planted garden; in that reverie, it was pleasantly free of any florid scents, a kind of memory where the smell was captioned, causing a half-smile. I snapped back to new-world with a brief blip of disappointment, then repeated my previous day's ascension sequence, ignoring the apparent abdomen-burster that was taking up residence in my gastro-intestinal tract, urging me to find a dollar slice or at least try a handful of pebbles.

I turtle-necked over the edge, expecting more glow-eyes, but it was clear, causing a volume of air seemingly trapped in my lungs for days to spontaneously release. I clambered over the lip, flattening myself up against a thick oak, craning my head around to scan the area. Nothing in sight: no wolves, bugs, or other megafauna anywhere. I determined where I was, roughly one-third of the way in to the park from the western edge, confirming my proximity to pre-events dog-murder location.

In the middle of the clearing ahead of me was an oversized maple, trunk probably twenty feet in diameter. I approached it, almost wanting to convince myself it was real. I knelt down and touched it; its bark seemed like any other bark, and the branches

 Leaves *and* Circles

and leaves above me did too, just magnified. I was on one knee and felt something solid, almost rock-like under the ground. I started to brush away some soil, and found what it was quickly: a line of bones, perfectly encircling the base of the trunk, another bone version of plastic tree rings. I felt a deep melancholy, and the furthest I'd ever felt from old-world.

I turned around and pushed out from the trees, getting onto a sloppy, pebble-dotted dirt path. The leaves around me were shades of brilliant emerald, momentarily forcing an awestruck and confused smile despite the situation. I brought myself back and started heading west, cutting through copses of trees and scrims of shrubbery.

I stumbled through some young shrubs, looking a satisfyingly deep green, knees padding down into the soft brown dirt. I lifted my head up and started to rise to my feet, but stopped, frozen. In front of me was a gibbet, latticed wooden bands partially cracked and protruding outwards in various directions. Inside was a heavily mangled robe-corpse, stained maroon and covered with tube-like, segmented creatures, distinctly reminiscent of maggots but with a green stippling along their sides in a long row. The creatures were wriggling over the robe, in and out of top-to-bottom rents in the body, which was pinkish aside from the blood, probably white-bodied but covered in human gore.

They were at least half a foot long, some longer. The body was disappearing quickly as the creatures made a meal of it from the inside out. I scanned around the park, looking for more, and instantly spotted similar scenes; one to the south of me appeared to have what appeared to be dead ringers for rats, but with segmented black and white eyes wide open and bodies already a foot long. They shrieked, feasting on what little remained of their meal, then hopped off and scurried further south out of view. More things were coming together; those gibbets, and the people within them, must have been incubators for new-world creatures, preserved until the world was ready to receive them.

I finally pulled myself up and continued my sprint, this time with twice the urgency, every bodily sense now demanding I get out of there and find somewhere safe, somewhere out of view of all of that.

I zipped right past a Watcher, then stopped myself short just a few feet in front of him, feeling myself surprised to see one of them not being torn into constituent limbs. I looked at him, slowly shaking my head, amazed. His eyes were electric green; cold; glowing; pulsing; the color of the bridges; to me having same beckoning, serene quality, covering the whole of the sclera. I forced myself to look away, feeling conflicted, calmed, astonished. Their eyes had changed, their patterns had changed, but they, unlike their brethren-turned-fodder, were here, still policing their grounds. I rubber-banded my neck just to get a quick glimpse, and he glared at me, and it became immediately clear: he recognized. *He'd learned.* His eyelids went wide and he stood there, taut, electric green irises speaking to me without a sound. Then, he opened his mouth but no sound came out, at least not that I could hear.

Sometimes, the dawn of understanding leads to a feeling of such terror that you lose all ability to conceptualize or even think about anything else in the moment, drowning everything else out, forcing the world through a lens of perception almost perfectly replicating the look and sound of viewing the surface above from underwater, but becoming instantly transparent as you emerge; *the sound of a dozen synthesizers, with every note being played at once, blared around me, shaking the grounds of the park.*

I ran, ran, ran, legs aflame, forcing them to continue going by sheer will, trying to bypass intermediate neural circuitry and instead demand muscle fibers and bone obey me directly. Left, right, then left again, one street after another, tripping over everything, stumbling down onto my palms, nearly slamming my face down onto the blacktop half a dozen times. Before I could even formulate a coherent thought, I was back in Red Hook, urged on by instinct and unmitigated fear. On that day, *I experienced a level of fear and panic greater than I'd ever experienced, forcing me to reevaluate what I thought were the limits of human terror.* I arrived back at the building, my would-be sanctuary, careering through the front gate, slamming it behind me, jumping multiple steps at a time to reach the top in the apartment, sealing all doors behind me. I made myself into a tiny bolus inside our sleeping bag in the corner of the apartment, in the corner of the neighborhood, in the corner of the borough, in a microscopic place in new-world, squeezed into as small a shape as I could possibly force my bones to comply with. It was warm inside, hot even, but I didn't feel it in that moment, too focused on willing myself into pill-bug form. I wanted to disappear. Then I was gone.

I woke up, disoriented, the echoes of terror from an unremembered nightmare giving my body that desynchronized feeling, like I was a few inches to the side of myself, a misaligned holographic overlay of consciousness. I crawled over to the window on all fours, elbows and knees really, bruise-feeling starting to return, peering out just the slightest bit from the side of the blackout. I left the curtain down, afraid that they could now hear me blink or breathe, just like back in that closet. Hunters, now larger than I remember them, roamed the streets, seeking, scanning, swinging their stretched-out limbs, even ganglier than before, in front of them while they hopped. Looking for me, I thought, probably correctly this time. My teeth were locked in place, jaw refusing commands, bruxism feeling like it might be a permanent condition. I barely moved, watching them operate in search mode from the sky blue of early afternoon to the soothing periwinkle of middle twilight before sighing and sliding myself down beneath the windowsill, feeling like a ragged, undersized mouse, trapped.

They weren't leaving. All I could think at that moment was that I was probably going to starve to death up here, alone. *Alone and without her.*

CH35
WE SHOULD BE CAUGHT UP NOW

I've been sit t ing her e f or nearly two weeks, biding my time, trying to come to terms with it all: the asymmetry of new-world that now exists along multiple dimensions; how to move around outside now that there's perpetual Hunter presence; what, if anything, that now grows outside is edible for me; and how exactly we went from cowl-clad murder cult stealing New York City's population and burying them in parkland to *this*. I'm not even sure they are—or were—a cult. It's just the term the media used, mostly because of the optics and a lack of information, and it stuck. In retrospect, it's clear that the Wordless were far more than a cult.

I've also been thinking about her. She's still missing, and my arm has started to ache again, I think sympathetically. I feel less hopeless now, though, having begun to get my head around it, at least parts of it. I've started considering new ways to find her, perhaps using the terrain to my advantage. Kat and I never tried to search police stations to try to acquire guns—with neither of us knowing how to use them—and we were always worried about driving due to noise risks, but now both of those things were worth revisiting. Our ancestors managed to hunt the mammoths to extinction with spears and bows; a double-barreled shotgun in a SWAT van could work wonders here, assuming I could teach myself to load and shoot one from a manual or something. I'm still mulling where to begin with this one, but I'm sure I'll come up with something. I'm also considering trying to teach myself to drive while both avoiding attracting the attention of Hunters and without crashing into an oversized tree trunk, though that seems like a very long shot.

The Hunters finally left the immediate area after roaming it for a while, looking for me, but they're never far away anymore. I still see the odd one in the distance every so often, proving that they don't go into "hiding" the way they used to, making scavenging s e e m much riskier than before. One of the main advantages I'd come to rely on, their lack of regular street presence, is gone. Now there's a "Hunter beat," but I still feel optimistic that I'll figure something out.

The nights are no longer illuminated by floating circles, as those objects clattered to the ground on Gaia Day, which means days are now more dangerous than nights. There are flowers in their stead, with the smallest bells several feet across, larger than the flowerpots that might have once contained them. The flowers appear in green, white, and purple, in a variety of patterns and shapes, resembling orchids, lilies, sunflowers, and a dozen other types at least. Beautiful, though with the too-familiar floral scent that I never grew to appreciate, sickly sweet and occasionally overpowering, worse now due to their incredible size.

Moonlight has returned to sometimes-cloudless skies, seemingly clearer and brighter than ever, a silent jewel of bone, at times feeling more familiar than the city I live in. Light-circle period now seems like an LSD-fueled binge era, remembered in fragmented thoughts that only half-qualify as actual memories, streaked from deep crevice of mind-corner to barest edge of perception, with bouncers replaced by Hunters and hypnotic synth lines replaced by earth-rumble and gutter-whispers.

I looked out the window yesterday, breathing in the new air, strangely pleasant, humidity having been dialed down to a comfortable level. In an oversized, but not monstrous, spruce a few blocks away, I could see leaves rustling, and branches shaking back and forth. Jumping down from a branch was what I was sure had to be a squirrel again, standing on its haunches as they do, head darting nervously from side to side, a whitish brown coat with a long white stripe running from neck to tail. Its body was thicker, too, than an old-world squirrel, likely to support its increased height and weight if I remember the rules correctly. It was at least six feet tall, reminding me of a BBC docu-drama featuring extinct giant sloths; at this point I wouldn't be surprised to see those, either.

The quakes and underground water rushes have stopped, with not a single one since the day at Barclay's, when the soaring trunks of new-world titan-trees broke through the substrate of the city.

I've seen other things. On top of the shipping cranes hanging over the bay, I've seen creatures with a strong resemblance to seagulls, at least twenty feet from wing to wing, white, but with a dark blue stripe on either side and beaks much wider—more like a pelican's—than an old-world one. They perch up there, several on top of the crane's mouth and others on its neck, scanning the area and occasionally gliding over the bay. I haven't seen any dive into the water, which I assume still lacks fish or other aquatic life. I also haven't tested it to see if surface tension has returned to old-world levels, but I am curious about it. There are pigeons, too, nearly identical to old-world ones, but at least twice the size, adorned with familiar grays, blacks, and tans in a myriad of patterns, with some having the familiar splotches of purple and green on their neck plumage. The pigeons seem to be a favored meal, with the peli-gulls diving down from above while both are in mid-flight, catching the smaller birds in their talons and quickly stuffing them into their beaks, swallowing them whole with a gulp.

On various trees on the blocks around me, I've seen what appear to be some kind of new-world beetles: six spindly black legs; short, jagged pincers out in front of the face; and hard, chitinous, deep purple shells, looking shiny and lacquered, almost resembling a motorcycle helmet stuck to a tree. They move slowly or sit motionless on the enormous trunks, sometimes a dozen to a tree. When they do

     Leaves *and* **Circles**

move, they leave clear, slimy trails resembling semi-watery mucus in their wake.

I occasionally spy a creature resembling a rat running across the cobblestones out front, other times on adjacent blocks. Six-legged, with the familiar tapered tail colored black, white, tan brown or silver-grey, scurrying north, presumably to find food, then returning some hours later, presumably after eating their fill. I've been thinking about how I could bludgeon them, maybe start using them as a protein source, though I'm of course concerned about new-world diseases. Still, with the level of risk involving in regular scavenging now, I'm forced to seriously consider it. If Kat were here, she'd give us medical options, at least those based on old-world knowledge. Which would be more than I have right now.

None of that is happening today, though. Today is quiet. Today I think about that leaf falling into the void of a sewer grate, vacillating from side to side as it goes, turning into a tiny circle as it passes through the grille. Now, unlike before, I imagine that it comes back out, and when it does, it's colored a deep shade of green.

That's the last of it. I stopped making any new observations a few days ago, opting instead to pore through my notes again, reviewing all the data and analyses, and revisiting my speculations and theories, trying to come up with more complete, more unified hypotheses for everything that's happened. If and when I do come up with something coherent, I'll add it; that's how I'll end this work.

For now, I'm curled up in the sleeping bag against the wall, holding the fabric close to my face, her scent still lingering on it.